Praise for Kevin Helmold's
Debut Novel

Echoes of Torment

"A novel from a fireman lures you into cliché, i.e. the narrative burns off the page, but it really does. A blistering powerhouse of a debut. Carl Braun, the hero, suffering post traumatic stress is absolutely compelling. The novel is also one of the best evocations of Vegas I've ever read. Rarely has a novel got it all…pace, compassion, thrills, style. Echoes does. It burns like all sheer talent does."
—Ken Bruen, Shamus Award Winning
author of *American Skin*

"Fast paced and tension ratcheting; Kevin Helmold's ECHOES OF TORMENT is a page-turner sure to satisfy even the most fickle suspense junkie!"
—Deborah LeBlanc, author of *A House Divided*

"Like a house on fire, retired Chicago fireman Carl Braun's life really heats up when he moves his family to Las Vegas… a minefield of Russian mobsters, shifty card sharks, and a sultry woman intent on making him forget his marriage vows. Cut the cards and pull up a seat at Helmold's poker table. I guarantee you're in for one fiery read."
—Evelyn David, author of the Sullivan Investigation series
Murder Off the Books

"*Echoes of Torment* pushes all the right buttons! …easy, rich prose and strong character development… Helmold zeroes in on your sense of honor and justice and produces a novel of suspense that escalates and twists until the unforgettable ending!"
—Luisa Buehler, author of the Grace Marsden Mystery series
The Scout Master

"*Echoes of Torment* follows firefighter Carl Braun as he moves from fire into the proverbial frying pan. Powerful images of a brutal profession that haunt beyond retirement. A gritty tale with descriptive prowess that holds the reader spellbound."
—Margot Justes, author of *A Hotel in Paris*

"The authentic voice skillfully combines a firefighter's world, high-stakes Las Vegas gambling, and the Russian mafia in a riveting tale of emotion and suspense."
—Grace E. Howell, author of *True Friends*

Also by Kevin Helmold

<u>eBooks</u>

Impossible Paradise

A World Left Behind

A Warmth in Bitter Cold

Echoes of Torment

a novel of suspense

By

Kevin Helmold

Echelon Press

Publishing

ECHOES OF TORMENT

An Echelon Press Book

First Echelon Press paperback printing / July 2007

Echelon Press

9735 Country Meadows Lane 1-D

Laurel, MD 20723

www.echelonpress.com

ISBN 978-1-59080-512-1

10 Digit ISBN: 1-59080-512-7

PRINTED IN THE UNITED STATES OF AMERICA

10 9 8 7 6 5 4 3 2 1

For Dad.
You've missed so much.

Writing this book would not have been possible without the support and patience of my family. Diane, Ed, Liz, Maria, and Rosie, thank you.

Special thanks to Debra LeBlanc, Terry Howard, Karen Syed, and Kat Thompson.

1

Carl pulled out of the driveway and pointed his truck at the growing light of another dank Chicago morning. The shock-jock on the radio did his best to get Carl's attention, but he heard nothing. He held his head low, only raising his tired eyes enough to see over the steering wheel. His mind deeply involved in figuring his odds. He wanted to get through today without absorbing another tragedy. *It could happen.* Every now and then the city gave him a break. He arrived at work hoping this would be one of those days.

He sat alone at his desk in the firehouse shuffling through paperwork, intent on avoiding eye contact with any of the guys. The jumbled chorus of camaraderie reached out to him from the kitchen. He sighed deeply and locked his hands over his ears. *Not now boys, I just want this day to be over.*

Carl managed to shut himself off from the noise. Just as he believed he might escape with a quiet day after all, fate intervened with a vengeance.

The alarm bells jolted Lieutenant Carl Braun to his feet, his pulse pounding. Three decades in this business and the adrenaline still rushed with each call.

A fire on south Haymarket. The address just two blocks from the firehouse.

The digitalized voice repeated its information and the men scrambled to their rigs.

"I think we got a hit," one of the men shouted. "I could have sworn I smelled smoke out back a few minutes ago." Carl didn't doubt his man. Sometimes it just felt like the real thing. A dispatcher enters information into a computer and the speaker doles it out in the same monotone way, whether it's a false alarm or not. This one didn't feel false.

They were good at this game. Too good. Some of them had been acting like cowboys lately. Take your eye off the ball or lose your concentration for only a moment, and the result could be cruel. Carl knew this only too well. He'd found out the hard way on a number of occasions, most of the guys who worked in this part of town did.

The men twisted and turned in the cab of the engine, jamming into each other while struggling into their heavy gear. Not much time to get ready; they would be in front of the building in seconds.

Carl looked over his shoulder at Kenny Broderick, the youngest of his men. His face beamed with enthusiasm and anticipation. It always did during a run. So far Carl had been able to shield him from the recklessness of youth. But who would look out for Kenny after today?

The engine burst from the firehouse making a hard right onto 75th Street. Black smoke billowed above the trees. The men fought to remain in their seats as the engine swerved onto Haymarket. They drove through a thick wall of smoke, and the rancid cloud poured into the open windows of the rig.

Frank Taglieri stepped out of the rig and turned to Kenny.

"How do ya like that kid? This one's trying to choke us right here on the street."

The fire roared through windows in the front and south side of the building. Flames stretched skyward in a wild frenzy, striving to invade the second floor. The lot to the south was vacant, always a good thing–no other buildings to worry about. One building on fire at a time was enough.

Branches sizzled from a tree in the front yard, dropping hot twigs onto the men as they frantically went to work. The whole neighborhood stood in a wide semi-circle around the scene, eyes gaping and filled with fear as the firemen entered the inferno.

Carl's men sprang to action without a word of direction. Frank led out the hose to the front door, while another pulled and straightened it. With everything ready, the engineer opened a valve and water rushed into the canvas-covered line making it jump and twist as it became as rigid as a stone. Kenny dragged the heavy supply hose to the hydrant.

Weighted down by ninety pounds of gear in eighty-eight degree heat, the men breathed hard and dripped with sweat before they reached the front door.

Brian Dunn pried at the flimsy front door with the pick of his axe until the wood around the lock splintered and broke free. Carl wedged the door open and the men turned their heads to avoid the smoke that flowed past them. The fire realized it had gained an additional source of oxygen and the flow reversed itself. Air pulled back through the door as the flames sucked in as much as possible. The men looked at each other in silence, recognizing this ominous sign. They had to move fast, had to slap this beast down while they still could.

The fire leaped in intensity, the heat they felt standing on the porch just a sample of the hell waiting for them inside. The beast taunted, gloating confidently in its growing strength. Almost in unison they reached for their masks and prepared to enter the battle. The beast beckoned, but didn't realize what it asked for. These guys weren't intimidated. They'd taken on tougher and knew this one would be child's play.

As the truck men raised the aerial ladder to the roof, Carl, Frank, and Brian masked up and crawled toward the source of the blaze. Frank dragged the hose line by the nozzle while Carl fed more hose as they advanced. They rounded a corner, only to be hit with the inevitable wave of heat.

Instinct implored Carl to back off, but tasting battle, he hunched lower and forced himself to inch closer.

Hungry flames engulfed two large rooms. The fire twisted and spun in a savage vortex, thrusting itself toward the broken windows in a life or death search for the precious air it needed to survive and grow. Drawn by the open door, the vortex sent groping fingers of flame over the crouching men's heads, the heat becoming unbearable as the flames moved in their direction. Carl watched as Frank braced himself for the incredible rush of energy he was about to unleash.

He opened the nozzle and over a hundred pounds of pressure caused the line to lurch. Carl had seen this release of pressure flip grown men onto their backs. Trapped air sputtered from the nozzle and a stream of water slammed into the inferno. It hissed like an angry python. The sudden temperature change caused the burning materials to snap and pop and shoot pieces of hot debris in every direction. Steam descended on the men, scorching any exposed skin.

"Goddamn it," Brian said. "This son of a bitch is a hot one."

They tried to escape the heat once again by dropping as close to the floor as possible. The cold water soon began to overpower the steam and the men slowly rose to their feet. Carl let out a sigh of relief.

The room, once brightly lit by its fiercely burning contents, went instantly black. With the fire darkened down, nothing remained but dense smoke and an utter blindness that no amount of sunlight could penetrate.

As Frank continued to work the line, Carl and Brian forced their way toward the windows, stumbling over furniture and rubble as they went. They located and shattered the remaining windows, increasing the openings to the outside and to fresh air.

Carl's radio crackled to life. He heard the battalion Chief through the noise and static. "What have you got in there, Carl?"

"Living room and dining room. Fires out. We're just starting to wash it down now."

The Chief barked out orders, "Truck 12 you can hold the roof–" too late, the guys had already cut a nice sized vent hole– "85 pick up your line, 51's got it."

Soon, the building filled with men pulling ceiling and opening walls, looking for places where the fire might be hiding. Frank had to open the pipe a few more times to extinguish remaining hot spots. They had to be thorough.

Sometimes it didn't take much for a fire to rekindle. No one wanted to come back.

The men stood shoulder to shoulder, trying not to elbow each other while working. More men now than were really needed, but everyone wanted in on the action.

Even though the heat and most of the smoke had lifted, the air remained charged with residual toxins. Tiny fiberglass particles, ash, soot, and heavy dust, floated in layers through the air. As the smoke cleared, the evening sunlight streaked back into the building and illuminated each particle, making them glow like dancing crystals. In spite of the tainted air, the men had already removed their masks. Some lit cigarettes.

The fight may have been over, but everyone still rode an adrenaline high. Rehashing of the frantic events began immediately and continued throughout the overhaul and picking up process.

The guys from engine 85 stuck around to help re-bed hose. A chorus of laughter rose from the street. More than banter from a group of men who shared a unique brotherhood, they laughed at everyone who wasn't them. They laughed at the firemen who worked in the outlying battalions and only went to a couple of fires a year. It wasn't their fault; many of them wished they could work in this part of town. The guys were lucky to work on these companies. They all knew it, and none of them thought of giving up their spots anytime soon.

After a fire, Carl usually placed himself in the center of this group, joining in the revelry. Today, he felt content to stand aside and watch.

He studied each man in turn, trying to emblazon each in

his memory, wanting to remember them at their best.

"Hey, Kenny, do they still have you on hydrant duty?" One of the guys from 85 took a stab at the new guy. "Haven't you ever felt that orange stuff up close?"

Kenny opened his mouth as if to say something, but looked away with a frown.

"Carl, what are you saving this kid for? Why don't you let him play with the big boys?"

Smiling, Carl dropped a fresh air cylinder into his harness and shook his head.

The laughter amped up a notch, but not truly directed at Kenny. Carl understood. He knew it was directed at any one of a million soft little men who sat all day in a cubicle, riding the same elevator, day after day, in his steel and glass high-rise. The only excitement he had to look forward to were his fantasies about the new receptionist, the one with the long legs and pert little breasts. He would let his mind wander, a dreamy grin on his face, only to look up and see the boss glaring down at him, wondering why the hell he wasn't pecking away at his keyboard, or holding a phone in his hand placing orders, or taking orders, or whatever the hell he was supposed to be doing. Who gave a shit? He wasn't doing this. He wasn't fighting dragons like one of King Arthur's Knights. He wasn't walking away from battle, his armor scorched black by the demons breath.

One day this soft little man would be eighty-five years old. He would sit in his overstuffed recliner, still thinking about the receptionist, but he would no longer remember why.

Carl looked at his friends and knew none of them would

ever see eighty-five. Most would never reach seventy-five. Theirs were live now, pay later existences. The soft little man may never have to pay much, but then did he ever really live? Not like this he didn't.

Yes, these men, his men, were truly lucky. Lucky to be aged beyond their years. Lucky to have their bodies corroded from the inside out.

Carl thought the trick was to live the life and put off paying until the distant future. He'd always been confident he could pull off the trick, but lately wasn't so sure. Lately, he considered he might have already started paying.

2

While washing the soot and grime off his face, Carl recognized a familiar tingling sensation. A quick look in the mirror showed him a blister rising from a reddened patch behind his left ear. Not an unusual occurrence for an engine guy. He nodded to himself and considered just how hot that relatively small fire had been. If they hadn't knocked it down so fast, it could easily have gotten away from them.

He stared at his reflection, his eyes settling on a faded scar. With his hands gripped tightly on the edge of the sink he allowed a familiar memory to return.

Mickey Fitzgerald was a mountainous red-faced Irishman with wavy brown hair and a deep bellowing voice. He ruled over a kingdom of jesters at a never-ending party. Carl had never met a more quick-witted man. He could let loose a barrage of insults in a blink, but Mickey's words came with a smile and the twinkle of friendship in his Irish eyes. No one ever took offense, in fact most found it impossible to spend more than five minutes with him and not become his friend.

They'd met on Carl's first day out of the Academy. Carl walked into the firehouse carrying his pristine new fire coat, and with apprehension, extended his hand. Mickey jumped from his seat, brushed aside Carl's hand, and grabbed him with a crushing embrace. He kissed Carl on the cheek and said, "So you're Braun's kid. I worked with your dad years ago. He's a good man. What happened to you?" Carl stood motionless, his mouth gaping. "I like your dad. I guess you can't always blame a guy for the way his kids turn out. I suppose I'll have to beat you into shape myself." Mickey pulled a twenty-dollar bill from his pocket and gave Carl his first order. "Walk over to 63rd street, kid, and get me a fifth of Jamesons. Clyde will open up when he sees the uniform. Make sure you tell him it's for me. I get a special discount." Then with a threatening glare that no one bought, except Carl, "And you better not try to screw me on the change."

Carl didn't quite have a year on the job when he got that first scar. They had just battled a fire in a cluttered one-room apartment, the ancient ceiling weakened by heat and water. The first chunk of plaster knocked Carl's helmet off. He flinched just in time to prevent the next one from ripping out his right eye. The razor sharp edge rode along his skin, slicing it from the corner of his eye to the bottom of his cheekbone.

He returned from the emergency room to find his Lieutenant waiting for him in the kitchen. Mickey looked at Carl's bandaged face, told him to sit down, and handed him a glass of whiskey. "Peel back that rag and let me see what they did to you."

Carl wasn't much of a drinker, but in 1978 drinking remained a favorite pastime in the Fire Department. Feeling as if embarking on a rite of passage, he picked up the glass and turned back the bandage.

"Oh, would you look at that for Christ sake. Wait till your little doe-eyed, dago sees that. You're not as pretty as you used to be. By this time tomorrow she'll be dumping you for some fair haired professor."

Carl put his empty glass on the kitchen table. "Kiss my ass, Mickey; I'm still prettier than you, and my wife teaches at a grammar school. They don't have any professors."

"Yeah, but they don't have anyone who looks like Frankenstein either.

"Did you guys hear this kid?" Mickey clapped Carl on the back with a catcher's mitt sized paw. "He hasn't said two words since he got here, and all of a sudden he's got a goddamned mouth on him. Everyone grab a glass; we have to drink to this."

When Mickey Fitzgerald told you to grab a glass, you grabbed a glass. Carl woke the next morning, his head pounding. The headache disappeared in time; the vertical line that hung from his eye never did. Whenever he looked at it, he thought of Mickey.

Mickey's last shift on the Fire Department came two years later. While driving home from work he careened his LTD wagon into a row of parked cars. They said he had a heart attack, said he was dead before he hit the first car. Mickey had been up all night battling an extra alarm fire with his men. Carl remembered how beat everyone felt that morning. Mickey didn't seem any worse than the rest of them.

Carl looked away from the mirror and whispered to himself, "Well, at least I made it longer than you, Mick." He finished washing up, then turned away without giving his burn another thought.

* * *

Later, he joined the others in the kitchen for what would be his last meal in a firehouse.

The room may have been full of loud men, but Carl sat alone with his thoughts. Twenty-nine years and now, on with the rest of his life. He sat at the head of the table, his head down and shoulders slumped. He pushed his food around with his fork, the dinner table mockery as brisk as ever, but tonight he had no desire to join in.

He looked up at his men, his second family. He'd been working with them for years, each one a respected friend. Once again he struggled to plant them in his memory. No one noticed the intensity of his gaze; he lowered his head before they could. He'd be moving on now. Retirement. Off to a more agreeable climate. Chicago's weather was brutal in summer or winter. He would rarely see these guys again. He thought about making a little speech, maybe raising his glass.

While the men continued to work their way through the prime rib and double-baked potatoes, their attention turned to Carl. "Well, that might be the last one for you, Carl." Brian observed. "The only fire you'll see from now on will be in your fireplace."

Carl made a quick reply. "That'll be fine with me. Maybe my lungs will clear out a little."

"Keep thinking that way, Carl. A couple months of that fresh desert air should make up for years of firefighting." Phil Miner, a two pack a day man with thirty-three years on the department and no plans to quit any time soon, joined in. "I'm sure you'll get more pension checks than anyone else ever got.

What's the average up to now, about twenty checks?"

Carl brushed off the sarcasm. He'd always been health conscious, working out almost every day and trying to eat right. Phil loved to deride his efforts, often saying, "What do you want to be, the oldest guy in the nursing home?"

Carl just went about his business with a smile, never paying much attention to him. In the back of his mind though, he knew Phil could be right. Most firemen didn't have long retirements. Carl's own father only lasted long enough to cash fourteen pension checks. That wouldn't stop him though. By staying as healthy as he could, he thought he might at least improve his odds.

Improving your odds, playing the angles, putting yourself in the best position possible, creating your own luck. Words to live by for Carl. They not only described his approach to health and work and to life in general, but they had become the guiding principles in his most passionate pastime, poker.

"Knock it off, Phil," Kenny said. "Just because you're making a beeline for the grave doesn't mean the rest of us are in any hurry. Now let's get this table cleared off and break out the cards. This might be the last crack we're gonna get at the master."

Kenny handed Carl a couple cigars. A going away present. His favorite brand, smooth and aromatic. Carl only smoked a few a month, if that. One small vice. He accepted the gift and slid the cigars into his shirt pocket. "Thanks, kid. Make sure you bring a few when you visit me in Vegas, but don't bring any of these jackasses with you. Leave them here where they belong."

Phil wouldn't let that comment pass. "Listen to you. By this time tomorrow it'll be Carl who? There ain't gonna be any visits, not from Kenny or anyone else."

"Don't listen to him, Carl. I'll be out there, as long as you introduce me to that cute daughter of yours. You can't hide her from me forever you know."

Carl dropped his head in surrender. He didn't feel sharp enough to mix it up with the guys tonight.

Frank made reference to Carl's uncanny knack for poker. "After today we should be playing on a more level playing field."

"Stop it will ya, Frank" Carl said. "Don't blame me for your failings. After today you'll just find someone else to give your money to."

Carl was the acknowledged man to beat, and a victory over him always tasted sweeter. Poker had been a tradition at 51 for as long as anyone could remember. Different incarnations of the game had been played, but hold 'em had grown to be the most popular by far. As soon as Carl transferred in, his level of play and style kept the others guessing. His advantage over them only grew when they started playing hold 'em. It got to the point that they continued to play in spite of him. As if he were just a handicap they had to overcome, like the house rake taken in a casino.

They kept the stakes low enough to keep most guys in. Even if some didn't win too often, they usually considered the money well spent for entertainment value alone. This didn't mean they treated the games lightly. Firemen are naturally competitive, and winning is always the goal.

With the suggestion of a poker game, Carl snapped out of his introspective mood and put his game face on. He loved playing cards and had all his life. He played whenever the opportunity presented itself, and usually he created the opportunity.

His talent for the game came naturally, like the rare musician who plays by ear. His professional world ability to make decisions quickly and without fear easily transferred to his card-playing world. Sizing up an opponent became second nature to him and he did it without realizing it. He seemed to push at the right time. Bluff, fold, call, slip out of a trap just in the nick of time. His firehouse and casino opponents alike found it maddening.

Casino poker meant low limit. Part of his success, he figured, came from playing against the average Joe, the casual enthusiast. Pros avoided low limit games like the plague. After all, he was just a fireman who wanted to raise his kids and plan for retirement. He had no business playing in a high stakes game. Once you started playing for more than you could afford, your judgment twisted a little, and before long you lost your edge.

After several medical runs and the fire, things began to quiet down. They only had three runs after dinner.

An automatic alarm came in shortly after they started the first card game. It proved to be nothing.

While halfway through their second game, Engine 51 was dispatched on an ambulance assist run for a stabbing victim. They spent five hectic minutes with a young man found doubled over in pain.

He clutched at a stomach wound, blood pouring through his fingers. A crowd gathered. Angry screams rose above the wailing and sobbing of some onlookers. It was a steamy summer night and the scene began to boil. Carl's muscles tightened from the tension and his thoughts turned to the safety of his men. He wondered if the police were coming.

They waded cautiously through the crowd, ignoring as best they could the shouts and jeers. "Why ain't you runnin? If he was your boy, you'd be runnin!" The stares, ripe with criticism and distrust, burned through the men as they laid the victim on the sidewalk.

Carl ripped the teenager's T-shirt up the middle and shook his head at what he saw. The wound wasn't minor. About two inches long, just below his sternum. Bright red blood flowed freely. Quite a bit had already congealed on the concrete.

Carl responded automatically, but his mind lingered, it released a torrent of thoughts that he kept to himself. *A few minutes ago this kid was just another tough guy hanging out with the gang bangers. Now look at him, a dispute with one of his own, and now this. What a waste. I suppose his buddy didn't have a gun handy so he had to use a knife. A little more up close and personal maybe, but just as effective. Now this tough guy is just a boy again.*

Lying on the sidewalk, the boy looked up at Carl, his eyes wide with fear. At fifteen, he was no stranger to the streets. He had probably seen others lose their lives to violence, but never considered that it could happen to him. Streetwise maybe, but just young enough to retain a measure of innocence and hope. Perhaps the hope left him vulnerable.

The police showed up and parted the crowd. Carl heard them scuffling with the more aggressive onlookers. Somehow their arrival didn't make him feel any safer. The shouting, now directed at the police, increased. Young men on the outskirts of the group flashed gang signs at the cops. The cops ignored them as long as they kept their distance. Carl's muscles remained tense, he wanted out of there, but they had a job to do. This kid depended on their efforts, but it didn't look good.

Carl applied pressure to the wound while Kenny set up the I.V. The blood flow would not ease up. A sticky red stream flowed from beneath the boy and soaked into the dirt that bordered the sidewalk. His shirt and pants became sodden; the air surrounding him grew pungent with an iron rich aroma. Kenny started the I.V., and let it run wide open. The boy failed to make the customary flinch when he inserted the needle. He had grown limp.

His respirations became nothing more than short, gasping efforts, the muscles and sinews of his neck bulged from the struggle. Carl moved to the boy's head and prepared to intubate him. The ambulance arrived at last. Still looking down at the boy, he saw the fear fade from his eyes. His pupils dilated. Carl inserted the breathing tube as the ambulance crew came with their stretcher.

The look of disbelief and shock had passed from the boy's face. Within minutes the paramedics began the race to the trauma center. Kenny went along to help. Carl doubted there was any use. This neighborhood could be unforgiving.

The blood on Carl and Kenny extended beyond their latex gloves and onto their forearms. While cleaning up at the firehouse, Phil approached to ask where all the blood came from. "Huh, another honor student that won't make it to college, I guess."

That goddamn Phil, Carl thought. Always trying to get under my skin. Sometimes he wasn't funny. Carl thought how nice it would feel to crack him on the jaw. The hell with it. It wouldn't matter after today.

A fire alarm came in just after midnight. It turned out to be nothing more than a pot left unattended on the stove. A little work with the five-gallon hand pump. Nothing more.

The slow evening allowed the guys to play three tournaments. Everyone participated in honor of Carl's last day. He didn't disappoint them. Initially, the guys thought he may have been losing his touch. He finished out of the money in the first round when he went all in with nines full of tens. Brian knocked him out of the game when he caught a queen on the river to make his three tens, tens full of queens. Carl took the setback in stride and made up for it in the next two rounds, finishing first both times. He went out with a victory and headed up to the bunkroom, smiling.

In spite of the long day, sleep refused to come easily. Carl left his windows open to allow the cool, early morning air into his room. The noise from 75th street, usually bothersome, brought a feeling of nostalgia.

He folded his hands behind his head and surrendered to the bout of insomnia. He filled his lungs with a deep breath of inner city air and realized his sleep would rarely be interrupted again. No booming car stereos or horns. No yelling or fighting or police sirens to make him toss and turn. No more alarm bells to jolt him out of a deep sleep and make his heart pound so suddenly that he thought it would explode. These were good things to leave behind, but tonight he knew they had become a part of him.

As he lay in bed and stared vacantly at the starless sky, he considered his decision to retire. Was he being too hasty? He did max out his pension. Twenty-nine years. But he was only fifty-three.

It would still be ten years before mandatory retirement. He knew it wasn't as simple as that. Firefighting had always been a young man's game and he didn't want to overstay his usefulness. He also had his health to consider. Why should he subject himself to the toxic environments in these fire buildings any longer than he had to? Or continue to run the risk of exposure to some disease on one of the endless ambulance assist runs they respond to?

He could have transferred to a slower fire company, but he couldn't picture himself merely sitting around watching the time go by. He'd played these thoughts over in his mind a thousand times while making his decision, and he guessed he would for a while longer.

In the end, it usually came down to one thing: life held more than just the fire department. He felt compelled to move on while he still could. He refused to address the possibility that he may have reached the limit of his tolerance for this work.

He rolled over, in anguish, as his mind settled on a reality. For the last several months, specters from his past had begun revisiting. The images of fires, some so big he could see the night sky glowing orange from blocks away. Others so small he found it hard to believe the extensive damage they caused. A lifetime of possessions erased from existence, not only by flames, but by smoke and water. The pain of human suffering and tragedy. Anguish on the faces of the innocent.

Then there were the children. Carl sat on the edge of his bed rubbing his temples at the thought of the children. Faces that would be with him always. Silent. Looking at him with searching eyes. Victims never of their own doing.

Over the many years they had become nameless and numberless, but they visited him just the same. Usually at solitary times like this, when he would pick one face out of the many and remember what his brief relationship with that child had been. It was usually a desperate time, and Carl stood as their only chance. Sometimes his efforts paid off. Sometimes he could do little. He found that the children also appeared at times when he was being put to the test. A critical situation at a fire or ambulance run. They might show up, their eyes pleading, imploring him to prevent another tragedy. "Get it right. It all depends on you. What are you going to do?" He tried to escape these thoughts by burying his head in the pillow. His blistered neck started to sting, adding a physical distraction to the mental ones keeping him awake.

He considered his personal injuries: the broken bones, the burns and scars, the aches and pains. These he would not be leaving behind. Some never faded and remained visible to anyone who paid attention, some he carried hidden away. He had given a lot of himself, mostly a little bit at a time. It all added up, and now he felt he had very little left to give. Yes, it was the right decision. Sleep finally came.

Seven o'clock that morning found him in the kitchen drinking coffee and making some final goodbyes. He shook hands with the guys from his shift and with the guys from the oncoming shift. Everyone smiled and wished him well. They told him how lucky he was, but he thought they looked right past him as if he were already gone, already a memory. And just like that he was. The door closed behind him, and his shoulders sagged to match his mood.

3

The sharp morning rays jabbed through the windshield. Driving east toward the Dan Ryan expressway, Carl reached for his sunglasses. Usually he allowed himself to be distracted by the chatter of drive time DJ's, but today he drove on in silence.

A collection of tight knots formed in the pit of his stomach. He tried to force them away with the heel of his hand. It had been a long time since he felt them. He used to get knots when he did something new for the first time. The paper route, high school, his first day in the academy, his first day as a lieutenant.

The fact that the knots had reappeared after so many years, and on the first day of his retirement, made him feel silly. What was there to be nervous about? It was all down hill from here. Nothing to do but enjoy the fruits of his labor. Collect his pension checks. Travel. Relax. Work at a casino just for the fun of it. He tried to shake it off by chuckling at himself, but the feeling remained.

As he drove away from his peer group he realized that he left behind more than just the guys in his firehouse, or his battalion, but all the guys. The final and permanent truth was that he was no longer a fireman. It had been his identity for almost thirty years, three decades. Now the department would go on without him. Someone new would lead his company.

They'd fight fires without him. The young guys would move up a notch in seniority. Occasionally, his name would come up while they sat around the kitchen table.

Often at first. Less as time went by. Then rarely. Now these damn knots seemed determined to stay.

He told himself he should look forward. Concentrate on the future, but his past kept demanding attention. At least he could try to guide his thoughts toward pleasant memories. Maybe he could loosen the grip this invisible fist had on his gut.

He exited the expressway a little sooner than usual and cruised by the house he grew up in. Driving past his childhood home was usually a sure fire way to pick up his spirits. Memories of long warm summers and Christmases with his whole family together.

He could see his father, still young and strong, pushing the lawn mower or working on one of his old station wagons. He remembered sitting in the shadows of the front porch kissing a new girlfriend for the first time.

His brother and sisters around him again. His mother, always there, always secure. Visions of a simpler time. All he had to do was drive past. Had he returned to that time? Was life going to be like that again? Simple. The knots remained, but they weren't little anymore and a lump appeared in his throat. He considered that driving through the old neighborhood on this day could have been a mistake.

With the sun behind him now and moving higher, he returned his sunglasses to the glove box, glad to be rid of them. He found wearing them a minor annoyance. He didn't like the way they sat on the bridge of his nose and caused sweat to build up, or the way they squeezed the side of his head, or the slight distortion they caused in his vision. He wasn't in a patient mood and didn't feel like putting up with anything annoying, no matter how minor.

The air felt heavy, muggy. This damn humidity, he thought. It would be oppressive by noon. Good old Chicago weather. *You can have it!* His frame of mind didn't improve. Another block. Almost home.

4

He parked at the curb in front of his house and looked up to see Gina opening the front door. She still wore her nightgown and summer robe and had been sitting by the window waiting for him like they were newlyweds again. She held a steaming cup in each hand and offered a warm smile, her eyes sparkling with expectation

Her love had remained the one constant thread throughout his adult life. Things changed. People came into their lives and went out again. Through sickness and health, near or far. Her warmth was always there for him and he felt it now. Just the sight of her made the lump in his throat begin to rise. Were tears actually welling up in his eyes? What was wrong with him? He squeezed his eyes shut for a moment and took a deep breath. He hadn't experienced a sudden wave of emotion like that since learning of his father's death. This felt different. More like when he looked down the aisle thirty years ago and saw her walking toward him, dressed like an angel.

A gentle summer breeze forced the satin clothing tight against her body. She did make him feel like a newlywed again. He swallowed hard and got out of the truck. Not as tough as he thought he was. He felt silly again.

She let him reach the top of the stairs, never taking her gaze from his face. She tried to pick up a hint of what he was feeling or thinking. Even though he rarely volunteered any of his thoughts, she knew him better than he imagined.

Over time she became adept at picking up his signals. Even if he hadn't realized it, she knew this morning wasn't going to be just another morning.

She handed him his coffee, reached up with a kiss, and without blinking, looked into his eyes with a girlish smile, and asked, "Weeell?"

He moved closer, drawn by the stark contrast she provided to the chaotic world he left behind. He closed his eyes and inhaled deeply, trying to breathe in her freshness.

His mind returned to a summer long past. Nineteen, and only a year out of high school. She was seventeen and going into her senior year. A little shy, but just his type. Deep brown eyes that seemed almost black when she became impassioned. High cheekbones, a little turned up nose, and dark brown hair. A smallish woman, only about five-foot two alternately lean or round in all the right places, more pretty, or cute, than beautiful.

By the end of summer, they had grown inseparable. He found himself always wanting to be near her, to be touching her. She made him want to be gentle. He discovered tenderness inside him. He kept it hidden from others; she alone enjoyed it.

Carl's rugged good looks and lean six-foot frame made it difficult for her to look away from him. When they first started dating she mistook his quiet nature for a kind of untouchable distance. As their relationship developed, she came to recognize his silent warmth for what it was. The power of it overwhelmed her. It may have taken her a little longer to completely fall for him, but once she did, she fell hard.

They could bear separation no longer and married over Christmas break four years later, with Gina still in her senior year at NorthWestern. Young and impatient, they managed to anger both their parents by not waiting until they were more established.

Gina completed her teaching degree and Carl entered the fire academy a year later. Like all couples, they had some hard times, especially early on, but they went through them and overcame them together, believing they grew closer than most couples because they stumbled along and became established as a team.

He smiled, wrapped his arm around her waist, and pulled her soft body against his own. He kissed her again and let his cheek linger against hers for a moment. The knots and lumps disappeared.

They sat on a weathered cedar bench and Carl answered her question. "Well, it was okay for the most part. We had a fire just before dinner and then played a few rounds of cards." He didn't mention the stabbing victim.

Gina noticed the blister on his neck, but said nothing, glad that it would be the last.

"We stayed in pretty much since midnight. I guess I had some trouble falling asleep, but other than that it was a good day."

She looked up at him and prodded a little more. "That's not what I meant. How do you feel now that you've really retired?"

He sipped his coffee and stared into the cup. Apparently

she wanted to discuss his thoughts and feelings. He wasn't used to this kind of thing, but knew he had to say something. The coffee didn't give up any answers so he figured he had better stop staring at it and say something. "I don't know. The drive home this morning was a little rough. I felt kind of low. A million things have been going through my mind. To tell you the truth, I'm a little dazed and overwhelmed. I know it's a ridiculous way to feel after all the thinking and planning we did."

"It's anything but ridiculous. No matter how much planning you do, it's still a big move. You were on the fire department for a long time, honey. You know it will take awhile to adjust. Just wait, you'll feel better when we start moving ahead with our plans."

Gina placed her hand on his knee and said, "You've got to admit, we've been really lucky so far. The house here sold in just two weeks and the place in Vegas was finished right on schedule. How often does that happen?"

"I guess so," Carl conceded.

"Now you're not going to mope around all day like an old retired geezer are you?"

"Ouch, how could you say something like that? Where's the sympathy?"

Gina coaxed another smile and asked, "What have you got planned for your first morning as a free man, Blue Eyes?"

Blue Eyes was what Gina called him when she felt romantic. Since their third and final child went off to college a year ago, he was sure he heard it more than Sinatra ever did. He had to admit that he'd gotten used to being an empty nester.

He figured he would get used to being retired as well.

She let him finish his coffee before rising and taking him by the hand. Her robe fell open. Carl glanced up; the thin nightgown did a poor job of hiding her figure. He wondered if the breeze played this trick, or if his wife was aggressively setting a mood. She watched him watching and tightened her grip on his hand.

They entered the house without speaking only to have the deepening spell shattered by a piercing electronic chirp. The sudden noise drew Carl's attention, and the caller I.D. on the handset display caught his eye. "Damn it, what do they want?"

5

"Just a minute, honey. I'll be right there." Carl picked up the phone and detected an apologetic, pleading tone in the poker room manager's usually gruff voice.

"Carl, listen I'm in a bind down here. I'm already running short one dealer and now Henry went home sick. Can you help me out?"

Carl's rolled his eyes, "For Christ sake, Tommy, this is the first day of my retirement. Gina and I were going to spend the day just soaking it in and hanging out."

Carl's tone suggested he might be willing to give in and he listened while Tommy turned up the heat. "C'mon, Carl, help me out today and I'll see what I can do about getting you off the schedule tomorrow."

"All right, Tom, but you better do more than just see what you can do about tomorrow. You know we're moving in a couple of weeks and I've got a million things to do. You already loaded me up on that schedule since I gave you my notice."

"Thanks man. I'm going to miss you down here. You know you've been my 'go to guy' since you got here."

Carl knew the patronizing tone. "Okay, Tommy, take it easy. I already said I'd come in."

"I know, I was just saying–uh when can you get here?"

Carl almost chuckled. It amazed him how the manager could go from beggar to tyrant whenever necessary. "I'll be there in about an hour; the drive to Joliet takes me close to forty-five minutes."

Carl knew Tommy would be pleased with himself, and could picture him grinning while he offered his gratitude. "Great man. Thanks again."

Carl had gone to dealer's school a little over a year ago. He had planned to get some experience in one of the local casinos and then hook up with a big Strip casino when they moved to Las Vegas. His oldest daughter had recently become a department manager at his favorite resort, one of the biggest and most opulent places on the strip. He intended to make it his first stop.

The casino action and environment never failed to invigorate him. He wanted to be a part of it, but didn't want to be one of those people who blew their pension checks every month. He figured dealing as the natural choice. So far he had been right. With his card handling skills already well developed, he flew through the school. Equipped with a long work history, engaging personality, and flexible hours, he found it easy to get work.

At first he had a little trouble reconciling himself to having a boss and being supervised. As a lieutenant on the fire department he called the shots and worked independently. Before long his bosses recognized his skill and popularity with the players. Soon, they considered him a genuine asset, a dealer who was there because he wanted to be, not because he needed to be.

Dealing put Carl in his natural element and it showed. His easygoing, lighthearted manner with the players and his skill with the cards made him stand out immediately. When he sat down at a table, the regulars welcomed him and the newcomers soon relaxed. He kept the play brisk and never got bored, relishing and anticipating each turn of the card as if playing himself. Tommy wasn't just patronizing when he called him his "go to guy." If he had a few more dealers like Carl, his job would be a breeze.

"That was Tommy, hon."

"Who else."

"I know, I know. He wants me to come in. They're really short."

Gina had a habit of curling the corner of her mouth into a wry smirk at certain times. Sometimes she did it in anger, sometimes in sarcasm, its cause didn't matter to Carl, the look never failed to amuse him. "Oh it's always something with that Tommy. Are you the only name on his list?"

Carl assumed a remorseful tone, "C'mon now, Gina, they've been great to me down there. They gave me a start and kind of depend on me and now I'm ditching them. I feel sort of guilty."

Gina rolled her eyes, the smirk appeared. "Please. You don't owe them anything. It was supposed to be a part time job and they ended up taking advantage of you."

He smiled and reached for her. "Well, you know what they say, a good man is hard to find."

Gina pushed away. "No you don't, Romeo. You had your

chance and now you're ditching me, too. You can't please everyone, you know."

Carl would not be put off. He set down his empty cup and caught her in his arms. She felt weightless. He bent and pulled her in close, tucking his cheek against hers. Standing straight, he brought her to the tips of her toes.

She sighed and hugged back hard, pressing full every opening between their bodies. "I'm glad it's over, Carl. Twenty-nine years is a long time to wonder if your husband will be coming home from work." Now, Gina tried to squeeze back tears. She couldn't. They escaped and rolled down her cheek. Carl kissed the side of her neck and slowly released her. She kept her head down as she pulled away.

She never let him know when she became emotional over the nature of his work. Turning quickly toward the kitchen, she artfully wiped away her tears with the back of her sleeve. "You better get going, Tommy's waiting."

"You okay, hon? I could call him back."

"Don't be ridiculous. It's not like you have to go to the firehouse tomorrow. We have nothing but time now. I'll see you when you get home."

Carl remained unconvinced. "Tommy did say he would see about getting me off the schedule tomorrow."

That snapped her out of it. She reached for the coffee pot and laughed out loud. "Stop it, you're killing me."

Carl's eyebrows arched in defiance of his wife's doubt, "Okay, okay, we'll see." As he walked toward the door, he called to her over his shoulder. "Don't I get a good-bye kiss?"

She wouldn't be taken in. "How about I save your kisses

for when you get home tonight, Blue Eyes."

He took a slow deep breath and pushed the screen door open. Her words caused an image to form in his head. Concentrating on the cards wasn't going to be easy with that on his mind all day.

6

Dmitri had been walking through a St. Petersburg slum for several blocks before his young companion finally mustered up the courage to question him. "Why are we walking to this guy's flat? We would be there already if we drove."

Ordinarily, Dmitri would have reacted with anger if questioned by a subordinate, especially one who had yet to prove himself, but in this instance he seemed pleased. Perhaps because it gave him a chance to lecture on a favorite theory of his. He expanded his chest and answered.

"My young friend, I am not unknown to the people of this neighborhood. Neither is the scum we are going to visit." Dmitri paused and furrowed his brow while collecting his thoughts. "This vermin has allowed himself to become addicted to our products. He has lost all control over himself and even though he sometimes could not pay, we satisfied his needs out of sympathy."

That statement caused the young man to glance at Dmitri. Out of the corner of his eye he could see the leering smile on the older man's face.

"He made the usual promises to pay us back, and sometimes he did. We never asked how he came by the money, but in time, he exhausted his resources. His debts grew and we no longer expect to recoup the loss. Now we come to the purpose for today's walk." Dmitri again paused. He looked into the young man's eyes and lowered his voice. "There is no more money to be had from this scum, but he will be useful to us yet. Many of these people are customers of ours. They know the man we go to visit and they know of his plight. Soon they will learn of his fate and will remember seeing me here today. This type of thing will make business in this area much easier. Surely you can see that?"

"Yes of course, but what of the police. So many people know you, aren't you afraid one will come forward?"

Dmitri let out a deep throaty laugh and replied, "No one will come forward. There will be no police."

Several minutes later, they entered a drab concrete housing complex, built as only the communists could build. They climbed to the third floor. The young man's breathing became rapid as his nerves got the better of him. Dmitri seemed determined to draw out every element of their mission, as if each moment was a rare delicacy. They continued along a dimly lit corridor until they reached the right door. Dmitri nodded his head and the young man beat on the door with his fist until a reaction finally came from within.

"What do you want?"

"It is your comrade, Dmitri. We need to talk."

The doorknob turned slowly. As soon as the young man heard the bolt slip back he shoved. Yuri Popov's emaciated body sailed backward and shattered a plastic coffee table. Dmitri followed his young assistant into the room and looked down at Yuri's terrified face.

"You must forgive me, Yuri, my friend, I misspoke a moment ago. Actually we no longer need to talk, do we?" The young man closed the door and stood in front of it with his arms folded. Dmitri reached out and offered Yuri his hand. His jacket opened slightly and Yuri's eyes settled on the butt of a pistol.

Dmitri followed Yuri's gaze. He pulled his prey to his feet, but did not release his hand. "Don't be concerned with that my friend. There will be no shooting today. I only bring that along in case things get out of control. You are not going to get out of control are you, Yuri?" Dmitri's hand closed like a vice and pain registered on Yuri's face.

"No, no of course not. Please my friend, hear me out. Let me explain about the money."

"Calm yourself, Yuri. The time for explanations is over. It is all over."

With the skill and strength of an Olympic wrestler, Dmitri flung the drug addict to the floor before wrapping a thick hand around his throat. He lifted the wasted little man by the neck and slammed his back against the cinder block wall.

Death was a new sight to the young man standing by the door, and the distinction between the struggling men's expressions made him recoil. Yuri's eyes bulged with fear, while Dmitri's became to narrow slits. The condemned man desperately tried to free himself by throwing feeble punches and kicking out. Dmitri set his jaw and watched his victim's face contort; he seemed oblivious to the blows.

A wet stain spread in the crotch of Yuri's ragged denim pants. His body grew limp. Dmitri held him against the wall for a while longer, never looking away from his eyes. Plainly, any hint of life had already drained from them, but Dmitri looked on. This was, after all, the rarest of all delicacies, and he would not deny himself any of its pleasure. His jaw relaxed into a grin and his eyes regained their normal size. He opened his hand and Yuri's body crumbled to the floor.

7

Sometimes the only tolerable part of an August day in Chicago is the early morning. Carl woke in the middle of the night, turned off the air conditioner, and opened the windows. Later, as the first red rays of light reached timidly from the darkness, he began to wake again. The sweet clean smell of the summer morning made him inhale deeply and take notice. The night air left a strong, refreshing chill in the room, the kind of chill that no air conditioner could duplicate. He became aware that Gina had tucked her body in tightly to his. Not just seeking warmth, she always did this. He'd grown attached to sleeping this way, dependent on it. Another reason he sometimes had trouble sleeping at the firehouse. The cool morning made her closeness feel especially nice.

He opened his eyes a bit, squinting in the dim light. Leaning over, he gently kissed the top of his wife's ear and thought about waking her. Perhaps start the day with an intimate encounter. She looked so peaceful. His thoughts faded. He put his head back on the pillow and allowed sleep to reclaim him.

Two hours later, with the sun beating in through the windows, the temperature in the room had become uncomfortable. Gina woke first. "C'mon, lazy. Lots to do today. Let's get started."

Carl's eyes opened slowly. "I know. I'm getting up."

Tommy, as good as his word, gave Carl the day off.

They dressed in light gym wear, had some coffee, and headed to the club for a morning workout. Gina had started joining Carl in his workout routine years before, going with him whenever she could, and then going on her own on the days he went to work. It had long since been a part of their lifestyles and was largely responsible for their seemingly ageless appearances.

While working out, they tried to put together a schedule for the day. "Maybe we should make a list, Carl. There's so much to do, I know we're bound to forget something."

Carl tapped the side of his head with his forefinger. "I don't need a list, hon, it's all up here. Call the lawyer, pick up boxes, start the packing, set aside things for the garage sale. I could go on, but you can see I got it covered."

Gina felt like adding, *separate from our memories*, but kept the thought to herself.

The next several days showed them just how much a family could accumulate. Every empty space had become a storage area. Often their work stopped completely as they reminisced over a piece of their past. "We have to stop taking breaks, Gina. We're on a deadline here. Just put the photo albums in the box. We can look at them in Vegas."

A pair of rolling eyes joined the smirk. "Sure, Carl, we'll look at them in Vegas."

Gina thought it would have been nice if one of the kids could have stopped by to help sort through things, but they had busy lives of their own. Jim's work at the Board of Trade demanded so much of his time, and now he and Lori were expecting their first child. Sandy had moved to Las Vegas three years ago and had just gotten her first promotion at the Majestic. With Therese already back at school, Gina and Carl found themselves wading through an ocean of stuff alone.

"Jim said he and Lori would be by on the weekend to help with the garage sale, hon."

"I know. I talked to Lori this morning. Funny thing you ending up on that casino schedule both days."

"Yeah, that's too bad. The garage sale would have been fun."

Gina let the comment go unanswered, believing it too ridiculous to warrant any other reaction.

By Monday, the only chore remaining would be to pack the U-Haul. They would hit the road early Tuesday morning.

Carl had the twelve-foot trailer hitched to the SUV before they went to bed. Their last night, in their house of thirty years, would be spent in sleeping bags. Nothing to do in the morning but get up, shower, and leave. Easy.

Daybreak Tuesday found them standing silently on the sidewalk staring at their home. Not as easy as they thought. Carl placed his arm around Gina's shoulders. She kept her arms folded tightly as memories flooded into her head like a torrential downpour.

She looked at the freshly painted, hunter green front door, the same door Carl pushed open for her as she carried Jimmy into their home for the first time.

The top of his round little head had been all that emerged

from the blue bunting. She had snuggled him to her cheek as she crossed the threshold. A baby soft aroma filled her senses; she could smell it still. Legally, it wasn't even their house anymore. The thought brought as much anger as it did misery.

She reflected on her grandmother's stories of the farm in Italy. Generations lived on the same piece of earth, working, living, loving, dying. America, in its vastness, had always been a country of nomads. A population descended from people who couldn't sit still. They possessed a collective restlessness that compelled them to move on. Grandma had said she never wanted to leave Italy, but women had very little to say about things back then.

Gina thought she would have been more than happy to stay here forever, and found herself wishing they had never encouraged Sandy to establish a career so far away. Come to think of it, there really was no they; it was Carl's idea. She thought about Jimmy again and about the grandchild who would be coming soon. Her legs felt weak and began to tremble.

Reluctantly, Carl spoke up, "C'mon, hon, we should go."

Without turning away, Gina simply said, "I know."

Neither of them felt much like talking. The endless activity of the last several days had taken their minds off the magnitude of the changes they were making in their lives. As they separated permanently from their home, it sank in sharply.

Carl stopped for coffee. Gina drained her cup and curled up on the front seat, falling sound asleep before they reached I-80. It always amazed him how quickly she could fall asleep. Clear conscience he guessed. Carl looked over at her, brushed the hair away from her face, and considered the fact that he was bringing an innocent soul to sin city.

8

The late morning sun rose high in the sky, and a cloudless summer day unfolded. With the cruise control set at eighty, the miles flew by. The diesel engine barely noticed the twelve-foot U-haul. Carl's face reflected his pleasure; he loved this truck. It cost a small fortune, more than they had ever paid for a vehicle before, but they preferred to travel on the open road. With a cross-country trip to Nevada and plans to travel more often during their retirement, it seemed like the time to take the plunge. Passing through the Midwest provided only one sight at this time of year. Corn. Everywhere. To the left and to the right. Fields pregnant with the promising harvest as far as the eye could see. To some, this might have been monotonous, but not to Carl, not today. The sun shined bright, and nothing but newness and adventure lay ahead. The somber feelings he'd had at the start of the day evaporated with the morning dew, replaced with eagerness and expectation.

Gina woke after a couple of hours, and Carl tested her mood with a question.

"There's a little town coming up just over the Iowa border. Do you feel like stopping for something to eat?"

"Yeah, okay. I wouldn't mind going for a walk, too. I feel like a slob. We haven't been to the gym in awhile." Gina wrinkled her brow and looked out the windshield, apparently at nothing.

Carl replied, trying to sound upbeat, "I know, hon, but give yourself a break; we've been pretty busy lately. We'll get back on track once we've settled in. It's turning out to be a beautiful day, huh?"

Gina turned her head and gazed blankly at the passing corn stalks. She made no reply. Carl let it go. He figured she'd come around in time.

They got off the interstate and drove beyond a landscape cluttered with fast food restaurants and budget motels. A couple of miles up the road they found what appeared to be a quaint diner. It stood in the middle of the town's main street, and from all appearances had been there since the beginning of time. Its imaginative name was 'The Main Street Diner.' Carl turned the corner and parked on the street next to the building. Taking up two parking spots didn't seem likely to cause a problem in this town.

A few superficial attempts at cheerful decorating failed to improve the interior of the modest restaurant. Gina couldn't decide if the red, white, and blue bunting was left over from the Fourth of July, or the diner was being made ready, prematurely, for Labor Day. They sat in a booth and she got a closer look at the bunting. Dust in the folds and thin cobwebs at the top suggested that the last effort to brighten the diner had taken place at least a couple of years ago.

"Coffee, folks?" A gaunt, blue jean clad woman complete with a Marlboro behind her ear showed up at the booth, a pot in each hand, one brown rimmed, one orange rimmed.

"Yes. Thanks. We'll both have regular." Gina turned her cup right side up grateful that it appeared to be clean.

"I'll be back in a minute for your orders." Without waiting for a reply, the woman moved on to the other tables.

Gina's eyes scanned the rest of the diner. Leaning forward, she whispered, "Maybe we should have picked one of the restaurants near the highway."

Carl grinned. "C'mon, it's just a little rustic in here. The food's probably great." Gina scrunched her nose. She wasn't so sure.

Sensing that his wife might need help coming out of her sour mood, Carl came up with what he thought was a sure fire idea. "It's about 7:30 in Vegas; Sandy should be up by now. Why don't you give her a call?"

Gina's eyes remained fixed on the laminated menu. "I don't think so. I'm sure she's busy getting ready for work."

Undeterred, Carl made his next move. "Well, I wanted to talk to her for a minute before she left. Let me have your phone; I left mine in the car."

Gina dug around in her purse for a moment and then lethargically handed her cell phone to him. Realizing now what Carl had on his mind, the familiar smirk formed in the corner of her mouth. She didn't think she required any emotional boosting. She considered her mood appropriate. Still, when the small electrical device emitted its wakeup beep, her heart lightened.

Never one to memorize phone numbers, Carl scrolled through the phone's directory until he found his daughter's name, then hit 'send.' A short ring later, Sandy's excited voice made him flinch and separate the phone from his ear.

"Hi, Mom. Are you guys on your way?" The wonders of caller I.D.

"Hi, hon, this is Dad."

"Oh. Where are you?"

"We're at a little diner in Iowa. We've been driving since about 5:30 Chicago time. Listen, I wanted to know if you had a chance to pick up the extra house keys from the builder."

Gina lowered her head and smiled at this charade thinking, "Really, Carl, the extra keys. Is that all you could come up with?"

Sandy answered, a confused tone in her voice. "Not yet, Daddy. I can swing by there on my way home from work, but I thought you weren't going to be here until late on Thursday."

Rolling her eyes, Gina looked up at her husband. "Oh, Carl, give me that phone, you dufuss."

Satisfied that he had achieved his goal, Carl proudly handed over the phone.

"Hi, sweetie"

"Mom! I can't wait till you guys get here. I was at your place over the weekend. We're going to have so much fun decorating and buying furniture."

Gina's eyes brightened and her lips finally formed a smile. "I know, hon, I can't wait, either. Now about those keys… I don't know what's on your father's mind, but please don't go out of your way. We'll pick them up ourselves when we get there."

"It's no trouble, Mom. You'll have enough to do."

"Honestly, Sandy, you've done enough already. Don't listen to your father. He's only been retired for a couple of weeks, and he's already going goofy."

"Okay, Mom, if you're sure."

"Of course I'm sure. Now I'll let you go. I know you have to get ready for work. We'll see you soon."

Sandy signed off by saying, "I love you," and directed her mother to pass along a kiss to her "goofy" father.

It only took Carl a few minutes to see the little restaurant in the same light as his wife, so expecting disappointment if they ordered anything in the least bit elaborate, they decided on oatmeal and grapefruit. The waitress seemed insulted. She jotted down the unusual request, and looking over the top of her pad, made a quick assessment of her customers. In mock exasperation, she turned and mumbled under her breath, "City people...should've stopped near the highway." Fifteen minutes later, they gladly left the diner.

"Do you still feel like going for a walk?" Carl asked.

"No, I guess not. Let's go a couple hundred more miles, then we can stop for a good long walk."

The tone in Gina's voice had become easy and pleasant. With sights set on the future and at least momentarily off the past, Carl knew they were on the same page at last.

Gina leaned over and kissed Carl hard on the cheek. "Sandy wanted me to give you a kiss."

Carl faced his wife. "No kidding? That one felt like it came from you."

9

As Dmitri had expected, business flowed with less difficulty than usual in the months that followed Yuri's 'passing.' Cash flowed in and he spent it with pride, flaunting his newfound wealth. Gold hung from his neck and rubies glistened on his fingers.

In time, however, the spike in his income began to abate. Any business could be like that, whether illicit or legitimate. A wise businessman, with a mind for the future, knew this and prepared for it. Dmitri may have been many things, but no one ever accused him of being a wise businessman.

Intelligent in his way, and coupled with an infamous ruthless streak, he managed to avoid any serious problems in life. That was about to change. Dmitri liked his new lifestyle, thought he earned it, and deserved it. When business dropped off, he proved unwilling to alter his habits. He opted instead to diminish the tribute he sent to the leaders of his organization. After all, he thought, I am the one who is doing the work and taking the risks.

Fluctuations in the tribute were expected from time to time, but in Dmitri's case, the word fluctuation did not apply. The amount merely dropped from one week to the next. The leadership looked into this disturbing situation and demanded an explanation.

Dmitri had long been a valuable member of the organization. Before he took on the narcotics end of the business, he ran the organization's gambling and prostitution interests. He always managed to show a healthy profit, so the organization felt it in their interest to accept his explanations. Weeks later, Dmitri provided another collection of excuses. Though the excuses seemed thin, they agreed that he would be given a little more time.

When no improvement seemed forthcoming, Dmitri received a third summons. As with Yuri, the time for explanations had passed. A replacement had already been selected. When the summons came, Dmitri understood the gravity of his situation.

His thoughts turned quickly to his brother, a wealthy and powerful man living in America. He had been trying to convince Dmitri to join him in his business. Dmitri knew he couldn't simply flee to America. He would never get out alive, unless he had the blessing of the organization. To get this blessing, he would have to show them that their investment in him still made sense, that he could establish an interest for them in America and repay his debts with the valuable American dollar.

Dmitri sat bolt upright, across from a cold steel desk, flanked on each side by men every bit as physically capable as himself. The office, nothing more than a glass-enclosed cubicle, overlooked a warehouse floor.

The warehouse workers took a break from their chores

and watched in anticipation as Dmitri was led into the office. He wasn't the first to be taken to the boss. The men sensed they might be in store for another show.

Dmitri came to the meeting confident that he still had room to redeem himself. He faced a brutal, single-minded man, but with the substantial numbers he intended to propose, he knew they would give him a chance. If it had been decided conclusively to remove him, he would have been executed without fanfare by some anonymous assassin.

The leader of the St. Petersburg organization, though similar to Dmitri in many ways, would never be described as a thug. Wearing a neatly trimmed beard and impeccable clothes, he rarely dirtied his hands on men like Dmitri. As young and aggressive as the fledgling organized crime world that he helped establish, he garnered respect and fear from all. In the post-communist environment, the spoils went to those who could think fast and act fast. When an opportunity presented itself, decisiveness counted most, and the young leader never failed to act decisively.

He looked at Dmitri with harsh eyes, but spoke as calmly as a judge. "Dmitri, you have let me down. You are so far behind in your payments that I can think of no way out for you."

Dmitri opened his mouth to speak. The man refused to be interrupted, and held up a hand. Dmitri remained silent.

"You understand that you can still be of use to me in another respect. You have long been one of my favorites. I had such hopes for you, everyone knew this. For that reason, if we use a firm hand in your case, the others will be so impressed that I doubt we would have this kind of problem again. Surely you can appreciate this, can't you?"

The man on Dmitri's right slipped behind him. Dmitri watched his reflection in the glass as he pulled a thin wire from his pocket and twisted the length between his hands.

Like a pack of hungry jackals, the workers crowded outside the office, craning their necks and pushing forward to gain a better view. The tension building, they fed off each other's excitement. It seemed they were in store for a show after all.

Things moved faster than Dmitri had expected. He had to speak up before his time ran out. He acknowledged the irony of his boss's words, but he was not Yuri. He had a well thought out plan, to not only make up the deficiency, but to set up a source of income that would grow and last. If unable to present his ideas, none of that would matter.

He took a quick glance at the jackals and understood the purpose of this meeting at once. They intended to make his execution a public display. His confidence plummeted and sweat began to soak through his shirt.

The reflection showed a pair of hands rising, the wire coiled tightly between them. Dmitri's eyes grew wide and he blurted out, "I have been in contact with my brother. He wants me to join him in America. Please hear me out. There is still much to be gained." His leader held up a hand once again but this time not to silence his guest. Dmitri watched in the glass as the hands lowered.

A frustrated look came to the busy man's face. He had hoped to take care of this situation without delay, but could not ignore an opportunity. "I remember your brother. It has been a long time. A KGB Agent, correct? What sort of business is he involved in?"

The boss stroked his beard and listened to the plan with interest. Dmitri continued to sweat, but he presented his ideas with as much conviction as he could gather. When finished, he clutched the edges of the desk and gazed intently at the person who would determine his fate.

The dire man before him sat still for what seemed an eternity and then slowly started to nod his head. He liked what he heard. Clearly, Dmitri could still be of value to him. Dmitri wiped his brow and began to breathe again. He watched as the man in the reflection rolled up the wire and put it away, no doubt to be used in the future on some other hapless victim. One by one, the disappointed jackals dispersed.

Dmitri nodded silently as he accepted the terms and the repercussions if he failed to meet them. The timetable given left little room for error. Deception would be impossible. The boss didn't need to point out that America's distance would provide him with no shelter. Finally, the discussion came to an end, and with the approval and assistance of the organization, Dmitri would join his brother in America.

10

They wanted to make it to Nebraska on the first day. Carl knew that he would have to turn the wheel over to Gina at some point. She wasn't necessarily a bad driver, but he considered this vehicle his baby. Oh, what the hell, he thought. He supposed a lonely stretch of mid-western highway would be safe enough. He could get a little rest and then take over again. He made a mental note to get a car for Gina ASAP.

They spent the next hour in light conversation, mostly thoughts on furniture and decorating. Carl feigned interest, but planned to leave those decisions to Gina and Sandy. All they brought from Chicago had either been packed in the Excursion or the trailer. Their fresh start would be almost complete.

During a lull in the conversation, Gina reached for her book. Sentimental and romantic stuff. Carl used to tease her about her taste in literature. One day she informed him that she needed to find romance somewhere. He knew he lacked a little in that department, but in his defense, he pointed out that as a man he had difficulty thinking like a woman. She shot him the smirk. Carl thought that perhaps it would be okay if she rounded out her romantic needs this way and decided that in the future he would confine his teasing to other subjects. With her legs pulled up and the seat tilted back, it wasn't long before the book fell from her hand, and she slipped off for a late morning nap.

The road stretched out like an endless black ribbon. Heat rose from the pavement in gently undulating ripples. What looked like pockets of water appeared and disappeared with each subtle rise and fall of the ribbon? Carl's thoughts meandered, and the car seemed to drive itself.

As usual, they showed up gradually, and before long a panorama of faces had filled the relaxed emptiness of Carl's thoughts. Each one an individual, yet all alike. Young and frowning, eyes wide, fearful, silently pleading. He closed his eyes and shook his head, trying to chase them away. They refused to leave. Unable to escape from his own mind, Carl had no choice but to follow along.

One face stood out from the many. He found himself in a familiar place in another time. The first warm day of spring, early April over twenty-five years ago. The city rebelled against the oppression of a long and unusually cold winter. The streets burst with activity as everyone embraced the suggestion of summer.

Soft blonde hair with dark blue eyes, only nine years old, thin and barefoot her clothes, dirty. He didn't know if it was because of the accident or because she had been playing outside all day.

It happened not far from the firehouse. Carl's engine took in the run along with the ambulance. They arrived simultaneously. He had been on the fire department only three or four years, but had already built up his emotional defenses. How could one function otherwise?

She lay near the curb in an unnatural position.

Assessment of the incident began even before the men exited their rigs. A quick survey of the scene provided an array of vivid, if incomplete data. She was on the street but against the curb. No skid marks could be seen. Blood streaked her small frame in several places. Her left foot twisted behind her back, her dislocated right arm wrapped around her neck.

Carl went to the little girl while the ambulance crew retrieved their stretcher. "What happened?"

An answer sprang from the crowd. "A bunch of them was running across the street. She was the last and got hit by a motorcycle. He was really flying. How could he drive like that with all these kids around? He must have knocked her about a hundred feet, she rolled forever."

Road rash stretched from her forehead, to her chin. Her right eye had swollen shut, but her left eye remained open. Her legs were broken in many places and blood seeped from both ears. Carl knew they couldn't stop that kind of bleeding. The paramedics immobilized her with a backboard and c-collar and wheeled her to the ambulance. Carl went along in the ambulance to help the two-man crew as much as possible.

Her breaths came in short, rapid gasps. The heart monitor indicated a rate of 120, but Carl couldn't feel a pulse anywhere. They started an I.V., and began the race to the trauma center. Even though the ambulance rocked violently from side to side, Carl managed to start a second line, both now running wide open. Surely they were replacing fluid as fast as she could lose it. Her breathing became a useless gulping motion. The monitor showed a pulse rate of 80 and falling. "Shit," Carl uttered. "I'm gonna start compressions."

The flow of blood from her ears increased with each compression and became thin and watery. He figured her spinal fluid had to be gone already and grimaced, realizing she had nothing left to bleed but I.V. fluids.

They used an ambu-bag and mask to aid respirations. The heart monitor showed asystole, flat line. Doing chest compressions with one hand, Carl helped them wheel the little blonde-haired girl into the hospital. They made their report, and turned her over to the nurses and doctors.

The medics cleaned and restocked the ambulance, making it ready for the next run. They left the hospital and that was it. Carl never heard another word about her. Never learned for sure of her fate, although he knew of only one possible outcome. He wondered briefly how her family would react. Would they be able to recover from this devastation? How would he cope if that were his child? Without much effort, he turned his thoughts in a different direction. He still had that ability.

He knew no good could come from following that line of mental pursuit. Carl spent maybe ten or twelve minutes with the little blonde-haired girl on that April morning long ago, then turned away and left. He didn't realize it at the time, but she never did leave him.

Her face rejoined the others in the panorama, and the ribbon of road reappeared. The sun, now high overhead, beat down unchecked. The corn seemed to bend away from the heat in silent objection. A gauge on the dashboard read 92 degrees, the temperature inside a comfortable 68. To look at Carl you would have never guessed; his brow dripped with sweat.

With his thoughts no longer relaxed, Carl considered a number of questions for the first time. *Why do these visions pursue me and will they ever relent? Are others visited in the same way? Perhaps some of the guys from my own firehouse.* If so, he knew they would never discuss the issue, just as he never would himself.

Carl understood that bad runs, like the one involving that little girl, had to be absorbed by the people sent to rescue her. They seldom discussed the incidents after the run ended. Perhaps the technical aspects might be reviewed, certainly never the emotional aspects. It wasn't affected bravado that led to this behavior. These guys really were tough, hard as nails when they had to be. They had no choice. Emotion could only be counterproductive to the efforts of those sent to perform a grim task. Emotion had no place in their world. Absorb it and move on. The next one was always just around the corner. Several, at times dozens, on each draining twenty-four hour shift. He wondered how large a man's capacity for this work could be.

Carl told himself that 'this work' was a thing of the past for him. He tried to convince himself that with a new life and a new start his mind would eventually clear itself of these scars.

He looked at his sleeping wife, content, peaceful, safe. He could ask for nothing more. They had shared their lives together, but he never shared the realities of his occupation with her, and never would. He couldn't imagine burdening her with the torments of his professional life. But more than that, he liked coming home to the cheerfulness she provided. He didn't want to poison that by exposing her to the horrors that took place just a few short miles from her orderly piece of the world.

"My God, Carl, it's already after one. I'm all slept out. I guess I was more tired than I thought." Gina rubbed the sleep from her eyes and informed her husband that he looked tired. "Let's stop at the next town and stretch out a little."

"Okay, hon. I could use something to eat, too. That wasn't much of a breakfast."

She straightened her seat and slipped her sandals on. "Sounds good to me. Are you going to let me do a little driving after lunch?"

Carl winched at the thought, but replied that he *guessed* he could use a break for a couple of hours.

11

Tuesday gave way to Wednesday. The miles passed, and eventually the cornfields passed from the landscape. With the mid-west behind them now, the mountains became visible through the mist of distance. Carl stared at them, numbed by their grandeur. Mountains on the horizon were a rare sight for a mid-western boy. He wondered if small town people were as impressed when Chicago's skyline came into view. The skyline might have been impressive, but to him the sight had grown common. He believed the mountains would never grow commonplace in his eyes.

One more motel, one more day of driving, and they would be home.

Hoping to break up the hours, they initially planned the trip to include occasional stops for sightseeing, but the sightseeing stops never materialized. Gina would have been willing, but didn't want to push the issue. Carl seemed open to the idea at first, but as Gina guessed, before long the trip evolved into a job. Not arduous and stressful, but a task nonetheless. Any job worth doing was worth doing right, and to Carl that meant efficiency and time management. Stopping now would be frivolous and would only serve to extend the job. Being retired meant they would have plenty of time for touring the country. Getting settled in had to be accomplished first.

Gina didn't really mind. They would arrive in Vegas hours earlier than originally planned, early afternoon instead of late evening. That meant a more relaxed first night. So why should she care? Carl did most of the driving anyway. She accepted that looking out the window would have to satisfy her sightseeing needs for now. As they progressed further from the world she had spent her whole life in, looking out the window did provide quite a spectacle.

Carl spoke with the enthusiasm of a child. "We're almost in the mountains, hon. I've felt like a tourist since we left Chicago. Isn't this great?"

Gina slapped the paperback to her lap. Carl had let his guard down, and she wasn't going to let the opportunity pass. "A tourist? Really? Maybe you should write a book: 'How to See America at Eighty Miles an Hour'."

A ridiculous look sprang to Carl's face. Unable to hide his confusion, he asked. "What do you mean? We could have stopped any time you wanted."

"Oh, please. Who do you think you're talking to, some stranger off the street? Once you got into that 'hell bent for leather' mood of yours, I knew any real sightseeing was out of the question."

Hell bent for leather? The ridiculous expression remained, and he realized he had to defend himself. "Hey, all you had to do was speak up; I'm not a mind reader you know. I'll do anything you ask me to. How about I turn around at the next exit? We'll go back and see whatever you want."

Not certain whether she was pulling his leg or not, when she reached over and, with a smile, squeezed his hand, Carl knew he was okay. "No, I don't think that will be necessary. You can parade me around America some other time. I'm anxious to get settled in myself."

After a minute of silence, Gina again turned to her husband, this time squinting her eyes, and using the most authoritative tone she could manage. At one time she had used this tone exclusively on her fourth grade students; it always left them searching for the right answers. If employed properly, it got Carl to scramble the same way.

"I would like you to answer one question, though. What happened to you last night?"

Bewildered, Carl's eyes moved back and forth as if he thought he would find an explanation to this question written on the windshield. "What do you mean, last night?"

Gina reopened her book and searched for the right page. She let his question hang in the air for a minute, an impish grin forming on her lips. She glanced up at him and answered his question with a statement. "Well, I can remember a time when you would get me into a strange motel room and do more than just sleep like a stone."

She had him hooked and now hoped she could reel him in. He struggled to defend his manhood. The fact that she had him on the defensive again, for the second time in just a few minutes, amused her to no end.

"Sorry, hon. It was a long day. We were up before dawn, you know."

Without sympathy she said, "I was up, too."

"Yeah, but you slept a lot during the day."

Gina felt a twinge of guilt for amusing herself at his

expense, but didn't let that stop her. A little guilt wasn't going to make her give up her fun.

"I'm just saying that if you find yourself too tired at night, maybe you should take naps in the afternoon or try 'Geritol' or something."

"Geritol? Are you kidding me? Look, you do realize that we're gonna be in a strange motel room again tonight."

She bit down on her lower lip, doing her best to keep from laughing, "I know, but be careful. You don't want to make any promises you can't keep."

Carl didn't think responding would get him anywhere. His wife was in the mood to amuse herself, and he figured it would be best to let it run its course.

She let out a muffled laugh at his silent surrender, and poking him in the ribs, tried to get him to re-enter the fray. Her efforts did nothing more than bring a cynical smile to his face. Knowing the game was over, she turned back to her book. He knew that while she had been playing with him, she also wanted him to get the message. As if to punctuate the encounter, she finished by posing a question. "Where do you plan on stopping tonight, Blue Eyes?"

Carl cleared his throat and responded without conviction. "I thought maybe a couple of hours past Denver."

They hit the road at 5:30 the next morning, excited to be only eight hours away from their new home and being close to Sandy again.

Carl doubted he could have convinced Gina to make the move to Las Vegas if at least one of the kids hadn't been there already. For years it had been his plan to retire to Vegas. With that in mind, he encouraged his oldest daughter to seek a career in America's fastest growing city. Good employment and the opportunity for professional advancement would be plentiful. Sandy took the idea to heart, and the cornerstone of his plan was laid.

It wasn't easy to leave Jim and Lori. Especially with a baby on the way.

Their first grandchild no less, but when they announced their plans to move, Gina quickly pointed out that she planned on visiting often and would come back to help when the baby came. With the offer readily accepted, and the due date only a month away, Gina's first stay in Vegas promised to be a short one. Sandy planned to ensure that it would also be a busy one, the second child, but the first daughter. It wasn't until she graduated from college and began her career that she and Gina became friends. From her earliest teenage years, she'd resisted any guidance or direction from her mother. The frequent fights never really became heated, but they had served to keep each of the combatants on edge for years.

The basic cause of this seemingly endless clash was obvious to Carl, the outside observer. They were like two peas in a pod. Cut from the same mold. Both pretty, vivacious, and independent. Sandy's eyes and hair were almost as dark as her mother's. Her siblings favored their father in appearance. Jim stood even taller than his father and Therese, the baby of the family, had grown taller than her sister and mother before she had finished her freshman year of high school.

Sandy not only shared her mother's slight build, but had

also inherited Gina's restless determination and energy, the kind of energy that others could rarely keep up with. Numerous attempts to point out these similarities in personality only earned Carl a barrage of smirks, and rolled eyes.

Abandoning his peace-making efforts, he stood by and let time do the job for him. From the years of struggle, affection and a sense of kinship had grown between Gina and Sandy. Their attachment to each other had solidified like well-cured concrete. Now that Sandy had established herself in the professional world, her relationship with her mother had reached a new level.

Sandy made enough plans to fill her mother's time indefinitely. Of course Carl would be welcome to join them, and Sandy might even have been naïve enough to think he would, but Gina knew better.

While Gina would miss any one of her children if one left the fold, an old adage she first heard as a young mother proved to be true, "If you have a son, you have a son until he has a wife. If you have a daughter, you have a daughter for life." Over the years, as she watched her children grow and develop, she considered these words a number of times, and sure enough things seemed to be playing out that way. Now if she could just lure Therese out here in a couple of years, things would just about be perfect.

Three o'clock in the afternoon found them turning the corner into a yet to be completed subdivision on the edge of Las Vegas, the streets freshly paved, not a pothole or patch job in sight. Every house gleamed with new siding, not a sign of peeling paint to blemish the appearance. No driveways stained by oil leaked from an old and neglected car, and just the sight of the palm trees had Carl wide eyed. Though young and recently planted, each one burst open at the top, green and full of life. The Braun's new home had been built on a corner lot, about a half mile in from any major streets. Carl insisted on a corner lot. After so many years in a crowded Chicago neighborhood, he wanted to be sure his new house came with a feeling of openness. Though rather upscale, the neighborhood appeared too inviting to be considered snobbish. The rules required large lots, red tiled roofs, and attached garages that couldn't face the street. This made backing in the trailer a little tricky.

While Carl put the SUV in reverse and considered how to navigate the challenge, Gina snatched the house keys from the glove compartment and headed up the walkway. With the car still half on the street, Carl pushed the gearshift to 'park' and dashed to meet his wife before she could unlock the door.

Glancing over her shoulder, Gina shot a smile at her husband, turned the key, and pushed. The air conditioner worked overtime on the 115-degree day, and a blast of cool air immediately carried to them the aromas of newness, of fresh paint, carpet, and woodwork. Carl wrapped his right arm around Gina's waist and stooped quickly to slip his left arm behind her knees. He swept her up before she knew what he was doing.

Kissing her as he stepped across the threshold, he reminded her that he had missed his chance to affect this traditional 'first entry' thirty years ago. He didn't know if he would ever get another chance.

He plopped his wife back to her feet, slapped her on the bottom, and told her he would be back in as soon as he unhitched the trailer.

Gina closed the front door, amused at her husband's rare display of playfulness.

She explored the completed tri-level house for the first time. The front door opened into a large living room/dining room area with vaulted ceilings, skylights and a real wood-burning fireplace, artificial logs and a gas flame just didn't do it for Carl. A few steps down to the right led to a family room. A flight of stairs rose from the left of the living room area to the bedrooms. Only a walled partition between the kitchen and the rest of the house broke the open floor plan. A pass between, adorned with maple louvered doors, provided access to the dining area from the kitchen. Gina loved this architectural detail. Almost unheard of in a Chicago bungalow, it had been added to the building plans under her specific instructions. The master suite ran the entire length of the back of the house. They still hadn't decided what they wanted to do with the other two bedrooms.

Gina went into the kitchen and found some keys and a note on the beveled granite counter top. "Hi, guys, I picked up your keys on my way home tonight and set the air conditioner so you won't roast when you get here. Give me a call when you get in and I'll bring over some Chinese food or something. Love ya, Sandy."

A dial tone confirmed that they had phone service. She punched in Sandy's cell phone number and waited. After three rings, the familiar sound of her daughter's voice popped through the earpiece.

"Hi, Mom."

"Hi, honey. Well, we're here. I got the note you left last night, and I see you picked up the other set of keys for us. Thanks."

"Oh, no problem, Mom. When did you get in?"

"Just a few minutes ago. Dad's still backing in the trailer."

"Okay. Well, I can leave in about an hour. I'll pick up some dinner for us and help you guys unpack. How does Chinese sound?"

Gina sighed in appreciation. "Honey, that would be great. We brought a bottle of champagne from Chicago. I'll open it when you get here."

Sandy suggested, "One might not be enough for an occasion like this, Mom. I'll pick up another bottle."

Gina agreed, "I'm sure you're right. You're father already seems a little giddy, though."

Sandy chuckled. "Well he should be. I'm excited, too. Oh, and tell him that I spoke to the manager of the Poker room again. She said she'd be happy to give him a job interview."

"Okay, honey, I'll tell him. See you in a little while."

Gina hung up, leaned against the counter, and losing herself in thought, surveyed her new house. She flushed from a wave of satisfaction as Carl stepped in and called out her name.

12

Gina called out to her husband. "I'm in the kitchen, hon. What took you so long? I've already been all through the house and talked to Sandy on the phone."

Carl walked into the room with a box under his arm and a bottle in his hand. "I wanted to get something from the trailer." Opening the box, Carl pulled out two champagne flutes. "Remember these?" He held up the crystal glasses, etched with the date of their wedding. Gina used to take them out on their anniversary. It had been years since she'd seen them, and she didn't think Carl even knew they existed anymore.

"Let's open this up and celebrate," he said, holding the bottle toward her, label first as if for her approval. "Oh, Carl, I already told Sandy we would wait till she got here before we opened the bottle. She's coming over with some dinner in about an hour."

Carl shrugged off this resistance. "Well, I'm sure she won't mind if we have the first glass by ourselves." He leaned over the sink and wrested the plastic cork from the bottle. It opened with a familiar pop, and Carl poured quickly before the wine had a chance to bubble over.

"C'mon, hon, we can sit on the carpeting in here and relax for a little while." He headed for the living room and sat with his back against the wall; Gina knelt facing him. He lifted his glass and made a simple toast. "To our new home and our new lives." She touched the rim of her glass to his and they drank.

"You know, hon, kneeling there in those tight jeans makes you look like you did twenty years ago."

Gina scrunched her nose and smiled like a schoolgirl. "Well, thanks for the compliment, but after three days on the road, I sure don't feel like I did twenty years ago. I feel strung out and worn." Not seeming to have heard his wife's remark, Carl drained his glass and watched with expectation as she emptied hers. He took her glass and set it along with his own on the sill of the bay window.

Gina grinned in anticipation as he moved closer and wrapped his arms around her. He kissed her with more fervor than she expected and in one smooth motion eased her onto her back. She offered no resistance, but in hushed tones made a half hearted objection.

"Carl, its broad daylight and there aren't any curtains up yet." She breathed heavily.

He whispered a response, being careful not to derail the building passion. "Honey, most of the lots around here are still empty; there's no one around."

Wanting to give in, but needing to feel comfortable, she had to confirm her husband's words before letting herself go. As his caresses became more intense, she rose on one elbow to look out the window. Now kissing the side of her neck and working to unbutton her blouse, Carl followed his wife's gaze.

A bright red Mustang GT convertible came to a stop at the curb in front of their house. Sandy, all smiles, sprang from the car, then bent to retrieve a white paper bag and a bottle from the back seat.

Scooting away from the window and from her frustrated lover, Gina hurried to her feet, trying to regain her composure.

Looking dejected, with an ironic twist on his lips, Carl mumbled, "I thought you said she wouldn't be here for an hour."

Gina finished tucking in her shirt and still a little breathless, responded. "I guess time flies when you're having fun. Besides, you poked around in that trailer for so long, who knows how much time went by." Then added, "Although, now I do feel twenty years younger. How long has it been since one of the kids walked in on us?"

Gina looked down at him with an expression that promised this session wasn't over, only delayed. Recognizing this and, without words, accepting the promise, Carl joined his wife at the front door. Still finding it difficult to break away from her, he put his arm around her shoulder as they welcomed their daughter.

"Well, don't you two look cozy?" Sandy came in, kissed her father, and hugged her mother. "C'mon, let's eat this stuff while it's still hot. It's from Moy's, a cafe in the hotel. I had them bring it over to my office. They got there just as I finished up–perfect timing."

Carl glanced over at Gina and agreed. "Yeah, perfect timing."

Gina elbowed him in the side, and informed them that she had sold all their everyday dinnerware at the garage sale.

"I'll go out to the trailer and dig out the china. We can eat in style." Carl started for the door and heard his wife express her doubts about the 'style' they would be eating in.

"That'll be nice, but we still have to stand at the counter while we eat."

Sandy looked around the empty house and realized with a grin how much shopping had to be done to furnish the place. "Listen, Mom, I'm off this weekend. If you can hold out 'til then, we can spend two days shopping and decorating. Most places deliver pretty fast. By the end of next week things should be comfortable around here."

Gina nodded, agreeing with the plan. "That's fine, hon. I just want to lie around tomorrow anyway. It shouldn't take long to finish unpacking the trailer. Then it'll be nothing but 'R and R' for the rest of the day."

The women chatted through dinner and later only occasionally stopped to help Carl unpack the trailer. They rarely called on him to join in the conversation. He didn't mind, it pleased him to see his wife and daughter enjoying each other's company so much. As he carried in one thing after another, his thoughts wandered elsewhere. He found himself feeling anxious to get something started at the Majestic. He wanted to keep his mind occupied, maybe even distracted. Left to its own devices, it always seemed to take him to the same place.

Working robot-like to set up the few things they brought from Chicago, Carl considered his brain's tendency to revisit his past. Consciously reviewing his career, he remembered a number of children who survived, almost miraculously, as a direct result of his skill and efforts. All too often though, he had witnessed tragic results. Still he did his best. He should have no reason to feel burdened, but he sensed a growing weight on his soul and it humbled him.

He worked quietly, only bothering the girls from time to time if he needed an extra hand. By late evening, he had moved the last box, leaving the trailer empty. Gina and Sandy finished the champagne while watching the sun slip behind the mountains. French doors off the kitchen led to a west-facing deck. They leaned on the railing, glasses in hand, and allowed themselves to be awed by the sight.

Before Sandy left, Carl told her he would stop by the hotel tomorrow and see about the interview. She tried to remind him that he was retired now and should take some time off. Carl smiled at this, kissed her goodbye, and said, "See you tomorrow, Sweetie, late morning."

Gina came to him and asked suspiciously why he had been so quiet all night. Carl brushed off the inquiry, "Somebody had to work while you two drank all the champagne. I don't think I could have gotten a word in anyway."

Not willing to be put off so easily, she watched his face closely and suggested they didn't have to put everything away on their first night. "We have all day tomorrow, Carl, what's the hurry?" He looked back blankly, and replied that he wanted to get the trailer out of the driveway and swing by the Majestic to set up that interview tomorrow.

Gina thought, "Already!"

Sensing that he didn't want to talk about it, she merely replied by asking if it would be okay with him if she slept in tomorrow morning.

He saw the look of surprise on her face when he told her of his plans for the next day and knew that she cut him some slack. Her understanding made him smile and he said, "Honey, you can sleep in every morning from now on. Maybe I'll even bring you a little surprise when I come home."

She reached out, placed her hands on his hips, and taunted him. "So you think you can buy me with gifts, huh?" Carl smiled and let her question go unanswered.

Sleep came fitfully to him that first night. More like a series of short naps with bouts of tossing and turning in between. He fought to resist his own thoughts. Finally, when the first glimmer of morning crept in through the un-shaded window, he gave up.

He made his way to the kitchen in darkness, thankful Gina hadn't sold the coffee maker. Minutes later, he took a seat on the small front porch, a hot mug of coffee in hand, anticipating the sunrise.

As the brilliant colors flared over the desert, he realized just how fatigued his restless night had left him. The coffee, although strong, wasn't having its intended effect. He emptied the first cup and returned to the porch with a second. Too drained to resist his own thoughts any longer, he found himself drawn, once again, to a forgotten time.

Late afternoon, summer. A car, red mid-sized, stopped in the middle of a residential street. All four doors opened and both windows on the passenger side shattered. Tiny cubes of safety glass strewn about the asphalt. No apparent damage to the rest of the car. The inevitable crowd gathered, mostly standing on the sidewalk or near the curb. A young woman, so skinny she looked unhealthy, stood nearest to the car. In hysterics and inconsolable, she shrieked, "In the backseat, she's in the backseat. Can't you run?"

Feeling the intensity of the crowd's emotion, Carl reached the car and raised his voice. "What happened?"

A woman, only slightly less hysterical than the skinny one, shouted back, "They shot her, they shot her! We was all in the car. I was drivin', and some gang bangers just started shootin' at us. She was sitting on her mama's lap; we was all afraid to touch her."

He looked into the backseat, and there, face down on the floor in a pool of blood, lay a little girl, dressed in a bright orange jumper. Carl gently reached down and picked her up. Someone had braided her baby short hair into several tight pigtails, each one adorned with a number of brightly colored beads.

She would have looked like a precious doll if not for the ugly holes in either side of her forehead. Blood had soaked into her pigtails and stained her beads. It seeped steadily from both holes, more from the exit wound than from the entrance wound. It hadn't started to run onto the orange jumper until Carl lifted her from the car and turned her upright. Her eyes snapped open, startling Carl. He saw they still had life in them and was surprised to find a strong, regular pulse.

The ambulance arrived. As the bystanders caught site of the child, most began shouting and screaming, men and women alike. One of the paramedics opened the door to the ambulance, and Carl carried the baby inside, laying her carefully on the stretcher. The child's situation seemed desperate, so Carl again rode along to the trauma center to assist in anyway he could. Even though she was very small, they managed to start an I.V. Her pulse remained strong throughout the ride; she didn't have any trouble breathing. Carl couldn't remember if her pupils had dilated or not, or if the tissue that bulged from her wounds was brain matter or just flesh from her scalp.

With the short ride to the hospital over, his connection to this child ended. In the aftermath of the run, he wondered how the child's mother could have fled the car, leaving her baby behind alone and bleeding. He wondered why she hadn't gone to her and held her after the gang bangers left. He found these troubling thoughts quickly pushed from his mind as his attention turned to the next run.

He never found out what became of the precious doll with the brightly colored beads in her hair. He never heard of her again. She became another of the innocents, unprotected and victimized by mindless violence. A life disrupted, possibly stripped away entirely. Remembered by whom? Missed by whom? The news media never said a word about her. For one reason or another, Carl remembered her again, after all these years. She became his, one of his own, one of many.

The sun, now fully above the desert landscape, made him blink and shield his eyes. He realized that his coffee had become as cool as the morning air. Just as well. Utterly exhausted now, he left the cup on the porch and returned to bed. He had just enough energy to hang a large bath towel over the brightest window before collapsing onto the mattress.

Gina felt her husband return to bed and instinctively moved her body against his.

13

Still rising before his wife, Carl went to the kitchen and found that the coffee maker had yet to shut itself off. Couldn't have slept too long, he thought. Retrieving his cup from the porch and refilling it, he quietly began making himself ready for his day. Drop off the trailer, go to the Majestic, don't forget to bring a resume, pick out a house-warming gift for Gina. He should be back by early afternoon.

Having disposed of the U-Haul without incident, Carl headed for the Strip. The mammoth resort hotels grew closer. He felt like a kid on Christmas Day, and had to continually check his speed as his impatient nature pushed him to go faster than the posted limits allowed.

He and Gina had been coming out here on their anniversary for the last several years, and prior to each visit, his sense of anticipation grew. Years ago he knew that one day he wanted to live near this constant stimulation and action, twenty-four hour action. A schedule, which thanks to decades on the fire department, his body would always keep.

He never spoke about it with Gina but knew he would never be able to live a sedate retirement. There would be no peace, couldn't be. His change wasn't going to be that complete. There would be no more fires or medical emergencies to get his pulse racing, but the energy of Las Vegas would fill the void. He felt it, knew it. Only now, the stimulation would be different. Excitement generated by the turn of a card, the passing of fortune, the thrill of the game. He could grasp the sensation; to him it was palpable. He felt it in this town whether in a casino or out on the street. Vegas generated what he needed most, and now he could soak it up. No more victims. No more horrors.

Chicago had a world-class tempo of its own, but that town was ruined for him. It had let him down, betrayed him like an unfaithful woman. He had spent too many years toiling in the misery of its underworld. The neglect and despair left him with a sour taste in his mouth. Chicago had missed every chance he gave it at redemption. He had finally placed himself where he wanted to be, and the time had come to fill his mind with new memories.

Dealing poker would be his primary contact with the action, but he would still play at the tables. Usually poker, perhaps sometimes less mentally challenging games like craps or blackjack. He needed to be part of the action. It had been his goal all along, the reason he went to dealer school and worked at the Triple Seven in Joliet. He wanted to be an insider in this town built on outsiders.

The air still fairly cool, he crept along the Strip with the windows down, to more efficiently immerse himself in the environment.

Each edifice appeared to reach out, groping at all who passed by. Tempting, luring, trying to stand out from the others, pushing their own version of the same fantasy. They held the promise of excitement and satisfaction to any who dared enter. In the morning, laid bare by sunlight and sobriety, the Strip's true identity could be seen, but only by those who wanted to see it. Carl grinned to himself, realizing that he had entered the world's largest red light district.

Allowing yourself to be blinded by the dazzle and brilliance was for others, for tourists, conventioneers, gamblers. Carl had no interest in being lost in it. He kept his eyes wide open, he planned to be a part of it.

He turned onto the Majestic's access road well before the hotel itself, at least by the standards of an ordinary city. The grand cobblestone drive stretched out for half a mile on either side of the gilded entrance to what was arguably Las Vegas's most impressive resort.

Sloping through two square miles of land from the entrance to the sidewalk was a creation conceived by a team of the world's most noted landscape architects. Numerous gardens, themed from exotic locations around the globe, linked together by a winding path laid with the same cobblestones as the drive. An enchanting floral scent permeated the breeze and drifted throughout the property.

On the hot, arid days of summer, a cool fine mist wafting down from spouts hidden throughout the garden refreshed visitors. Cupolas and a few small cafes had been strategically placed along the pathways. After all, even a walk through paradise could be improved with the drink of your choice, available for a small price.

The building itself had become one of the most pursued tourist attractions in town. Camera toting crowds stood at the stone railing surrounding the property and snapped pictures without end. The spectacle they pursued cost over two billion dollars to construct.

It stood forty-two stories tall, with three giant wings holding over three-thousand luxury rooms and suites. Two of the wings stretched north and south along the drive with the third reaching west toward the mountains. Designed to resemble a traditional country manor house, the bottom third of the building was constructed of various colored fieldstones, the upper portion of red and yellow brick, enhanced by architectural detail not used in a century. A mansard roof topped the building with dormers protruding at regular intervals to provide an unmatched view for occupants of the most lavish suites.

As always, Carl shunned the idea of valet parking. He located a safe, distant spot in the vast underground lot. With the car's security system set, he made his ascent to the casino.

Years of research went into the art of stimulating casino patrons from the second they passed through the front doors. Carl loved the rush it gave him and was glad those anonymous marketing geniuses knew what they were doing. With a tuxedoed doorman eagerly opening the door for him, he entered.

This was the reason he came to Vegas. He paused for a moment to take it in. He had stepped onto a casino floor countless times, but each time seemed like the first. Every human sense bombarded from every direction: color and sound, lights glittering, slot machines simultaneously purring and clanging, shouts from the craps tables, moans from the blackjack pit. Tantalizing cocktail waitresses, each one more stunning than the last, paraded to and fro in costumes that surely sprang from a lonely man's dreams. Always smiling, always for you.

Time lost all meaning; it no longer existed. In here, the fantasy became real. It had to be–so much depended on it. A monumental investment demanded it. This one resort employed thousands. If you could be convinced you were someone else, you would have no inhibitions, no conscience, all your desires presented to you in one exciting package. That's where the profits came in. If you didn't know this, you didn't work here. Not for long anyway.

As overpowering as these surroundings may have been, Carl kept his wits. This ability usually put him a step ahead of the competition. He wasn't immune to these seductive attractions, though. He could feel the allure, was aware of it and impressed by it, but rose above it.

He moved briskly, and with confidence, through the casino maze toward the poker room. He felt comfortable here and knew his way around. Since it had opened a few years ago, the Majestic had become their resort of choice. He had spent many hours, usually while Gina slept, fighting one opponent after another at the hold 'em tables.

He wasn't walking so quickly that he failed to notice a shapely young waitress walking past with a tray full of drinks. She smiled up at him; a suggestive gleam sparkled in her bright hazel eyes. Did she exaggerate the natural swing in her hips just for him? Yes, they did make it easy to feel comfortable here, everyone on the same team, perpetuating the illusion.

14

Carl already had an acquaintance with the poker room manager. He always booked their rooms through her in order to get a player's rate, and made a point of stopping by after each visit to thank her. However, they only came once a year, so he figured she would not remember him. Sandy had told her he would be coming in, so he didn't feel completely out of line just popping in. He wasn't looking for much today anyway, just an introduction and an appointment for an interview.

When the waist high railing that surrounded the otherwise open area of the poker room came into view, Carl's step lightened. Action at the bean shaped poker tables looked rather subdued. The late night crowd had mostly filtered away, and the day players hadn't started to show up yet. Only about half the tables were in use. By mid-afternoon the room would be full, with a growing waiting list.

The manager's office stood at the back of the poker room, door open. Actually, Carl didn't recall ever seeing the door closed. Behind a large plain desk, cluttered with the debris of business, sat Meagan O'Meara, 'Meg.'

The Irish name failed to match her features. A striking woman in her mid thirties, she had tanned skin and light brown eyes. Her jet black hair reached beyond her exposed shoulders and made Carl recall the phrase 'black Irish.' She stood above average height with a lean athletic figure, the muscles in her shoulders and arms taut and formed. The sleeveless top she wore indicated that she was not only proud of her appearance, but perhaps used it to project an image of strength and authority.

He stood on the threshold and rapped lightly on the doorframe. Meg rose with a smile and an extended hand. "Carl. Sandy said you would be coming in this morning. Have a seat."

He accepted her hand. "I don't want to take up much of your time. I know you're busy. I just thought I would stop by and make an appointment." Carl was gratified that she remembered him even if Sandy had jarred her memory a little.

"I have a few minutes now. Things haven't picked up yet."

He took a seat and, with a grin, said, "To tell you the truth, I'm a little embarrassed that my daughter bothered you."

With an easy manner, Meg reassured him. "Don't be silly. You can't blame her for wanting to help her dad. Besides, she just stopped in for a second to drop off your resume."

That piece of information made Carl chuckle. "I didn't even know she had a copy of it. You see what happens? You spend your whole life taking care of your kids, making sure they get into the right schools, helping them find jobs, whatever. Now she's turned the tables on me. I'm not used to having someone look out for me like that."

Still smiling, Meg said, "I got the impression she was excited that her dad might be working here, too."

"Yeah," Carl agreed, "she's always been a sweetheart."

Meg nodded "I'm sure that's why she's doing so well here.

Attitude is everything."

"Now, I looked over your resume. I see you're looking for a part time position, and you have some experience at a gambling boat in Joliet. We do take on part timers. How flexible are you on hours?"

Carl informed her that he was pretty available and that she could call on him in an emergency to fill in. Meg seemed to like what she heard and asked when he could come in for a trial shift. All business, small talk kept to a minimum, no beating around the bush, Carl liked her approach. He thought he had better spend these first couple of days with Gina, so he asked if Monday or Tuesday would be okay.

"How does eight o'clock Tuesday morning sound?"

"Great," Carl replied.

"Okay, you'll have to fill out this Gaming Board application. You'll work with a temporary registration for awhile." Carl completed the tedious forms and returned them to Meg. She rose, and he thanked her as they shook hands.

One of Meg's floor supervisors came into the office. She used the opportunity to introduce Carl. "I'm glad you're here, Dmitri. This is Carl Braun. I'm going to start him out in your area on Tuesday."

Dmitri shook Carl's hand saying, "I am sure you will work out fine. Meg would not take you on if she did not think you good enough."

A stocky man, two or three inches shorter than Carl, thick necked with a powerful grip, he looked Carl up and down as he spoke. His words were friendly, but his demeanor spoke of suspicion. Carl detected the hint of an eastern European accent. He knew that a Russian immigrant who had worked his way up through the ranks ran the Majestic. Carl wondered if the two men had a connection. Perhaps, thought Carl, I've just misinterpreted his demeanor. He attributed it to foreign mannerisms and put it aside.

Carl wound his way back through the casino floor enroute to Sandy's office. She had recently accepted a promotion to shift manager for hospitality services and moved into a large office in the main lobby. Along the way, Carl found himself resisting the urge to compete at the tables, telling himself that there would be plenty of time for that later. He crossed the ornate mosaic tiled floor of the lobby in time to meet his daughter, who invited him out to lunch.

They sat on the terrace outside of Vito's, a fine Italian restaurant that overlooked the gardens. Vito had been handpicked and imported from a small town near Naples where he ran a modest but respected restaurant. The Resort's major investors had been traveling in Italy in search of renaissance art and were so taken in by the atmosphere and cuisine of his restaurant, they made Vito an offer. It was so generous that Vito and his family now lived comfortably in Las Vegas. The chefs at the Majestic's two other world-class eateries were lured to Las Vegas in similar fashion. The emphasis on these acquisitions was placed more on unique quality, rather than star status.

Both the host and the waiter greeted Sandy by name, and she lost no time introducing her father. During the short walk to the restaurant, Carl couldn't help noticing that his daughter waived to or said hello to several different people. Surely most of these people fell outside the scope of her responsibilities. It made Carl proud that she used her people skills to network and make a name for herself.

He always thought she might have been overly friendly, perhaps too outgoing. Sometimes the trait had worried him. He feared that it might leave her vulnerable, but now he saw that it had paid off.

Carl told her about the meeting with Meg and gently admonished her for the way she paved the way for him. Sandy smiled at him and said, "That's just the way it is, Dad. Get used to it."

Carl shrugged his shoulders in acceptance, recognizing the futility of resistance. They moved on to the subject of a gift for Gina and discussed it at great length.

Over the years, Carl had shown that he wasn't always the most proficient gift buyer. His heart always in the right place, his selections usually earned him more laughs than kisses. Now that they had embarked on a new stage in their lives, Carl wanted to give his wife a gift worthy of the episode. He trusted Sandy and knew she wouldn't let him down.

With a list of specific instructions, Carl pulled out of the parking lot positive his mission would be a success. One hour and almost a thousand dollars later, he got out of the SUV with Gina looking on. "Go back inside, hon, I have a surprise that you're going to fall in love with." She didn't look convinced, but followed his instructions and returned to the kitchen. Carl followed, an ear-to-ear grin on his face and an unwrapped box in his hands.

15

The familiar smirk curled the corner of Gina's mouth as Carl approached with his mysterious box. "All right, let's see what you've got there." He handed over the box, noting the doubt in her voice. It failed to diminish his enthusiasm.

Gina had little time for guessing. Bigger than a shoebox and made of thin cardboard, it had an unfastened lid. She considered its weight, jumped when it moved on its own, and her heart skipped a beat as the lid flipped off and two bulging eyes looked up at her from a fawn colored head.

To say she was surprised would have been an understatement. "A puppy! Carl, are you crazy? We're not ready for this. Oh, my God. What kind of dog is this? Carl!"

He heard what she said, but paid more attention to her body language.

Once a mother, always a mother. Since Therese had gone away to school, Carl became aware that Gina no longer had an outlet for her maternal instincts. Now that he had retired and they made their big move, he didn't want her turning to him to fill this need. Attention is a good thing, but he liked the status quo, and didn't want their new situation to change things.

Her eyes softened. The box fell to the floor, and the little dog curled up in her arms.

"It's a pug, honey. He just turned seven weeks old, still a baby. Look how much he likes you. I think he's found a new mother." Carl talked fast, trying to seize the moment. "I didn't just buy the pug, hon. I got all the accessories and equipment we'll need to make raising him easier. A little cage, his bowl, a harness and leash, and a book on raising and caring for the breed."

As Gina nuzzled and petted the excited, squirming ball of fur, Carl went on to explain that this breed is very low maintenance. "They are the ultimate lap dog. They just want to sit near you or on you. They are bred solely for companionship."

The smirk returned in a snap. "I thought that's what you were for."

Carl brushed off the wise crack. He could see that he had sealed the deal. This gift hit the mark.

"I had lunch with Sandy and talked it over with her. She was all for it, said she's been wanting a dog, too, but with work and all, it's impossible for her. She said she would love to watch him when we take trips or whatever."

By now Gina no longer needed the sales pitch. "You can ease up, Carl. I think he's adorable. I love him already." Then as if to secure a concession before she lost her chance, "But you have to help train him, too, you know."

Starting to relax and feeling proud of himself, he reassured her, "Of course, hon, I told you they are very low maintenance."

Carl retrieved the rest of the items from the car. They discussed names while he knelt on the kitchen floor to set up the cage.

Gina said, "He's cute, but kind of funny looking." She

furrowed her brow and held the pug's face close to hers as she considered a name. "What do you think of Charlie?"

The question was rhetorical; they both knew it didn't matter what he thought. "Sounds great to me, hon."

With the turmoil generated by Carl's surprise beginning to abate, Gina asked about his visit to the casino. "It went great. Meg is all business. She liked my resume and is gonna give me a trial run Tuesday morning."

"Tuesday!" Seeds of irritation grew in Gina, and she began to doubt her husband's motives for buying her a dog. Perhaps he just wanted to give her something to occupy her time while he went off and started a new life?

"Meg. I suppose she's young and pretty."

She bit her lip after the words escaped. Jealousy rarely got the better of her; she didn't like giving in to it. She knew Carl never gave her cause to be suspicious, but stranger things had happened to recently retired men who thought they still had to prove themselves.

Her muscles tensed and her thoughts ran free. *In all our years together, he never once displayed a healthy dose of jealousy. These damn firemen, so cocky. 'Not my wife.' Huh, there have been plenty of men over the years who have 'given me the eye.' Even flirted with me, and he knew it. It would have been nice if he'd shown a little jealousy. Such over confidence, they think they can walk on water. He's come home busted up enough times. You'd think that would have taken him down a notch or two.*

She stood silently after making the remark about Meg. Carl knew she was heating up about something. He figured she probably got a little irked that he moved things along so fast and considered that it might look like he planned to leave her behind. All at once, he went from thinking he had just scored big in the endless game of marriage, to realizing the need for some fast damage control to prevent a full-scale eruption.

He rose and placed his arms around her, the puppy wiggling between them. "Look, honey, I know it seems a little fast, but I need to be established in something. I won't let it take over our lives. It's just going to be part time."

Without looking up, Gina said, "I thought you were established in our marriage."

Searching for the right thing to say, he decided to address her earlier comment. "I am, honey. You're still my type you know. Yeah, Meg's pretty, but she's not my type. You know how attracted I've always been to you. No one's ever going to change that. Why would you even go there? Give me a little time, hon, please."

The puppy's wiggling became frantic. Gina decided to give her husband a break. He really was the same old Carl. Busy, fidgety, always up to something. Retirement didn't appear to be mellowing him yet. "Okay, Carl, but don't forget where you live."

He squeezed her in spite of the puppy. "Never, hon."

"Yeah, we'll see." She pulled away. "We better take Charlie outside for awhile. Where's his leash?" Carl went for the harness and leash, not sure if the storm had passed or not.

As promised, he did help with the puppy. In fact, he read the book Friday night and spent most of the weekend working with him, completely taking over the task of training. The training actually turned out to provide an unlooked for benefit to dog ownership. It gave Carl the excuse he needed to avoid the big weekend shopping spree.

Dragging him along had been Sandy's idea anyway. Even though she grew up with her parents, she obviously didn't appreciate the dynamics of their marriage. She thought her dad's input and opinions on the purchases might be valuable. While Gina would have enjoyed his company, she knew the thought was ridiculous. Carl saw his 'out' and took it.

"I should probably stay and work with Charlie. You guys will be gone a long time. I don't think he should be in his cage that long during the day yet."

Gina allowed herself to be convinced without an argument. She didn't want the little fellow locked up all day either. He had spent a lot of time crying and whining in his cage that first night. Carl had to restrain her from going to him and bringing him to bed. He convinced her that in time Charlie would get used to his cage and come to think of it as his own private den.

No, Carl wouldn't have to go shopping. However, Gina wanted to let him know that she was on to him. She replied to his assertion without trying to hide the sarcasm. "Yeah, right, Carl. It's all about the puppy. Okay, I'll let you off the hook this time for Charlie's sake."

He did spend a good amount of time with the puppy and also scoped out a couple of gyms in the area to see which one would be suitable for them. Over an hour went into practicing his card handling skills. He hadn't touched a deck since he left the Triple Seven and wanted to be sharp on Tuesday.

The job wasn't a lock yet. Although Meg seemed agreeable, he knew that most of the big resorts liked their new dealers to have more experience. So far everything went along according to his grand design. He liked the Majestic and wanted this job. He didn't want to start out at some hole in the wall just to gain more experience.

The women returned well before dark and turned over their 'doggy bags' to Carl. Thankful that they both ate like birds, he found more than enough to eat. They allowed him just enough time to finish before directing him in the task of hanging various pieces of artwork.

When he finished with the last picture, Sandy subjected him to a review of brochures and flyers. "Sit down, Dad, I'll show you what we picked out."

Carl saw the pride in his daughter's voice and didn't have the heart to refuse. "Sure, Sweetie. I can't wait."

Gina opened a bottle of merlot and looked on with a grin. She had long since given up trying to spark his interest in her shopping trips. "Yeah, Carl, sit down. You're going to love the stuff we picked out. Sandy made sure she got pictures of everything we looked at today."

Sandy picked up her mother early Sunday morning for what promised to be another long day of shopping. Carl overheard them making plans to reserve Monday evening for car shopping. He thought he had better tag along for that one.

Tuesday morning found him getting into his SUV, now parked next to a used, or rather, 'previously driven'

Thunderbird convertible. It looked light green to Carl, but Ford labeled it 'vintage mint green'. Not exactly what he would have picked out, but Gina never had anything like it before and it was a sharp car. When she drove it home from the dealership she could barely control her joy.

Carl spent his drive home from the Majestic that evening trying to decide if he had cause for concern. Meg and the floor supervisor seemed satisfied with his ability, maybe even impressed. By the end of his shift, she had him on the schedule through September. Just two or three times a week, day shift only. No weekends yet.

He should have been elated. He fell right into the swing of things. He had returned to his natural element. The players fed on his enthusiasm and the action stayed lively. This wasn't lost on Meg, who kept an eye on her new dealer as much as possible. His immediate supervisor, Dmitri, watched Carl, too, but without concern. He apparently had no complaints, but had a non-committal attitude, remaining aloof and distant.

In spite of the day's success, something didn't seem right. When Carl sat at a table, he became involved, whether dealing or playing. He tried to get a feel for each player and made mental notes. A number of players won more than he thought them capable of. It went beyond the standard run of good luck. He couldn't shake the feeling that something just wasn't right and decided to return as soon as possible to sit on the other side of the table. As a player, he wouldn't have to rotate from table to table. He could follow the action more closely and see if his suspicions had any merit.

16

Carl walked into the kitchen still preoccupied over the observations he had made at the tables. His attention moved closer to the present when greeted by the yelping, leaping puppy. He scooped up the popeyed animal and looked around the newly furnished kitchen.

Gina called to him, her voice carefree and light. She sounded pleased and sounded as if she wanted Carl to be pleased as well. "How do you like it, honey?"

"It looks great. You really know your stuff. Sandy wasn't kidding; they do get this stuff delivered in a hurry."

"That's not all, come on in here and see what else I've got for you, Blue Eyes."

His attention moved completely into the here and now. He stopped at the fridge to retrieve last night's unfinished bottle of chardonnay, "Okay, honey, I'm having a glass of wine. Do you want one?" Carl received an enthusiastic reply and a moment later stood shocked and surprised by a provocative sight. He tried without success to control the leer in his eyes.

Gina lounged amidst a collection of throw pillows on an overstuffed couch wearing nothing but a new, revealing, pink tankinni, the matching cover-up, unbuttoned and draped open. He sat next to her, and detected the aroma of coconut scented suntan oil. Beginning to suspect the way her day had been spent, he handed her the long stemmed glass.

She affected a pout. "Look at me would you; I'm going all to pot. Can we make it to that new gym tomorrow?"

Carl grinned at her sarcastic assessment of herself and ran a finger, moistened in wine, up and down her abdomen. "Sure, hon, but it'll have to be early. The cable guy will be here around noon."

Gina reached up and pulled him close saying with a smirk, "Oh, Carl, I love it when you say romantic things like that." She gave him a sultry kiss and nipped at his lip in protest when he pulled away.

"Listen, hon, I feel all grimy from work. I haven't been lying around all day in my bathing suit, you know. Let me take a quick shower." He wondered if her devilish mood indicated she had been at the wine already.

Gina replied quickly, "I hope you're not scolding me. I had to do something while I waited around for all those delivery trucks. The patio furniture came first, so I thought I would work on my tan."

Carl, already on his way to the staircase, turned to survey his wife. She held her head low, but glanced up to meet his eyes, still using the pout.

It didn't take the sun long to reveal her Italian heritage. Her soft olive skin and taunting brown eyes made it difficult for him to continue up the stairs. He forced himself away, finishing the wine in one gulp.

He entered the master bathroom and undressed. A spacious shower stall enclosed on two sides by a clear glass door and matching panels was set in the corner of the stone tiled room. Two shower heads combined with several wall-mounted jets to produce a pulsating showering experience, usually reserved for guests of the most exclusive resorts.

Carl thought this upgrade a little extravagant, but Gina insisted. After a few days, he was glad she did. With each jet working its magic, Carl stepped in and the day's concerns melted away.

The rhythmic sound and vibrating massage of the jets lifted him to a hypnotic state. He closed his eyes and let his mind wander. His thoughts found Gina and began to build a fantasy. He indulged himself so deeply that he was unaware she had entered the room until she opened the shower door.

He turned in surprise to see her tan-lined body rapidly becoming wet from the spray. Water blended with tanning oil to make her skin glimmer like fine silk, her breathing, deep and rapid, the playful pout gone from her lips. She moved toward him with a flash of unrestrained passion in her eyes.

"All that sun and lotion have made me feel grimy, too. Mind if I join you?" He watched her approach, completely taken, even before she wrapped her arms around him.

17

That night, Carl watched the hours tick by, adjusting his pillow time after time and rolling back and forth. Gina didn't seem to notice; perhaps she had grown accustomed to his bouts of insomnia. He heard Charlie's occasional whimpers over the hum of the air conditioner.

The whimpering became less pronounced with each passing night. Carl had raised dogs before and knew the fussing would cease altogether before long. Charlie's whining usually didn't bother him. Tonight the whining combined with reflections of the day's events caused him to succumb to the distractions.

His thoughts ranged widely, stretching from the excitement of his first day at the Majestic to his concerns about some of the players. He realized that it would be days before he'd have the opportunity to investigate those concerns on his own. On top of everything else, his head still spun from Gina's smoldering performance.

He looked at her, curled up in sleep, and rested his hand on her waist. She'd always been a good lover but sometimes she outdid herself. He wanted to caress her, perhaps get something started again, but decided it might be better to savor this evening's encounter and let her sleep. It had been quite a day; reliving it now was keeping him awake.

* * *

He became acquainted with some of the other dealers, before long coming across another dealer from Chicago. Brian Bartman was a robust man with a thick beard, the same height as Carl, but easily eighty pounds heavier. Carl learned he came from the north side of Chicago but proved willing to forgive him this infraction. They struck up a conversation and Carl asked him, with a laugh, if he might be related to the Bartman of the now infamous Bartman ball incident from the Cub's '03 playoff run. Brian, nicknamed BB, said no but confessed that people asked the same question all the time when they learned he came from Chicago.

BB knew a few firemen from back home and asked Carl if he ever worked with any of them. Carl did know one of them and the conversation flowed seamlessly. After turning the discussion to a more immediate subject, Carl learned that, as suspected, Dmitri had a connection to the casino's general manager. In fact, he was Al Beria's younger brother.

Carl already knew something of the elder Beria's reputation, but BB, and some others, filled him in on a lot of things. By the end of his shift he had learned a lot about his new boss.

Aleksandr Nikolaevich Beria had emigrated from St. Petersburg, Russia in the early nineties. An educated man, who presented a veneer of refinement, he had a storied past. His ability to bring great intelligence and energy to bear on a problem was legendary. No solution had ever proved to be beyond his grasp, and rumor pointed to a ruthless pursuit of success.

He maintained an earnest expression at all times. With

close-cropped blond hair and average size, there was nothing particularly notable about his appearance, except perhaps his style of dress, professional and conservative. He shunned the designer suits and jewelry worn by most men who had attained his stature.

He came from a family deeply entrenched in the Party. A great uncle had been one of Stalin's right hand men. Through clever political maneuvering, the family managed to retain its station despite the whirlwind that followed in the wake of Stalin's death.

After completing his formal education Aleksandr did a stint as an officer in the Russian Navy. His skill, ingenuity, and loyalty did not go unnoticed. The naval elite decided that his talents would be of better use elsewhere. They recommended him to the KGB and persuaded him to join. Working diligently, promotions came as a matter of course, and before long, all recognized him as a rising star. Inwardly, he even contemplated political possibilities. Then the unthinkable happened: the social climate of the Soviet Union changed dramatically. Aleksandr could see the writing on the wall.

Because of his history, both personal and professional, he sensed he would be an unwanted figure. A future once filled with opportunity now began to dry up. A criminal class, long dormant under the iron fist of communism, poised itself to reemerge with vigor. Because of his involvement in certain 'domestic projects,' while with the KGB, his name was not unknown to these people. In fact, he no longer felt safe in Mother Russia.

Aleksandr had an acute sense of duty to his family. His

parents were old. His brother, much younger than him and rather wild, he feared would prove to be a bit too much for them to handle. The decision to leave did not come easily.

After much consideration, he accepted only one solution to his predicament: America. Like all who go to America, he would go with the intention of providing any children he might have with a future full of promise, a future that no longer existed in Russia. Although still a single man, he longed for a family of his own, but he knew his parents would not leave Russia. He decided he would send for his brother once he had attained success. They could raise their families together; establish a new way of life for the Berias in the new country. He would work without fail until the day came when he could reunite with his brother.

Over the years, he had made an in-depth study of the United States. Although required of any agent who hoped for advancement, with Aleksandr it went beyond requirement. While always a loyal Party member, he could not help but be impressed by the wealth and success of the American system. He didn't fail to appreciate the similarities in ideals that sparked their countries' respective revolutions, 'Government of the people, by the people, for the people.' At that point, however, the similarities disappeared. With the grand experiment over, the time to move on had arrived.

His visa processed quickly. The authority's willingness to assist him with his emigration took him by surprise. The government must be glad to be rid of him, he surmised.

Within a year of his arrival in America, Leningrad became St. Petersburg once again and there could be no turning back.

The path he chose in America would have seemed harsh to some, but Aleksandr never recognized this. His research told him where to head. Las Vegas was ripe with opportunity. He accepted any menial job in any hotel or casino that would have him. As always, his employers took notice. Aleksandr showed up earlier, stayed later, and worked harder than anyone they had ever employed. No matter how dirty or distasteful the job, he completed it efficiently and without complaint.

Again, promotions came, but he continued to push. He worked non-stop to improve his situation, moving to new jobs in better casinos, taking classes at night to improve his understanding of American business. His hands no longer got dirty, but that didn't matter; he continued like a driven man.

The opening of Vegas's first mega resort, the Mirage in 1989, brought a building boom and tourist frenzy that continues to this day. Aleksandr rode this wave to the pinnacle.

With the Majestic still under construction, the young company's CEO came to call. Aleksandr held the position of casino shift manager at one of the Strip's largest and most plush resorts. Aleksandr's shift ran smoother and more efficiently than the others, arguably smoother and more efficiently than any shift, anywhere in town.

The people at the Majestic knew his reputation and offered him the position of general manager. He would answer to no one but the Board of Directors. The board wanted to ensure success in an ever-competitive business, and signing on Aleksandr gave them an ace in the hole.

Aleksandr accepted the position, but declined the

invitation to name his own price. Money never seemed real to him; it was just a tool of the modern world. He had enough already. The Board of Directors implemented a salary and system of incentives that would have been considered overly generous by most in the industry. Aleksandr never batted an eye. It would make his wife and kids happy and perhaps make up, in part, for his continual absence.

Some might have considered they had finally arrived. Not him. Upon assuming his new responsibilities, he pushed himself even harder. He refused to let up until he was sure everything that could be done to ensure perfection in his new resort had been done. He wanted his hotel to rise above the others, and he left no stone unturned.

As patrons of the resort, in one of its first months of operation, Carl and Gina recognized the differences. The new resort did stand out from the others, and like many, they decided to make the Majestic their only choice when staying in Las Vegas.

To any observer Aleksandr's indefatigable efforts had produced flawless results. In fact, his work was flawless. However, one small aspect of his labor festered, causing decay, unrevealed and unnoticed, except by Carl Braun.

18

Al Beria might have been considered aloof, maybe even cold and callous by some, but he did have a soft spot and he reserved it for his family. Marrying an American did make obtaining his citizenship easier, but that factor never mattered to him. He truly fell in love. Robin was as beautiful as any showgirl in town. She was tall, stately, and blonde with a classical, statuesque figure.

They met while he still worked as a pit boss and she as a cocktail waitress. A whirlwind romance ended in marriage within six months. Robin gave him two sons, born a year apart. They were now active primary school kids. Al loved to share their energy, and never grew tired of their antics. His incredible workload kept him away most of the time. Often, the casino would call him back as soon as he arrived home from an already long day.

Complaint was not thought of. Al knew the magnitude of his responsibilities, aware that the success of the resort depended upon his policies and leadership. The livelihoods of so many families were in his hands. He would not let them down. The Majestic came first. It pained him at times, but that's the way it had to be.

Robin, for her part, understood full well the extent of her husband's responsibilities and took his absences in stride. She knew his love for her and the kids went deep. He would be with them always, if he could. Instead of being resentful, she admired his sense of conviction and tireless devotion to responsibility.

She managed to make up for any emptiness she felt by indulging herself and the kids in the benefits of their growing wealth.

Al left all the domestic decisions to her, and Robin set herself up in opulence. They owned a gorgeous house in the most exclusive area of Las Vegas, a live-in nanny helped with the boys, and a maid took care of the household chores. If Al could not play the part of dotting father and husband, Robin made sure she and the boys wanted for nothing else.

With his paternalistic instincts fully activated, Al's concerns turned back to St. Petersburg, back to his only brother. Dmitri had been just eighteen when Al left the country. Thoughts of those he left behind never drifted far from his mind. He sent what he could, more as he made more, and his parents did their best to attend to Dmitri's needs.

Al kept in touch sporadically and learned that his brother had managed to make his way in a struggling world. His parents could never elaborate on their younger son's professional endeavors, but related that he seemed to be doing well. When Al thought of it at all, his thoughts became clouded in doubt. A young person, growing up in the tumultuous modern Russia, could easily head in the wrong direction.

Trying to establish himself in America and with a new family proved an all-consuming job for Al. A sense of guilt built up inside him, born mostly of a feeling that he had abandoned his family when they needed him most. He thought of redemption and atonement.

By the time Al assumed his position at the Majestic, his parents were gone. It took some persuading, but he managed to convince his brother that with his help he would find a better life in America. Dmitri did need persuading. He argued that he did quite well for himself and that Russia treated him in a princely fashion. He would not go into detail concerning his means of support. No fool, Al easily read between the lines.

Al argued that Russia might be a democracy now, but their prisons remained some of the harshest in the civilized world. It was just a matter of time.

Dmitri knew this without having to hear it from his brother. Actually the law was the least of his problems. He considered that his brother could provide him with a way out of a more dangerous concern.

Al pressed him to get out while he still could. One day, without explanation, Dmitri relented and Al felt he had moved a long way toward redemption.

Dmitri arrived with Al's sponsorship, and upon completion of a course at a local dealer school, took a job at the Majestic. Most people wouldn't have figured them for brothers. Although blond and about the same height, Dmitri was huskier and projected an image of robust strength. Almost universally disliked by his coworkers, they tolerated him because he was the boss's brother. His gruff demeanor and coarse personality gave the impression of a man always on the verge of losing his temper, which he often did.

Some took offense when Al promoted him to floor supervisor so quickly. In fact, he simply offended people. He often made comments about lazy or wasteful Americans. His favorite pastime seemed to be pointing out the shortcomings of American society. When Al became aware of this behavior, he put Dmitri on the day shift and advised the poker room manager to keep an eye on him. After a couple of conversations with her, Dmitri seemed to toe the line. Al stopped hearing complaints and became confident that his brother had finally come around.

Dmitri did come around, so to speak. By the time he convinced Al to push through his promotion, he had too much to lose. He didn't like working under that 'American whore,' but he swallowed his pride. He had to. As floor supervisor, he could kick his operation into high gear. If he played his brother right, he might even be able to move in on Meg's job, and then the sky would be the limit.

The floor supervisor's job involved finding an open seat at one of the many tables for anyone interested in playing. Shortly after his shift began Monday morning, Dmitri found himself directing his newest dealer to an open seat at a $4-$8 table.

Carl came to play. He had finally managed to finagle a little time out of his schedule. Now he would see for himself if these young men just possessed incredible luck or if they were teaming up to cheat the game.

19

With his head reeling Monday morning from another night spent indulging in alcohol and strippers, Dmitri found getting out of bed difficult. Heather still slept next to him. He never thought twice about the money he spent for her, and on her, but when the night ended and he no longer needed her, he always felt the price had been too high.

America, Dmitri knew, held many temptations, and there could be no getting around the expense. The more pleasure each temptation promised, the higher the price tag it carried. Dmitri had the money. He knew how to be successful, how to work. But the allure of all that success proved more than he could resist.

The dangers he left behind in Russia became faded memories. They meant no more to him than old scars. He still sent payment, but in recent months he had found it impossible to send as much as he should.

He had created the Las Vegas enterprise out of nothing and decided it belonged to him. Surely he had made up for past indiscretions. How long could they expect him to continue paying such a heavy tax? He deserved the right to enjoy the fruits of his own labor. He would keep sending money, but they had to be more reasonable.

Dmitri pushed the blankets to the edge of the bed and forced himself to stand. The room spun and he tried to focus.

Heather's nude body reacted to the sudden chill. Dmitri managed to focus on her. His eyes raked over her with greed and lust. She was exquisite. Expensive, but exquisite. He reached down, almost tumbling with the effort, and slapped the pale skin of her backside. A sound like the cracking of a whip sprang from her flesh.

Heather's body twitched and she voiced her objection with a sleepy groan before reaching for the missing comforter. Her reaction made Dmitri laugh. Later, men in various stages of inebriation would stand before the catwalk and gape at the beauty gyrating around the brass pole. Many would wonder about the beet red handprint.

A shower and strong coffee rejuvenated Dmitri as much as possible. Before leaving for work he checked his e-mail. He rarely heard from St. Petersburg anymore, but when they needed to contact him, the message came by e-mail. Because of the time difference, the messages arrived during the night.

There was a message from back home: "I am sure you remember the terms of our agreement. We fear that you are falling back into an old habit. We are sending Leonovich to evaluate your operation and to collect the full amount owed to us. Expect him in about a week."

Dmitri re-read the brief message. Nothing for weeks and then this. Short and arrogant. Apparently they weren't prepared to be reasonable yet. He tried to control his anger as he considered how to handle things.

His head ached, and concentrating on this problem did not help. After rubbing his temples for a few minutes, he thought he had a solution. If he put aside all the revenue gathered in the entire week, he should have enough to satisfy Leonovich. It would still be short of the amount they expected, but it would be a considerable sum. One sure to impress. He would just have to put off paying the team for a week. He could make it up to them later. Satisfying St. Petersburg had to be done first. He knew he would hear no complaints from his team members.

The operation ran smoothly. Surely Leonovich would recognize its value. No, there shouldn't be a problem. Perhaps he had better deny himself for a time. Take business matters more seriously. America, and her sinful pleasures would still be there waiting for him after he had placated the people back home.

In spite of the long night and disturbing e-mail, Dmitri arrived at work full of energy, his mind cleared of the cobwebs left by the alcohol. He met with Peter, the leader of his team, and told him to inform the other members that there would be a delay in receiving this week's salary. Peter considered asking for an explanation, but thought better of it, simply telling Dmitri that he would pass on the information.

When Carl came into the poker room and approached the sign-in desk, Dmitri almost didn't recognize him. After all, he had only been working at the Majestic for a short time. They had a brief conversation about a seat at a $4-$8 table, and Dmitri left him without giving him another thought.

A couple of days later they conversed once again. Stunned after this second conversation, Dmitri rarely thought of anyone else.

20

Carl and Gina sat on the deck sipping coffee Monday morning when Carl suggested she might want to spend the day shopping and maybe have lunch with Sandy. Because of the way he beat around the bush and stuttered his suggestion, she assumed he had to be up to something. She figured he probably wanted to find something for her to do, so he could go off and play poker with a guilt-free conscience.

She did have a lot of shopping to do, but began to feel like he was always trying to put something over on her. "That sounds great, hon. I did want to pick up a few things. What will you do with your day? I know, why don't you play a little cards? You must be tired of just watching everyone else play."

The sarcasm stung and Carl quickly returned it. "Oh, I never thought of that. Maybe I will. Come get me at the poker room when you're done with lunch and we'll head home together." With his day arranged, Carl guessed he had four or five hours to get to the bottom of things.

Carl drove to the casino distracted by thoughts of what he might find, but the electrified room, ripe with the allure of action, cleared the fog from his head and infused him with life.

He took his seat, stacked his chips, and reviewed the mental catalogue of things he suspected. The suspicious players conducted themselves in a quiet and reserved manner, talking only amongst themselves. This in itself was not unusual; some players were like that, but he noted other peculiar similarities in their play and appearance.

Always at least two per table, young, early twenties. No matter where the action was at the table, they looked at each other and usually kept to a three-word vocabulary: "check," "raise," and "call," depending on the situation. If they wanted to fold, they simply tossed their cards toward the muck pile. The infrequent speech made it hard for him to be sure, but Carl thought they shared a similar foreign accent.

Their most notable characteristic was their steady winnings. Hesitant and unsure of themselves, they seemed new to the game. Of that, Carl was certain, and they had no business winning with such regularity. If they did cheat, their technique, without doubt, depended on ease and subtlety. Try as he did, Carl could not spot their method while dealing.

Running the game meant he couldn't concentrate on their play alone. Without giving up his suspicions, he asked BB for his opinion on the quiet young men. BB said they didn't seem unusual to him, but that he did believe them to be foreigners. "Nothing unusual about that. The town's full of them."

Carl worked two more shifts before coming in to play, and by then his instincts had him convinced that something was up. He would always be a player first and dealer second. Years of experience couldn't be wrong. Novice players don't get lucky every day. What did BB know anyway? He claimed he never played the game, just dealt.

He took the last available seat at any of the $4-$8 tables. Things were picking up early and Dmitri started taking names for a waiting list. Before he started, Carl knew he might have to move to another table if he didn't find what he was looking for at this first table. As it turned out, that wouldn't be a problem. Reluctantly, he donned a pair of dark glasses. Annoying or not, he didn't want anyone to follow his gaze today.

He recognized one of the young foreigners right away, and within the first few hands spotted his partner. The unfamiliar one religiously stuck to the three-word vocabulary. If he intended to hide his accent, he wasn't doing a very good job of it. Definitely eastern European, early twenties, pudgy, and soft. Carl got the impression he had never known physical labor.

The other one Carl had seen play twice before. He had more confidence and sat at ease. Not one of the ones Carl considered a beginner. Older, maybe thirty and more talkative than the others. His speech seemed very American. Only occasionally, and with the use of certain consonants, could his accent be detected.

Both men, as with most poker players, fidgeted with their chips. Rifling them together and adjusting the stacks, an absent-minded practice usually done to pass the time. With the new guy, however, the practice appeared to be more deliberate, if only a couple of times. Early in the game, Carl decided to concentrate most of his observations on the new guy. The fact that he seemed less polished assured him that the guy would give up the most information.

Almost three hours passed and Carl's brain continued to analyze the bits of information he managed to pick up. A few times the new guy glanced down quickly and adjusted the position of a top chip. Once or twice he seemed to glance at his stacks and then back at his cards as if to confirm something. Subtlety seemed to be the key. Over a period of hours, and with an obvious novice, Carl only managed to spot this small thing, but it was enough. They were signaling to each other.

Carl didn't know yet what the signals indicated or how the partners knew which stack was the designated 'signal stack' or if they used multiple stacks. They seemed to move their chips around as much, and as innocently, as any other player. That didn't matter, though; they knew what they were doing.

Carl watched both men now, trying to see if they would give up some previously missed clue. Some cheating teams incorporated betting patterns into their schemes. The teammates worked together to run up the pot on a third and hopefully a fourth bettor. Sometimes they bet so aggressively that the mark would fold and lose his investment. This practice was usually not done recklessly, and if the hand went to a show down, one of the conspirators at least would have a strong hand and take down his share of pots, but at an inflated price.

Carl couldn't spot anything this common. The foreigners seemed to bet independently of each other, sometimes even going head to head in earnest. He remained convinced that while some coercion in the betting probably occurred, it wasn't the main tool of the system. He was sure that the conveyance of information had to be their main game.

Knowing just one of the other player's hole cards would, over time, give a talented player an invaluable edge. He could calculate odds and adjust his betting with more accuracy than his opponents. Seeing through a bluff would be child's play if you knew, for a fact, your partner had the card your adversary tried to represent. The applications for this information could be limitless.

But why the measly $4-$8 table? Surely this technique would reap much bigger rewards at the high limit or no limit tables. Almost as soon as this question occurred to him the answer slammed into his head. A testing ground for the team. Of course, the clumsy new guy and the polished pro. That's why they could afford to be subtle, usually just doing a little better than average. In a twenty-four hour town, with a large enough team playing in any number of high stakes games, the take would be immense. Little bits at a time; it was all relative.

No one notices a twenty or twenty-five percent win over a few hours of play. Those percentages didn't add up to much when sitting at a $4-$8 table. But plug those numbers into a high stakes game and you'd make a fortune. Bit by bit. Employ a work ethic, be subtle, avoid greed, and detection.

Stunned, Carl rose to go to the washroom and casually surveyed the other tables. It was as though he had developed x-ray vision and he saw thieves everywhere. Quiet young men at every table, stealing his game, ruining it.

The elation he expected at discovering the cheater's methods didn't materialize. The suspicions had been on his mind for a week and were the only reason he showed up today. Instead of elation, his mood soured. The Majestic, his handpicked home away from home, with all of its tasteful glamour and luxury had become dirty to him. He felt dirty himself.

21

Carl returned to the table, his shoulders slumped, feeling like a clipper ship robbed of the wind that only moments ago propelled him with great energy. He pushed his glasses carelessly over his forehead and took his seat. He had seen enough for one day. Realizing for the first time that he was down about a hundred dollars, he decided to keep his mind on the game and try to make a recovery.

He noticed that a very attractive young brunette had taken the seat next to him. Actually, she had been sitting next to him most of the morning. Ordinarily he would have taken notice right away. Her low-cut halter-top did little to hide the soft flesh beneath. She could certainly turn heads. That, of course, was the point, and Carl smiled to himself wondering if one of the oldest distractions in the book might have been the cause of the 'trainee's' mental lapses.

"Give up on the glasses, Blue Eyes?" Hearing Gina's romantic pet name for him coming from the lips of another woman, especially one as young and tempting as his brunette neighbor, startled Carl. He turned to her, and even though his eyes wanted to drift lower, he made an effort to maintain eye contact at all times. He got the impression she was testing his resolve. How could he possibly resist sneaking a peek?

Her eyes, large, green, and moist, were as lovely as the rest of her, and looking into them was an easy undertaking.

"No, I just think they're making my eyes tired. Besides, I'm down a little. I have to do something to change my luck."

She patted his knee, leaned close, and whispered with a flirtatious laugh, "That's funny; I was just considering how lucky you could really get. How about buying me a drink?" Apparently sensing Carl trying to stand firm, she had decided to turn up the heat.

Buy you a drink? They give *them away in this place*. He found himself completely incapable of reply. He had been with Gina for over thirty years and spent most of his adult life working in a man's world. Any meager ability he possessed to flirt with the opposite sex had long since been lost. In spite of the fact that he knew what she was up to, she had achieved her goal. He found himself thoroughly sidetracked. Getting his head into this game just became a little harder.

Carl turned to look at his newly dealt cards, wishing Gina would show up so he could get out of there. The hell with the hundred bucks. This wasn't his day. The brunette gave his knee a final squeeze as if to punctuate what they both knew just took place. He turned toward her; lips set tightly, arms folded against his chest, and gave a nod of acknowledgement.

What he saw made him blink. Apparently she was more than pleased with her performance. Her little charade caused her cheeks to flush pink, and the halter top now had matching protrusions straining to force their way through the flimsy material.

Her sudden transformation in body language had Carl fuming. Really satisfied with yourself aren't you, he thought. It never occurred to him that he might have misinterpreted the encounter. For him it was all about the poker and she was just an opponent trying hard to knock him off his game. With effort, he returned his attention to the cards.

A pair of kings, very nice. The best starters he had picked up all day. He raised from early position, testing the waters. The brunette re-raised without hesitation.

An immediate re-raise? After her well rehearsed production? Did she actually believe she put me on tilt that easily? Is she insulting me? The hand quickly became personal. He knew it was a mistake to feel that way, but, after all, he wasn't a machine.

The aggressive, early action forced most of the others out, including the foreigners. Good, Carl thought. He had already decided to drop most hands they participated in. Only the big blind called the double raise. Not wanting to chase the two remaining players out before the stakes doubled on the turn card, Carl only called the raise himself. The contenders anticipated the flop.

Ten, ace, king. Perfect. Carl suppressed his satisfaction with ease and quickly assessed the possibilities. He figured either the brunette or the big blind for an ace. Now one of them made top pair but would lose hard to his set of kings. There were no flush possibilities and only the big straight to worry about. Unless, of course, one of them held pocket aces, in which case he was dead in the water. With the best hand he'd had all day, he figured he wouldn't worry about pocket aces and would go for broke.

Carl opened the betting, and with some hesitation, the brunette raised. The big blind had seen enough; he mucked his cards claiming the flop was too scary for him. Carl didn't want to chase her off, but he sensed she had become emotionally involved in the hand, so he took a chance and re-raised. Again, with a show of hesitation that he now doubted, she came over the top with another raise. The ace he put her on did start to look like a made straight. Or was she being overly aggressive? Forcing her hand.

Maybe she really had made Carl a genuine offer and was thrown on tilt herself when he remained silent. He considered that she had patted him under the table and whispered her message to him quietly. If she had wanted to thoroughly rattle him, wouldn't she have made her taunts openly in an effort to embarrass him?

He recalled someone telling him once that all men over thirty-five are invisible to all women under thirty. It made good sense to him, so he adopted it into his belief system. Could this woman have actually found him attractive? Maybe she had traveled here on business or vacation and wanted a little extra excitement. Carl never wore a wedding ring. How could she know he had a wife at home? Who knows, maybe she was over thirty; he never could tell. Retrieving his mind from its wanderings, he called the bet and waited for the turn with a growing feeling of doom.

A harmless seven, still no flush possibilities. Not wanting to show that he had begun to lose confidence in his hand, Carl led off with a bet. She calmly raised. Carl called the raise, disgusted that he may have allowed himself to be trapped.

The dealer flipped over the river card with a snap. An ace. Her eyes flared. Carl caught the reaction. He knew he had her. She had been betting her top pair all along. Another ace wouldn't have garnered any reaction if she had been sitting on a straight, not that that mattered now anyway. He didn't put her on four aces. His only real concern was that her other hole card matched one of the board cards giving her aces full. The possibility existed that she held the remaining king along with her ace. Holding 'big slick' would explain her hard betting in the first round.

But he didn't sense it that way. She seemed disturbed, as if she wanted to inflict pain with her aggression. He decided to go with the idea that her antagonism was driven by emotion. Certain now, and even a little flattered, he knew he'd misinterpreted her flirtation. He would have to remember this incident. His usually dependable instincts seemed flawed when applied to women.

No, he was sure his kings full would stand up. Her three aces were only going to break her heart. When the final round of betting began, Carl knew it would go to the limit, and less than a minute later, it did. She proudly revealed her cards out of turn. An ace and a jack. Three of a kind. As expected. What happened next Carl had not expected.

He turned over his pocket kings and the winning hand. When the realization hit the brunette, her deportment changed in a hurry. The flushed hue in her cheeks became a red-hot glow. The halter-top, no longer under assault from behind, was quickly hidden beneath a nylon jacket.

Rising abruptly, she stuffed her remaining chips into her purse, glared at Carl, and almost screaming said, "Where do they find monsters like you anyway? I've never been treated like that in my whole life. How could you just sit there and ignore me? Take your big pile of chips. I hope they make you happy!"

Carl was relieved when the slap never came. If it had, he

wouldn't have objected. He'd taken a lot worse in his day. In a way he wished she had slapped him. He was sorry for her. He must have come across like an ass. Maybe hitting him would have made her feel better. He could have prevented this tirade if he hadn't been so dense. Simply declining the drink idea and explaining that he was married would have been enough. He felt like a fool.

Poker must have been just a side diversion to her. No skilled player would have lost that much in a limit game. Apparently, she had other motives for sitting at the table.

She stormed off, all eyes on her. The dealer pushed a considerable pile of chips towards Carl. He pushed several back, making a generous tip. Still following his heated opponent's retreat, he saw Gina jump out of her way to avoid being trampled. The brunette turned to her as if to apologize, but seemed too upset to speak. Gina spotted Carl and moved in his direction.

He started racking his chips. Time to go. Thank God. This trip to the casino turned out to be more than he bargained for. The other players tried to talk him into staying, assuming he was leaving because of the scene made by the brunette. He realized they were unaware of her whispers and flirtations. They must have attributed her outburst to a case of poor sportsmanship.

Carl saw that the commotion had drawn Meg from her office and she was headed for his table. He looked to Dmitri for a reaction and saw him laughing, his face twisted into a cruel, mocking sneer. He enjoyed the poor girl's pain. All at once, Carl decided that he didn't like Dmitri.

22

Gina reached the table and commented on her near collision. "That eye candy was sure in a hurry. Did you see her?"

Carl finished racking his chips, and turning toward the cage, replied, "Yeah, she sat at this table."

Gina looked at the empty seat and realized the woman had been sitting next to her husband. She put her hands on her hips and took a deep breath. "I never saw any poker players that looked like her at the Triple Seven. What got her so ticked, anyway?"

He feared that on top of everything else, he might be in store for a bout of wifely jealousy. He held up his chip racks and answered her question. "These are why she's so ticked." It may have been a little white lie, but he saw no up-side to explaining what really happened.

"Cleaned her out, huh? That's no way to treat a lady. She sure was a looker, too. They must attract a different breed of card player in Vegas."

Carl could see Gina trying to suppress a pout and thanked God she hadn't arrived in time to see the brunette patting his knee, wearing just the skimpy halter top. "They have more of a 'touristy' crowd here, hon. To tell you the truth, I was so caught up I didn't really notice her until a few minutes ago."

Gina put her arm through his and smiled as they walked

toward the cage. She accepted his statement because she knew how intensely he played poker and because she knew that when it came to women, he was rather naïve. "Didn't notice her until you took all her money, huh? That's my Carl." He put his racks on the counter and sighed, realizing he had dodged a bullet.

Meg broke away from a dealer she was talking to and approached the couple, holding out her hand to Gina. "I saw this beautiful woman walking up to you, Carl, and I knew she must be your wife. She looks so much like Sandy." She took Gina's hand. "I just wanted to come over and say hello. I'm Meg O'Meara. I'm the poker room manager, and we are very pleased you allow us to borrow your husband from time to time."

Gina smiled at the flattery and replied. "Nice to meet you. I'm Gina. I'm glad Carl's working out, but go easy on him; he is supposed to be retired, you know."

Meg accepted the friendly advice and assured Gina that she understood. "I know. A long career as a fireman, right? Well rest easy; we won't have him doing anything as rough as that."

Carl decided it was time to speak up. "Okay. Now that you ladies have my future all set up, maybe its time we should be heading home." Gina, with her arm still wrapped through Carl's, shared a laugh with Meg.

His chips had been converted back into cash. He picked up the bills and looked at Meg. "Well, that's enough for me today, Meg. I'll see you tomorrow morning."

Still wearing a pleasant smile, Meg said, "Yeah, we'll see

you tomorrow, Carl. Hey, what was all that commotion at your table?"

Carl replied in an off hand manner. "She took a bad beat. Fell in love with her trip aces. Should have played it more cautiously with a pair on board."

Meg shook her head and shrugged. "That's too bad. We like everyone to have a good time here. I think she's a guest at our resort. Part of a big convention group that arrived yesterday. They're here for the whole week."

Carl grimaced at this information and left saying, "I hope I don't end up dealing to her tomorrow." Meg assured him that that situation could be avoided.

They stopped by the concierge desk to pick up the results of a successful shopping spree. Carl had withdrawn into himself. At first, Gina didn't notice. A pleasant morning of store hopping and lunch with her daughter had put Gina in a lighthearted mood. She held onto her husband's arm and leaned against him while softly humming a Dean Martin love song.

She was glad she had met Meg and could put to rest any concerns she had about Carl's pretty new boss. She seemed outgoing and friendly. Not the man hunter type, always on the prey for unsuspecting goofs like Carl.

They walked to the T-bird virtually without speaking. Attempts to engage him in conversation were met with one-word responses and no eye contact. Apparently, his day hadn't been as pleasant as hers. She gave up.

She had seen him like this many times before, usually on mornings after the firehouse, and had learned early in their marriage that, if left alone, by afternoon he was usually himself again. It troubled her that he kept so much inside. She loved him deeply and wanted to help at times like this. With years of baggage built up inside, the silence could not be healthy. She wasn't going to let this go on much longer and had decided she must get him to open up, to let her in. She just needed the right time to try.

She watched him driving the convertible in the hot desert sun, his sunglasses still perched above his brow. He looked straight ahead, deep in thought, squinting against the intense afternoon glare, unaware that his glasses still sat on his forehead. Gina thought these episodes were a thing of the past. She hoped that once retired, and removed from the hostility of Chicago's streets, he would begin to shed his burdens. It must still be too soon, she thought.

She took his hand in hers, squeezing gently. He left his hand there, but did not return the squeeze. Gina looked at the passing scenery. They drove on in silence.

Carl's mind wrestled with a dilemma. Now that he knew the foreigners were cheating, what should he do? The rules said to inform the floor supervisor of any suspected irregularities in play, but he knew he didn't have much. He couldn't direct them to anything specific. Even if they did review hours of surveillance tape, they wouldn't be able to see anything concrete. The team was too reserved, too patient, their method of signaling almost undetectable.

He needed more, needed to further his study, and needed to learn how the system worked before he could spell it out for Dmitri. Once he had it all figured out, security could follow the action with precision, even predict the cheaters' moves. Then they would have them.

Now, fixed on a course of action, Carl relaxed. He pulled into the garage and discovered his hand in Gina's. He pressed his wife's hand to his lips and kissed it saying, "I can't wait to see what you bought today, hon. Go let Charlie out and I'll bring the packages in." Gina smiled and rolled her eyes at the same time. They both knew his assertion was ridiculous. He couldn't have been less interested in her purchases. He simply became reacquainted with the idea that he was, in fact, married and had just driven all the way home ignoring his long suffering wife. Now he wanted to make up for it.

Gina enjoyed showing off the fruits of her labor. Carl kept up a good front and she appreciated it. Charlie got tangled up in discarded tissue paper, boxes, and bags. The little fellow's antics had them both in stitches.

Carl went to bed that night well after Gina and found her curled up in sleep with the light on and a book next to her hand. He turned off the light and slid in next to her, lying on his back. The silent darkness allowed the day's events to creep back into his mind. Afraid rest would not come easily, he hoped he could unravel this puzzle.

Still sleeping, Gina turned and forced her slight frame tightly against him. The gentle pressure of her supple body and the deep rhythm of her breath on his chest soon had him lulled near sleep. He drifted off, released from thoughts of the next day's possibilities.

23

Tuesday morning, Gina rose early along with Carl. She wanted to share some time with him over coffee before he went to the Casino. She had started this practice after Therese was born and she left the teaching profession to be a stay-at-home mom. Usually the only peaceful time she had all day, things got more and more hectic, as with all young families. By the time the children went to bed, she was so beat that the peace and quiet of evening meant nothing to her.

For the last couple of years, however, once Carl went to the firehouse, or to the Triple Seven, she was simply left alone. Keeping house for two took practically no time. By then, they had begun to make retirement plans. So Gina endured the occasional spells of boredom by telling herself that they were only in a transitional period. As the light at the end of the tunnel got closer, she became more and more eager to start her new life with Carl.

She really liked Vegas so far, but Carl seemed to reject the whole retirement thing. They usually had good times when alone together. For a man who could be as hard as stone, Gina knew he had a soft heart. She wanted more of *that* Carl. She didn't want to be pushy or overbearing, but she deserved more of his attention. She didn't know how much more slack she would be willing to cut him. It seemed as if he didn't want to warm up to the idea that they were supposed to be starting a new, easier life.

After some morning pleasantries, Carl again became quiet. Gina quickly gave up any attempts at meaningful conversation. Without looking up Carl broke the ice. "Listen, hon, I know this may sound funny, but I think I'm going to have to go back to the Majestic again tomorrow to play hold 'em for a few hours."

The frustration boiled up inside her. The time for giving slack had come to an end. "What do you mean have to? Am I really that hard to spend time with? Maybe I'll get a job, too, then you'll never have to be with me," Gina nearly shouted. Charlie scurried to the protection of his cage.

"Please, Gina, you know it's not that. I came across a problem at the tables, and I can't work it out while I'm dealing. I have to be on the other side."

Gina rose and stood at the edge of the table trying to make the most of her limited physical stature in preparation for the battle. "Problem! What problem? Carl, you're retired now. You don't need anyone else's problems anymore. Don't you get it? You can walk away now. This time is for you, it's for us. God knows you gave more than your share already. When does it stop?"

Carl remained seated, his eyes never leaving her face. She was a strong woman, and he knew it. He could sense her fighting back emotions, trying to present her case without allowing herself to break down. He grasped the seriousness of her feelings. She wasn't just blowing off steam. Genuine unhappiness lay just beneath the surface. He couldn't allow things to get that deep.

He sipped his coffee, trying to project an image of calm and ease, even though he felt neither, "Honey, I know I've been distant from time to time since we got here, but let me work this thing out and then I promise I'll slow things down. I'll even ask Meg to schedule me only twice a week for a while. C'mon, Gina, I never walked away from a problem in my whole life."

Gina leaned over him now, still trying to make the most of physical positioning.

If the situation weren't so serious, Carl would have been amused by this posturing, but her need to feel intimidating made him see just how desperate she had become. It made him feel that much more sympathetic.

"All right, Carl, solve the world's problems, but don't make empty promises to me. I don't care if you have to quit that job when whatever it is you're up to is over!"

"Okay, honey, I'm not making an empty promise. It will be done by tomorrow afternoon." He rose and went to her.

She leaned away, defensively, displaying her displeasure with the change in their physical dynamics. He wrapped his arms around her and squeezed tightly, perhaps overdoing it with the bear hug. With her arms folded and her face pressed against his chest, she tried in vain to maintain some stature.

He let up, kissed the top of her head, and said, "You know I love you, hon. You're everything to me. I promise I'll come around soon."

He slid his hands to her shoulders and looked into her eyes.

Gina stood firm and with a scowl on her face did her best

to avoid his gaze.

Carl thought he saw her eyes soften just a bit and kissed her once again before leaving the room.

Gina pulled the puppy from his cage and watched her husband's SUV turn the corner. She flopped on the overstuffed couch and buried herself in throw pillows before letting herself cry. Charlie licked at the tears, not giving them a chance to roll down her cheeks. That was all she needed. The little fellow had her back to herself in no time. She decided on a quick workout at the gym, followed by a day of sunbathing. I'll pamper myself if he won't, she thought.

Carl took a seat at the first table in his rotation. First things first. He scanned the room for yesterday's angry brunette. Not here. Hopefully she'd be caught up with convention obligations all day and wouldn't hit the tables until his shift ended. He did spot a number of men he either knew, or suspected, to be, part of the cheating team. They were seated at various tables around the room. He didn't have the best view of the high limit area, but thought he spotted the 'polished pro' at one of the no-limit tables.

His own table was free of the foreigners, but even so, he had to force himself to be engaging and friendly. His mind remained elsewhere. He knew that soon he would be confronted with the cheaters. Rotating from table to table made it inevitable.

He already knew the first team he encountered. The new guy from yesterday, who seemed to recognize Carl but said nothing, and another young man he had dealt to once before.

He decided not to waste time trying to spot the signaling. He knew they were doing it. The *how* would come later. Instead, he thought he would try to make a mental note of the cards they revealed and then try to match a signal to a given card.

Time passed slowly, but Carl remained sharp in spite of the tedious effort. The cheaters gave up little. Moving from table to table throughout his shift, Carl had the chance to observe many different combinations of cheaters and possible signals. The team members themselves even switched tables on occasion and joined up with different members. This enhanced the illusion of casual play.

They were good, but after a few hours, Carl began to get a feel for their methods. He tested his impressions over and over again, and by the last half hour of his shift, he knew he had most of it down. He began predicting their cards with unfailing accuracy.

The method was simple but ingenious. He considered that an even more advanced system could have been developed, based on the same principles, and employed by more experienced members at the higher limit tables. The guys at the $4-$8 tables only signaled aces, kings, queens, and jacks. The signal stacks were the last stack used to bet from in the previous hand and the one to its immediate right. One stack for each of the two hole cards. Having only two hole cards made Texas hold 'em the perfect target for this system, much less info to convey. If no signal was to be given, the player simply cut the designated stack and rifled the chips back together; or if he hadn't mastered that skill, he simply restacked the chips.

The position of the top chip in the signal stack indicated

the value of the cards. Face up, with the design facing forward meant an ace. Face up and backward meant a king. Face down with the flip side design facing forward indicated a queen, and facing backward, a jack. Before the flop, they casually rifled or restacked the signal stacks. The signals were given quickly and then obliterated. Only some memory work and practice made a beginner team worthy.

Carl realized that these combinations could be altered at any time. Like switching the wheels on the Nazi's 'enigma' machine used for sending codes during World War II. A more advanced system, put to use by better players, would be even harder to spot. He was certain, however, that he understood the method employed at the $4-$8 table well enough to pick up any adjustment they might make to the system.

He imagined that there must be peripheral signals as well. An abort signal maybe, or time to switch tables. Whatever. The other signals were unimportant to him. He had enough already.

The Nazis considered the 'enigma' code machine unbreakable, an attitude that helped lead to their downfall. The Allies eventually cracked their enemy's code. Carl thought he had done a fine bit of code cracking himself. Tomorrow he would sit in with these thieves for a few hours to test his theories once and for all.

His shift over, Carl went to the employee lounge to change back into his street clothes. Lighthearted for the first time in days, he figured it wouldn't take him more than a couple of hours to confirm his theories and lay it all out for Dmitri. He might even be home by noon. Gina should be happy about that. Then he thought, I'll take her out to a nice place for dinner, just the two of us.

Carl shook off his thoughts for the next day when he realized that ten feet away, and walking unavoidably towards him, was a brunette in a conservative business suit. Not just any brunette–the brunette from yesterday. If this got ugly, Gina may not have to worry about him working at the Majestic. They wouldn't look too kindly on a new employee having an altercation with a guest, whether he caused the altercation or not.

His eyes fixed on her, Carl couldn't help noticing that she was somehow quite a bit more attractive in the skirt and business jacket than she had been in yesterday's revealing halter top.

24

Carl watched her approach, her eyes warm and wide, lacking any hint of anger. He relaxed even before she spoke. Looking her up and down, trying not to be too obvious, he reconfirmed his assessment from their last encounter. She was lovely. The business attire only served to enhance her supple curves. It also lent an appearance of primness and propriety. Possibly even prudishness. The forbidden fruit. Attainable yesterday, unattainable today. Perhaps that would explain his increased attraction. Now, seeing her dressed as a professional, Carl could see that she was indeed at least thirty years old. His belief system remained intact.

"I hoped I would run into you again," her voice soft and inviting. "Please give me the opportunity to apologize for my actions. Let me buy you a drink. I feel I have to explain. I'm really not like what you saw yesterday." Again, Carl was made speechless by this woman. He didn't want to seem like an ass all over again, so he agreed to the drink.

She led the way to a lounge, and Carl hoped Sandy wouldn't spot him with this alluring woman. He didn't feel like making an explanation to his daughter. He didn't want Meg to see this either. You never know what people might think. Now that Meg and Gina had met, and seemed to hit it off, he imagined that they had established some kind of feminine bond. Meg would surely think less of him if she suspected him of something tawdry. This didn't look good.

The brunette positioned herself on an upholstered divan in a dark, secluded corner of the lounge. The darkness would make it difficult for any outsiders to see them, but if seen, they would appear guilty of something. There was plenty of room next to her on the divan, and her expression inviting, but Carl opted to sit across from the cocktail table on a small, uncomfortable wrought iron chair.

A waitress took their drink orders and hurried away. Carl thought she gave him a knowing glance before leaving. *What have I got myself into?* What he thought was going to be a quick drink began to take on the appearance of an illicit tryst.

"Let me introduce myself. I'm Mindy Edgerton." She offered her hand.

He shook it gently and responded. "Nice to meet you. I'm Carl Braun. I'm sure I have some apologizing to do myself."

She turned his hand over and held it between her own. "Pretty meaty paw you have there, Carl. What do you do for a living, bend steel?" She released his hand, thankfully. Flirting seemed to come naturally to her.

"No, nothing like that. Listen, I am sorry about yesterday. I knew you were in over your head and I took advantage of you."

She seemed impressed that he managed to get his apology in first. "Don't, Carl. I'm a big girl. I know the rules of poker but that's about all. I didn't sit at that table for poker. I think you know that. Maybe you didn't at first, but you did by the time I left. Let me explain myself."

Carl couldn't understand where she was going with this, so

he interrupted her. "Please, Mindy, that's not necessary. What happened, happened; I'm fine with that."

She wouldn't be put off and seemed determined to have her say. "Please, as I said, I'm not like that, and I feel I need to explain myself." Carl looked into her eyes and nodded. She continued.

"I'm the newest, youngest, and only female senior vice president at my company. Most of the men resent me because they think I got the position only because I'm a woman, and the women resent me because they think I only got the position because of the way I look. They think I slept my way to the job. I can assure you, that wasn't the case.

"Anyway, for the last year, I've felt this incredible pressure to produce top level results. I've worked tirelessly, but along with the results, I got a reputation as a bitch. Now they've transferred me out here and asked me to host this convention. It's the closest thing I've had to a vacation in two years, and nobody I know will speak to me."

Carl remained silent; it was obvious that she had a lot to get off her chest.

"I'm lonely. I admit it. I haven't had time for boyfriends, and most of my coworkers have become just plain mean. So yesterday, after the opening ceremonies ended, I decided to look for some excitement and companionship."

Carl just had to ask. "So you picked me?"

"Well, not at first. I sat at that table because of the guy sitting a couple of seats to your right."

Carl nodded his head and grinned. The polished pro. "Yes, he would seem more appropriate for you."

Mindy frowned, "Yeah, well, he gave me the creeps. He was good looking enough but something didn't seem right about him."

Carl agreed. "Yeah, I don't think he's right either."

Mindy continued, and Carl wondered if this story had an ending. He ordered another round of drinks. If she weren't so easy to look at, one round would have been enough. He was sure appearance had something to do with her promotion.

"I won a few hands so I stayed. After a couple of hours, I began to notice what a gentleman you were. So quiet and polite. Kind of mysterious, and if you don't mind me saying so, I noticed how well you filled out your T-shirt. I sort of let my thoughts run wild, and when you left the table for a minute, I made up my mind to approach you with some kind of proposition. I had never done that before. Maybe I was a little clumsy, but my heart was out on my sleeve, and when you ignored me, I kind of lost it. And for that I apologize."

Carl smiled at the flattery and only managed to say, "I see." He paused and gave Mindy the opening she needed to continue her monologue, entirely missing his chance to mention his wife.

"Look, Carl, I realized after I calmed down a little, that what I said went right over your head. I already had you pegged for a gentleman. I should have been more subtle. In any case, I spent another day alone. I'll be moving to this town soon and I don't want to exactly pick up where I left off."

He reached for his fresh drink and she caught his hand again. Their eyes locked; he felt her drawing him in. She tempted him with a second offer, making him feel weak for the first time in his life. "Carl, I have a suite here. It's beautiful. A private spa. A fully stocked bar. A king size bed. Come upstairs with me now."

Nothing like this had ever happened to him before and he sat as if entranced. This young example of feminine perfection had just invited him to make love to her. He looked her up and down again in the sultry dim light and gathered all the strength he had left.

"Mindy, if I knew where you were going with this I would have stopped you. I'm married. I've been married for over thirty years. And I'm sure I'm much older than you. I'm sorry."

She continued to hold his hand and look into his eyes. "You couldn't be that much older than me."

With his ego swelling again, Carl informed her that he was fifty-three.

"Well, I just turned thirty-six. What's the big deal?"

"It's not the age difference, Mindy. I'm married, and I love my wife. I'm sorry you're lonely, but I could never hurt her. I'm sure you won't have any trouble finding companionship. You're a gorgeous woman."

She smiled. "I don't want to just find someone. I found you. And you did turn out to be what I thought you were. A gentleman, kind and considerate. Your wife is very lucky. I'd like to meet her and tell her so. I hope she appreciates you. I wonder how many men now-a-days would have turned down my offer, married or not. Where are you folks from?"

Relieved that she seemed to be turning down the heat, he said, "We're from here now. We moved from Chicago a couple of weeks ago. And you did come close to meeting my wife.

She was the one you almost bowled over when you stormed out of the poker room yesterday."

He left out the info about working part time at the Majestic. He didn't think he could handle the temptation of meeting her again.

"That pretty little thing was your wife? Well, age can't really matter to you. She didn't look much older than me."

It made Carl glad to hear this assessment of his wife by one so attractive. "I told you we've been married for thirty years. She'll be fifty-one this month."

Mindy's eyes opened wide. "Well, maybe you're the lucky one. I'm sure she works hard to keep herself looking so good for you. That's one way to keep your man home, I suppose." Her voice became as sultry as their surroundings, and she probed Carl with another question. "Does she work at anything else to keep you around the house?"

He suddenly became uncomfortable and thought the time to leave had arrived. He answered by saying. "You'd be surprised."

He wanted to leave it at that. As he stood to leave, he wished her well and told her to hang in there, and not to sell herself short. Love would find her. Her shoulders sagged, and a frown appeared on her face. It did nothing, however, to diminish her beauty; it only served to draw Carl in once again.

Although certain he was playing with fire, he made a gesture, almost involuntarily. "Look, Mindy, we're both new to this town. Everyone needs friends. Let me give you my cell phone number. Call me if you ever want to talk or something." He scribbled his number on a scrap of paper and handed it to her.

She finished her drink and stood up reaching for the slip of paper. She accepted it and caught his hand at the same time. She seemed to be rather good at that trick. Carl wondered if he had made the trick easier for her by letting his hand remain longer than necessary.

Squeezing the paper and his fingers, she reached up to kiss him on the cheek. The squeeze and the kiss lingered longer than Carl would have liked. "Thanks, Carl. I'll bet you're gonna make a good friend. I will call you, and I'll keep my mind on the 'or something'."

She released him and walked away. He watched her leave, her silhouette becoming more visible as she moved from their dark corner into the light of the casino. She was completely fascinating. The kind of woman that men wanted to possess, devour, and hide away selfishly. She passed out of sight and a shiver ran up his spine. He felt he should pinch himself. *Did that really just happen and did I really give that woman my number?*

He surveyed the rest of the lounge for the first time and realized he was out of place. He found himself wishing he were home with Gina. He thought that by allowing Mindy a glimpse of his relationship with Gina, he had betrayed her in some small way. He had been working at the Majestic for less than two weeks but already felt he needed a vacation. He couldn't wait to finish with this cheating thing and turn it over to Dmitri. Let him deal with it.

Cheaters and temptresses. Carl knew they were a part of Vegas, but he had never seen this seedier element before. This whole Mindy thing was uncharted territory for him. He didn't like feeling out of control. He thought of the character Glen Close played in *Fatal Attraction* and it made him shudder. He told himself that he did nothing wrong. Just extended friendship to a lonely person. He knew Gina would have trouble seeing it that way.

He turned into the driveway and saw Gina standing near the sidewalk holding Charlie by his leash. She wore her new bathing suit and cover up, looking as good as ever. She smiled and waved to him. She always smiled at him when he came home, even if they had been fighting. That incredible woman radiated love for him unfailingly, and he just had a drink with another woman. Even allowed her to kiss him. Feeling somewhat corrupted, he wondered if he might be coming under the influence of America's 'sin city'?

He left his car in the garage and met her at the sidewalk. He hugged her tightly and told her that everything went well. "By tomorrow afternoon it'll just be the two of us for a while."

She smiled up at him, and shot him the smirk. "Okay, Carl, if you say so."

Just being near her made him feel refreshed and cleansed. Arm in arm, they entered the air-conditioned coolness of the house. Charlie followed along, doing his best to tangle their feet in his leash.

25

They spent a quiet evening together, speaking little but remaining close. They took Charlie for a walk after the air cooled down a bit. The only remaining light came from a sky turned deep magenta by the sun's last feeble attempts to reach over the mountains. Carl listened to more than an hour of girl talk while trying to get through a magazine. Gina lay on the couch, her head in his lap, and called each of her girls in turn, speaking to Lori the longest.

She received a complete update on the pregnancy and learned that she would probably be needed in Chicago in a week or so. "I can't wait, honey. I think your father-in-law wants to get rid of me anyway." Without looking away from his magazine, Carl protested this remark by giving her a slap on the thigh. Gina responded by pressing the mute button and saying, "Prove me wrong then."

That night Carl took his wife with a passion that surprised even him. Gina responded in kind, releasing the emotion pent up since that morning's fight. The encounter said more than "I love you" or "I'm here for you." It reaffirmed a lifelong commitment and a mutual dependence born of confidence and comfort.

With her soft, tanned cheek resting along side his, Gina, physically and emotionally spent, fell asleep on top of her husband. Carl, exhausted from the tumultuous day, folded his hands over the small of her back and gave himself up to sleep. His last thoughts were of confiding in her.

He walked into the poker room the next morning full of confidence and eager to put this thing behind him. Dmitri didn't bother coming over and directing him to an open chair. He simply waved his arm in a wide gesture indicating that Carl should take his choice from the many open seats.

A quick scan of the room showed him that only three $4-$8 tables were up and running. He didn't see anyone he recognized at any of them. Must not be a training day he thought. Looking to the $10-$20 tables, he spotted one of the young men at a table with an open seat.

He considered his options. $10-$20 were higher stakes than he liked to play, but Gina was waiting for him. He might spend all morning waiting for the team to hit the $4-$8 tables, if they came at all. No empty promises. It had to be today.

He bought in for six hundred dollars and sat down. When the attendant converted his cash to chips, the increase in table stakes lost its impact. Chips were chips and Carl knew what to do with them no matter what color they happened to be.

He waited for the big blind to come around before entering play. By then, he had already figured out who the young man partnered with. It wasn't hard. Only one other young foreign man sat at the table. He found the method of sending info to be the same as the one he had picked up on the previous day. The signals may have been the same, but these two implemented them in a much smoother manner. If Carl hadn't known what to look for, he surely would never have spotted them at work.

He played with increased caution for a while, concentrating most of his efforts on observation. The two foreigners used their system to good effect, but it didn't take Carl long to realize that the extra info they passed to each other was the only advantage they had. They didn't seem to be natural poker players. Their body language and consistently hesitant betting styles spoke volumes. Carl's sense of confidence rose.

Initially, he didn't consciously recognize he exploited his unique situation, but before long, Carl routinely used the intercepted messages against the conspirators. He incorporated the illicit information into his decision making process as naturally as if he had picked up a 'tell' from a careless player. Very often he knew the hole cards of two or three players, his own cards, and the cards of one or both of the cheaters. This information, coupled with his natural propensity for the game, proved more than enough to make him a dominate force at the table.

In time, the lucrative results made him completely conscious of what he was doing, and it intrigued him. Armed with the awareness of his exclusive and advantageous position, Carl pushed hard. He felt invincible. A veritable superman. Between hands, he considered the possibilities.

These guys didn't know he was on to them. He could run with them as often as he liked and beat them at their own game. Talk about temptation. He turned the idea over in his head for a while. It made the hair on the back of his neck stand on end, but what of the other six or seven players at the table? From them it was just plain stealing.

Most of them were tourists who expected to lose a certain amount anyway and probably wouldn't think twice about the incredibly 'lucky' guy at the table. That didn't make it right, though. Goddamn it, he spent his whole life trying to undo the damage caused by criminals and now he considered cashing in on their activities himself.

This town, the one he thought he was familiar with, the one he'd chosen for his new home, could certainly poison your soul if you let it. In the last two days alone it had presented him with a taste of adultery and a taste of cheating. Two areas he had never ventured into before. He knew that if he had crossed the line either time, he would have destroyed something precious to him, his relationship with Gina, and the thrill of competing at the card tables.

Enough was enough. He was stronger than this town. He could control his own destiny here. He would not be led into despair anymore. The pitfalls here were different. More hidden maybe, but more immediately damaging on a personal level. He knew Chicago had him on the ropes, but not this town. This would be child's play. He would address his new 'friendship' with Mindy later. First, he would deal with the cheaters.

After three and a half hours, he decided he didn't need to see anymore. He racked his chips without counting them and signaled to Dmitri as he walked to the cage.

Looking around as he moved through the room, Carl saw that things had picked up quite a bit. The 'new guy' had taken a seat at a $4-$8 table. Must be a slow learner, Carl thought.

Dmitri met him at the window.

"What is it?" Carl ignored Dmitri's gruff and condescending tone, speaking quickly and earnestly, but being careful not to let the girl behind the counter hear what he said. "We've got a group of cheats working this room. I can point out a lot of them, but I'm sure there are more."

Dmitri looked astonished. His bull like face turned red. "You are crazy. Not under my nose. How do you know this?" His accent became more pronounced as his agitation grew.

"It wasn't that hard, Boss. That young guy over there tipped me off. After I caught his act, I kept my eyes open for a couple of days and figured out the whole system."

Carl turned to the teller and picked up a thick stack of bills. He counted for the first time. "Look, Dmitri, you saw when I came in. I sat down with six hundred, and in just a couple of hours it's thirty-four hundred. I'm pretty good, but not that good. I read every thing they sent to each other. I'm telling ya, it was like I couldn't lose."

Dmitri stood nodding his head, his eyes burning into the young man seated at the $4-$8 table. "Tell me more. Tell me all you know. Come this way."

Would-be players gathered near the sign-in desk waiting to be seated. Dealers were looking toward Dmitri to fill the empty seats at their tables. Smoldering, Dmitri saw none of them. He led Carl to a quiet corner and listened intently as Carl laid out the whole operation.

"Review the tapes, now that you know what to look for. You can't miss it."

Dmitri crossed his thick arms over his chest and stood

nodding his head. His eyes bore into the carpeting as if drilling for answers.

He didn't seem to doubt Carl's assertions, but responded only by saying "good, good." With that, he turned from Carl, as if to dismiss him, and went to his post at the sign-in desk.

Carl left the poker room at just past noon. He took a deep breath and considered what had just occurred. *Dmitri seemed pissed. I'm sure he'll see to it that things are cleared up. It must be embarrassing for him to have this going on, under his nose. Maybe he thinks he's let his brother down. BB said a lot of people didn't like it when Al made him a floor supervisor.*

Only two things kept Carl from feeling completely satisfied and at ease: the roll of bills in his pocket, and the persistent feeling that his extension of friendship to Mindy couldn't help but cause problems.

He took care of the bills first. A Catholic church was located just south on the strip. He and Gina attended services there, at her insistence, whenever one of their stays in town extended over a Sunday. A brief walk later found him standing in front of a box labeled 'For the less fortunate'. Carl peeled six bills from the roll and crammed the rest into the slot thinking 'For the lest fortunate' a strange choice of words to use in a church located in the heart of a city built on the less fortunate.

Curious to see if Dmitri had taken any action yet, Carl walked back through the Casino and looked into the poker room from beyond the rail. Dmitri was gone, as was the 'new guy.' Apparently he hadn't wasted any time. Other teams still worked the tables, but all in good time. Soon Dmitri would have them all. Carl knew that he had given him enough.

26

Viktor, the pudgy young novice card cheat, sat in the passenger seat and held the left side of his fleshy face, wincing in pain, the marks from Dmitri's fist already turning purple. Viktor was not used to being shouted at, let alone punched.

"I saw the way you looked at that tramp. Your mind should have been on business. Your carelessness could have cost us everything. You are a long way from earning your keep here. I will have to stop operations. Every day we are not at the tables, we are losing money. Do you know what it cost to bring you from Russia?" With effort, Dmitri managed to gain control. He couldn't afford to lose his temper. This was a time for action.

Viktor had only been in the United States two weeks. Throughout his life his family had been one of the few who prospered under Russia's infant capitalist system. Unlike many in St. Petersburg, Viktor had never wanted for anything. He didn't know what his father did to provide for his family. His father rarely came home. Viktor's mother, a plump woman with ruddy cheeks and dull eyes, doted on him, and Viktor led a contented existence.

Two years ago, things had changed overnight. Viktor's father stopped coming home at all. His mother didn't know what happened to him, didn't know if he had left with another woman, had an accident, or was taken away by the police.

While the days of Stalinist tactics had ended, the occasional 'mysterious disappearance' was not uncommon. Information could be hard to get in Russia and Viktor's mother proved ill prepared for its pursuit. Without fanfare or emotion, she went from mother to provider, taking a job as a maid in a nearby hotel. It was a nice place, serving tourists in St. Petersburg's fledgling new industry.

Viktor was eighteen then, and for the first time, left to his own devices. He had no thoughts of, nor encouragement to find work. His mother thought him too soft and unprepared for the rigors of the world. She would try to combine the responsibilities of mother and provider until she considered her son ready to enter the wide and dangerous world.

Before long, idleness led Viktor to the company of petty thieves and minor criminals. He spent his days in smoke-filled rooms or running errands for the lower echelon of criminal society. He came home one evening expecting a plate of sausages and potatoes to be waiting for him as usual, but instead found a young man, dressed in a bellhop's uniform, sitting on the broken stoop in front of the dingy apartment house.

Viktor and his mother had no phone, and the bellhop was the only employee the hotel could spare to convey a message. Without ceremony, he informed Viktor that his mother had suffered a heart attack while scrubbing out a bathtub, and had died.

The sudden change in his life shocked Viktor, but the possibilities of his increased freedom intrigued him.

He didn't ask where his mother had been taken or what arrangements needed to be made. She was gone. He considered that he would have preferred that she weren't but she was gone, and that was all that mattered. He assumed arrangements for her would be taken care of, and they were. No one ever asked him to claim the body. He stayed in the small apartment until the rent came due. At that point, he packed up what meager possessions he thought important, and became further involved with St. Petersburg's underworld.

Viktor could be rather clever at times, but was something of a dreamer who tended to cut corners and succumb to laziness. Not much of a criminal, he learned that the law was interested in him after he botched a small job. Petrified at the possibility of going to one of Russia's brutal prisons, he used what connections he had to seek options.

He recalled hearing stories of a local man named Dmitri Beria, and learned that he occasionally took young Russian men to America to work in a growing and lucrative venture. Viktor had never heard of Las Vegas, but with the right recommendations and assistance, he found himself there.

The scheme seemed simple enough. After several hours practice for several days in a row, more work than he had ever done in his life, Viktor was deemed ready for a live training session.

A young man not much older than himself, drove him to the casino. The man dressed in an expensive suit seemed wealthy, very sophisticated, and very American.

Viktor entered a casino for the first time and was dazzled. With his mouth gaping and a hand held up to shield his eyes from the glittering lights, an array of unfamiliar and alluring sounds invaded his ears. People hurried about in every direction wearing expressions of glee, determination, despair.

The atmosphere, while stunning to the young man from Russia, was quickly overshadowed by his next discovery. Something more captivating than anything he had yet encountered in America: the women. So striking they seemed magical, untouchable, more perfect than images from his most secret dreams. They were everywhere in this lavish place. Every type of beauty represented–dark skinned, light skinned, tall, small, thin, shapely. Each one clearly dressed by wealth and carrying themselves with a pride he had never before witnessed in a woman.

The older man saw Viktor's reaction and tried to steady him. "Take it easy kid, pay no attention to them. They're a dime a dozen, and remember, they build these places like this for a reason. They want to distract you so much that you won't realize they're taking all your money. Don't fall for it. We are here to do the taking."

Viktor heard and understood. But the women, he had to force himself to get over them. They were all so wonderful. The only women who would have anything to do with him in the streets of St. Petersburg had been the ragged whores, and he rarely had money even for them.

Dmitri sat them at a low limit table and things progressed well. Then an American woman sat at the table. Viktor was dumbfounded. The most beautiful one yet. And the way she dressed! Viktor's companion barely gave her a second look. He was smooth. Such control. In spite of the distraction caused by the woman, Viktor thought he executed the system well. After a couple of hours, the woman lost a big pot and stormed off in anger. He found concentrating easier, and left later that day feeling pleased with himself.

He had never actually spoken to Dmitri Beria before, but knew of his reputation for ruthlessness. He knew this brutality was largely responsible for his success back home. Viktor understood that Dmitri had taken an opportunity given to him by his brother, and now was set up here in this place of luxury. Though pleased with himself, Viktor was scared to learn that Dmitri was not. He kept his mouth shut as Dmitri explained what they must do to solve the problem caused by his carelessness.

With his temper under control, Dmitri drove away from the glitter of the Strip. "We are going to burn their house tonight while they sleep." He pointed to a small case of tools and continued. "Those will get us in. It should be easy. These Americans do not lock their houses the same as we did in Russia. Back home they knew we were coming, and it was more difficult to get in. Here, they all live in a dream. I saw a cigar in his pocket once. He must smoke. I will make it look good, like an accident." Viktor sat silently, holding the left side of his face, unmoved by the horror of Dmitri's plan.

Hours passed without a word. Dmitri seemed to be in deep concentration. Glad that his companion had gained control of his temper, Viktor left him to his thoughts.

Darkness neared when Dmitri brought the car to a stop

down the block from the Braun's house. "We will wait here until the lights are all turned off. Then we will give them two or three hours to fall asleep deeply before we go in. Do you think you can be quiet?" Viktor assured him that he could, but added that he had never done this sort of thing.

"None of you have, or I wouldn't have to do it myself. All they send me anymore are children like you. And I can't waste time looking for someone else to do it. I'm lucky he came to me first. He is a good American," Dmitri added with scorn. "Always follows the rules. But he will not wait forever. Next, he will go to that bitch. We have to move fast. Done like this, we can get rid of them both and nobody will ask questions."

Viktor wondered what he meant by both of them. "Do you mean we are to kill his wife as well?"

The question brought a silent sneer from Dmitri.

Viktor persisted. "Why must his woman also die?"

Dmitri answered with impatience. "You fool, these American men talk to their women about everything. We cannot take any chances. Don't tell me you do not have the stomach for killing a woman. I saw you gawking at them like an idiot. Do not be impressed with the beauty of these women. They are not like at home. They are all spoiled and want to control everything, especially their men. I will not think twice about killing one."

Dmitri's simmering temper began to rise again. He clenched his jaw and managed to control himself. He surveyed the neighborhood and considered the matter at hand. "This is a good area. Not many homes yet. We can work unseen." He turned back to the Braun's house and pointed. "Look, they are going out. Good, we can go in and look around. Make sure there will not be any surprises."

Even though they parked up the block, Viktor recognized the man he came to kill. It was the man who took the big pot from the beautiful woman. He remembered that Carl looked strong, with wide shoulders, lean, tall, and had a rugged appearance. Viktor was glad they would be killing him in his sleep. A confrontation would not have gone well, even with Dmitri there. He recognized the woman, too. She had come to the poker table before the American left. Another pretty one. It would be a shame.

Dmitri waited to be sure Carl and Gina weren't returning and then, as he predicted, the two men entered the house without a problem. He looked around. Charlie yelped and barked. "Sounds like a small dog." They followed the sound and saw Charlie in his cage. "There, in that little box. Such an ugly dog." Charlie stopped barking and frantically wagged his curled tail in anticipation of going out. "Not yet puppy. We will deal with you later." Dmitri looked at him with a wide grin.

Viktor risked another question. "Will he be a problem?"

His answer came with a measure of patience. "I do not think so. He is not very loud, and we know where to find him. I will silence him quickly. If he does wake one of them, we will do what we must." Dmitri opened his sport coat and revealed the butt of a 9mm automatic. "But I do not want it to go that way. Let's look around quickly and get out of here."

"Smoke detectors! I forgot about them. Very uncommon back home. Go to the window and watch, this may take time."

He searched the house for smoke detectors, removed the batteries from each, and disabled their wiring. A tedious process, but he wanted to make a clean job of it. He then closed all the doors on the second floor with the exception of the master bedroom. They exited through the front door. Dmitri was cautious and certain that in the darkness of the sparsely populated neighborhood they had not been seen.

Once back in the car, he unveiled his completed plan. "Their bedroom is at the back of the second floor. If we are careful, they will never hear us. I closed the other doors so the fire will have a clear path to their room. I doubt they will notice such a small thing as that."

Dmitri grinned and spoke with growing confidence. "When we enter, I will go to the dog and silence him. The cigar will already be lit, all I will have to do is spread some newspaper on the sofa. That should be enough to get things started. It will spread fast. We will open a window to make sure it has enough air. I doubt anyone will notice that either. The firemen will break all the windows anyway. By then, it will be too late for them. I do not think we will have any problems."

Encouraged by Dmitri's patience with his last question, Viktor posed another. "What do you want me to do?"

Dmitri lowered his voice and answered gravely, "I will need you to help me control the situation if we are discovered. If we are heard, I expect only the man will come to investigate. I will shoot him. You go to the other and stop her from fleeing. It may take more than one shot. Or I may miss. There could be a struggle. You see how difficult the problem you caused may become?"

Viktor did not like the way Dmitri looked at him.

"I do not want this to become sloppy. I do not want any questions. Even if I have to shoot them, we will burn the house, try to cover things up. But that, I think, the authorities will notice."

An hour or so after the Brauns left, Dmitri and Viktor watched Sandy enter the house and leave quickly carrying Charlie with her. Dmitri became rigid, his face twisted with concern. "That does not make sense. Why would she take the dog? I do not like this."

27

Carl turned away from the rail and headed for the exit, smiling to himself. He had done a good day's work. His game would remain clean and unspoiled. He looked forward to his day with Gina and maybe a romantic dinner at Vito's. It didn't matter to him, whatever she wanted. It was her day.

As he approached the exit, he ran into his new friend. Mindy seemed bubbly and pleased to show off her escort. "Hi, Carl, this is Sam. He works in our local office. Sam, this is Carl. Carl just moved here himself. We're going to be the new kids on the block together." Carl shook hands with a tall, thin man.

In a manner somewhat less than cordial, the man said, "Pleased to meet you," and did nothing to encourage further conversation.

"We're off for a late lunch, talk to you later." She smiled and waved over her shoulder as Sam led the way into the resort.

The chance encounter irked Carl a little. *'New kids on the block together.' What the hell did that mean? She could have said Carl and his wife just moved to town. Maybe then Slim wouldn't have seemed so irritated. I don't know what her game is, but I don't like it. What difference does it make? At least she found someone. I hope he has the cure for her loneliness.*

He found himself hoping Gina would pick some place

other than Vito's. He'd had enough of the Strip for one day and didn't feel like coming back again in the evening.

He arrived home later than he thought, but still early enough to show Gina that he took his promise seriously. "Okay, hon, I'm all yours. What's it going to be?" Carl found Gina in the final stages of washing her T-bird. As she leaned over, sponge in hand, he noticed that the pink tankinni, free of its matching cover up, was splashed wet in places. He couldn't look at her, dressed like that, without feeling the call of temptation. No other woman stirred him like this.

"Well, you can pick up that towel and help me finish up here for starters." Carl, anxious to please, did as told. "Then I thought you could make us a couple of frozen margaritas, and we could sit on the deck for a little while. Not too long, though; it's already pretty hot."

"That sounds great to me." His eyes traced her figure once again and he asked, "But what about later?" Leering now, the suggestive tone in his voice betrayed to Gina the effect her wet tankinni had on him. She grinned, inwardly satisfied with herself for teasing him. Thirty years of marriage hadn't caused her to forget how to play the game.

There would be no afternoon delight for her neglectful husband on this day, and she did not intend to don the cover up any time soon. She wanted him to see her like this. Let him sweat a little before earning his reward.

"Not so fast, hot shot. I think after the drinks, you can give Charlie a nice long walk while I get dressed to the nines. Then you can throw on whatever rags you call dressy and take me to Vito's. I want to dine overlooking the gardens tonight."

He gave no indication that Vito's wasn't also his first choice. Charlie's ears perked up at the sound of his name. Carl wondered how much of a walk the puppy could handle in this heat. He considered his chances of giving Charlie a short walk and then catching Gina before she started primping. No, he realized, short walk or not, Gina wasn't going to let him play it his way. The seeds of frustration started taking root. Damn it, he thought, she looked good enough to eat.

Gina requested more than one round of margaritas. The sun had started to make its descent before she thought it was time to shower and prepare for her romantic evening.

Carl hadn't eaten all day and the drinks had brought on a slight buzz. He allowed himself to become encouraged with the idea that Gina may be a little buzzed as well. He reconsidered his chances and gave her a few minutes' head start before following upstairs with Charlie scampering at his heels. He crept through the master bedroom, the sound of the shower drawing him to the bathroom door. He reached for the doorknob and tried to turn it without making a sound. Locked!

She may have been buzzed, but it would take more than that to throw her off track. She seemed intent on having her day, her way, and if Carl had to suffer a little bit, all the better. He turned to Charlie. The puppy cocked his head and looked back at him with confusion in his bulging eyes. "I guess it's just you and me for a while, little fellow." Carl sighed and went outside in search of the leash.

He dressed in a fraction of the time Gina took. In spite of his aversion to suits, as Gina alluded to with her 'rags' remark, Carl could clean up his act when he had to. Some nerve, he thought. *'Rags?' She's the one who picked out this suit.* He knew full well what she expected at Vito's, so he called Sandy and asked if she could get them a reservation at 'just the right table.'

"Dad, you're so romantic. I'm proud of you."

Carl thought his daughter sounded surprised. "What did you think, honey? I've been at this a long time. I ought to know what makes your mother tick by now."

Gina emerged from the bedroom tightly wrapped in what she knew to be Carl's favorite dress. The white strapless number didn't quite reach her knees and seemed to remain in place in defiance of the laws of nature. The color of the dress made her already browned skin appear even darker and more exotic. Her eyes, smoldering like coal, were offset by luminous pearl eye shadow that matched her earrings and necklace. With her hair pulled back elegantly, the soft features of her face stood out and begged to be caressed.

She watched for his reaction and would have laughed at his expression, but she didn't want to spoil the carefully planned effect. His face said it all. He was putty in her hands. It would be some time before he neglected her again.

Clutching a small handbag to her chest, she coyly walked past with lips pouted. "Aren't you ready to go yet?" His eyes had been following her form, visually stroking the soft, round contours that the dress accentuated and offered up so well. His frustration grew as he realized his hands and lips would have to wait jealously for their turn to caress those well-known curves. Patience and waiting never strong points with Carl, it was going to be a torturous evening for him.

Her words brought him to his feet. "My God, honey, you look incredible." He reached for her, as if wanting to touch the dream, ensure that she wasn't an image from some deeply hidden fantasy. She slipped away from his outstretched hand. She knew how she looked. Good or bad, every woman did. Apparently, she knew what made him tick, also. The game continued.

Their table sat at the edge of a stone balcony, the only light came from a flickering candle. A sweetly pungent aroma rose from the gardens. They chose rather light meals, neither finished, opting instead to enjoy the cabernet, maybe more than they should have.

The soft glow of the candle reflected back at her from Carl's warm, blue eyes. She was becoming hot, maybe a little light headed, and wondered if there was more to this feeling than the wine and desert air. Growing impatient with the game herself she grew eager for its passionate conclusion.

Carl refilled their glasses one last time, emptying the bottle. Gina felt she might try to turn the conversation toward whatever it was he considered so important at the casino. Perhaps emboldened by the wine, she thought it might be time to take a shot at bringing their relationship to a new level. She wanted him to let her in, wanted to feel what he felt.

She prodded with hesitance, and he responded nonchalantly that he had discovered a cheating scam and wanted to be sure before he turned the guys in.

Gina looked at him with concern, "Won't they be a little ticked at you?"

Apparently Carl never considered that possibility. "Well, I don't think they'll be too happy, but the authorities are on it. They won't even know who I am unless I have to testify." Gina accepted his words with skepticism, but let it go with a shrug; what did she know? Casinos were his business.

To Gina's surprise, Carl continued. Maybe this opening up thing would work after all. He looked up from his wine and peered deeply into her eyes. "Gina, I want to tell you something, get something off my chest."

Uh oh, she thought, be careful what you wish for.

Carl gave her the whole 'Mindy' story. From the halter-top, (he left out the part about the protrusions) to the kiss, (he emphasized cheek) to the meeting this afternoon with Sam.

His eyes remained locked on hers throughout. A wave of pain may have flowed across her face, but it rapidly turned to anger.

"Let me see if I got this straight, Carl." Her words came with precision and control. "This woman propositions you twice; you tell her you're happily married. She tells you she's lonely and makes you feel sorry for her. You tell her you'll be her friend and give her your number. As soon as she gets it, she starts hinting at sex again. Then this afternoon she uses you to make some other goof jealous, or vice versa. Does that about sum it up?"

Carl seemed unable to decode her signals. "Well yeah, hon, I guess. I guess that's about it." He knew he looked stupid. She looked so impressive tonight and now he felt unworthy of her. He kept his eyes on hers but hung his head in shame. Another first.

"Look, Carl, you're one of the smartest people I know, and I used to work with teachers who carried their advanced degrees around like trophies. None of them could hold a candle to you. But when it comes to women you're like a lost boy."

Carl wasn't sure what to think now. Was she about to let him off the hook? "This woman sounds like the consummate predator. Didn't you see that?" She didn't give him time to come up with a ridiculous answer "You turned out to be a better catch than she initially thought. That's why she kept trying to reel you in. Married thirty years, faithful since high school. It would have been a double kill for her. Ruin your unblemished record and spoil another woman's marriage in the process. She obviously doesn't hold the institution of marriage in very high regard. Well, I'm glad you at least had the sense to tell me before this woman lured you to bed."

Carl raised his head. Apparently he knew what to say now. "C'mon, honey, there was never any chance of that. I just felt sorry for her."

Gina got the impression he didn't see this thing from all angles. "Carl, don't you think that I, of all people, am aware of how active your libido is. I'm your wife, I love you. I love making love to you, but this woman could have come between us if she had caught you at the right time. You're only human, you know. Carl, I don't think, that after all these years, I could have lived with it if something had happened."

Carl tried again. "I know, hon, me either." As soon as the words came out he thought, what is that supposed to mean? I have to do better than that. His cell phone chirped, denying him a chance to rephrase.

"Damn it," he mumbled, "I should have left that thing home."

Mindy's voice still bubbled. "Hi, friend. You'll never guess what that Sam guy did at lunch. He wanted me to pay for my own meal. He said I make more than him, it was only right. He even suggested I pay for his, too. He cited the women's movement or some nonsense. I know you would never treat a woman like that."

Carl, embarrassed by her untimely call, had no intention of pursuing a conversation. "Mindy, I'm at dinner with my wife. I'll talk to you tomorrow."

Gina looked up with a snap and held out her hand for the phone. "Okay, Carl, hand it over. I'll show you how we're going to deal with this."

Carl chewed on his lower lip, but handed her the phone without pause. "Hello, Mindy. This is Gina, Carl's wife." Carl had tossed pocket kings onto the table all over again.

A pregnant silence followed, perhaps indicating that Mindy sensed her control of the situation slipping away. "I don't appreciate your attempts to sleep with my husband." Carl's eyes opened wide, no beating around the bush there. "My husband has more friends than a man has a right to already, and so far, they all respect him. I'm here to make sure it stays that way. He doesn't need any friends like you. Make this the last time you use his number."

This time Mindy responded without hesitation. No wife had ever spoken to her like that, and it seemed she did not intend to let this one get away with it. "Carl's a big boy; I think he's capable of choosing his own friends."

She was no match for Gina. "The fact that I'm speaking to you at all should tell you that he has made his choice, but here, talk to him yourself if you like."

She handed the phone back to her husband feeling more than pleased with herself.

"What was that all about, Carl? You didn't say she was the jealous type. We're still going to be friends, aren't we?" Her voice regained that 'woman in distress' tone.

Carl, with his eyes still trapped in Gina's, replied, "I never could understand women, Mindy. I've got the only one I need, and I'm going to defer to her judgment on this. Goodbye." He folded the phone shut without waiting for a reply.

Gina looked at him, the smirk in the corner of her mouth took on a devilish twist. "I saved your ass that time, Carl."

He rarely heard her use language like that. Then again, she rarely had so much wine. He had never seen her on the attack like that. Her verbal indiscretion caused an impish smile to brighten her face. She had defended what was hers and scored a victory over sin in a town with a reputation for iniquity. Carl could see that the sparring session and victory had excited her.

He watched her sip her wine, a prideful gleam in her eyes, and considered that she really had 'saved his ass.' Mindy had all the tools and knew how to use them. He just might have broken down in time. He had spent the better part of thirty-four years looking out for Gina, thinking of protecting her and sheltering her. Now in Las Vegas for less than two weeks and she had become his protector, all one hundred and six pounds of her. The world had turned upside down. He couldn't imagine what might be next.

They finished their wine, declined coffee or dessert, and then looked out over the gardens one last time before walking out, arm in arm. Gina rested her head against his shoulder. Carl leaned down and kissed her as they strolled through the resort's shopping complex.

It pleased him to see men staring at his wife as they passed by. He wondered how many of them turned to obtain the complete image. He never got over the feeling that he was lucky she chose him. This feeling waxed and waned over the years, but had never been stronger than tonight.

The sunset had not brought much relief from the heat, and after sitting on the balcony, the air-conditioned atmosphere of the shopping complex must have given Gina a chill. She folded her arms in front of her and Carl tenderly caressed her bare shoulders in an effort to bring her warmth. He proposed an idea that had first come to him while they sat in the restaurant. He knew his wife well enough to know she would readily accept the notion.

"I think we probably had too much wine to drive home."

Gina's grin showed that she knew what he was getting at, but apparently she wanted to play with him a little longer. "I think you're right, hon. Why don't we walk up the Strip and let it wear off a little?"

He looked down at her; the expression on her face told him that she was still having fun. "I have a better idea"

"I'll bet you do"

Undeterred by his wife's jibe, he continued. "Why don't

we stop at the wine shop, pick up a bottle of that cabernet, and take all night to let it wear off in a room overlooking the gardens?"

Carl paused in front of the wine shop and waited for an answer. "That sounds great, honey, but what about Charlie?"

He wasn't about to let a detail like that stand in his way. "I called Sandy when you went to the washroom. I'm sure she's already back at her apartment with him by now."

The smirk reappeared and they both knew the game was speeding to a close. "Pretty confident, aren't you? I suppose you already have us checked in." Carl reached into his pocket and pulled out the keycard.

"I made that call next. Great things these cell phones. I got the key when I said I was going to the men's room."

Gina seemed to lose her desire for light-hearted banter and became quiet. She slid her arm through his and clung to him tightly. Carl picked out a bottle and bought a small corkscrew. As they rode up in the elevator, he looked at her reflection in the polished brass doors thinking no woman ever looked so beautiful.

Standing in front of a hotel room door, always gave him a feeling of anticipation. The feeling grew when the electric lock clicked open and allowed them to enter. He pushed the door open and Gina brushed past. Now it was his turn to complete the image.

Carl pulled the cork and poured generously into a pair of long stemmed glasses. Gina watched him, her eyes wide and black as night. This wine would remain untouched.

* * *

Dmitri and Viktor waited until two in the morning before Dmitri announced the obvious. "They are not coming home, and even if they did, it would be almost light before we could go inside. We will have to come back tonight. I don't like this. Much can happen in the course of a day."

Dmitri dropped Viktor off at a convenient corner near the Strip and told him to sleep and meet him back at the same corner at dusk. "Do not make me wait for you. I am growing impatient already."

28

The air conditioner easily overpowered the hotel room, and Gina, with no nightgown to fend off the chill, wrapped herself in the blanket and tried to burrow under her husband's side for warmth. Carl, surprised to be struggling with insomnia once again, pulled her close and took stock of his day. It had been a good day.

Both of his concerns were resolved. Gina remained unbelievable in every respect. He couldn't get over how radiant she looked in that dress. His eyes fell to the floor where the dress laid after being carelessly tossed. His own things, cast off just as hurriedly, lay next to it.

He stared at the ceiling, his mind refreshed and free for the first time in days. He stroked Gina's smooth skin, felt her warmth, felt her at rest. The lights from the Strip filtered through the sheer curtains and set the room softly aglow. Carl saw the untouched wine glasses on the table near the window. It was good wine. Perhaps it would help him sleep.

He slid out of bed, doing his best not to disturb Gina, and took up a glass. Immune to the room's chill, he opened the sheers just enough to look down on the Strip and the gardens.

In spite of his care not to wake her, the loss of his warmth made her aware that she was alone. She opened her eyes and saw him sitting by the window, saw him raise the glass to his lips and swallow hard. She watched as he gazed blankly. The glass remained in his hand, but did not return to his lips.

At first he saw the glittering signs, traffic, people all reduced in size by the height of twenty stories. Then two small faces, alone at first but soon surrounded by the nameless many, neither on the inside of the window nor the outside. They were just there. Carl couldn't help but focus on them, and soon the Strip faded from his sight. He didn't bother trying to shake the young faces away. He knew it was useless to try. Instead, he drank heavily from the glass and braced himself. Why two of them? Which children were these? The others faded and only the two remained.

They faded, too, and Carl found himself back at the firehouse. Mid-autumn. A chilly evening. He was not yet promoted, but seasoned and experienced. Dispatched to a fire, they turned the corner to see the street glowing orange from the middle of the block. The alarm office spoke to them through the rig radio. "Engine 131, police are on the scene confirming a fire. We have reports of people trapped inside. We're giving you a box."

Boxing a fire meant extra engines and truck companies. Carl's officer replied to the message. "Yeah, we're in front now, southbound, two and a half story frame, fire on all floors. Exposure building to the north starting to go."

The men jumped off and the officer shouted orders, "Go off the back boys, lead out the two and a half's on this one." The officer referred to the larger gauge hose carried on the back beds of the engine. The men knew what to do without direction. This officer just liked to hear himself scream. It wasn't the only screaming they heard. People standing on the sidewalk shouted that there were kids inside the building. Two of them. The screaming and shouting continued, but the voices blended to become a confused mass of background noise.

Carl was the pipe man that day and led out the hose to the front lawn. He couldn't reach the porch before the heat forced him to recoil. Anyone trapped in there was in real trouble.

He stretched out the hose as fire burst from the front windows and door, engulfing the porch in flames. He could see the second companies arriving in the rear. Tony Bach led out a second two and a half inch hose to the exposure building, racing to prevent it from becoming fully involved in fire itself. At this point, manpower was stretched to the breaking point, and the men worked furiously to make an attack before it was too late. Carl's line jumped and lurched as it was charged and became rigid. He opened the nozzle and directed the stream to the porch, trying to clear the way of fire so they could enter the building. The burning wood snapped and popped as water washed over it. Hot debris and steaming water splashed back at him.

With the flames beaten from the porch, Carl and his officer masked up and forced their way into the heat. With the limited manpower they struggled to advance the line, trying to prevent it from getting snagged or kinked on the porch. Carl pushed forward, hitting the churning inferno with water as he went. It protested in anger and pushed back. At first, the water stream seemed ineffective, but he knew that if he could lower the room's temperature enough, he would start making progress.

Power saws roared on the roof, the second companies beat on the back door, trying to make an attack from the rear. Box companies started to arrive, the extra help making progress easier.

The kitchen door burst open and the second companies joined the attack. With the roof cut open, much of the heat and smoke began to lift, permitting Carl to advance the line further. They gained the advantage. He carried the fight to the second floor, leaving the remaining first floor work to the other engine company. The truck men had already started their search for the missing children, but so far were unsuccessful.

Carl pressed his way to the top of the stairs and found a closed door burnt away at the top. He kicked, and weakened by fire, the door fell easily. He crawled under the smoke, finding a victim a few feet into the room. It wasn't a child, though, it was a grown man, his skin burnt away and barely recognizable as human.

The second floor, much smaller than the first, and now being well ventilated, Carl could walk through and work the line with relative ease. The fight may have been won, but the children had still not been found. The truck men continued their search, extending it to the second floor.

Carl stood by a shattered window and directed a water stream through the opening to draw out the remaining smoke and heat. A truck man lifted the door that Carl had kicked in and called out, "Here they are. I found them."

Turning to face the gruesome discovery, Carl's body shuddered with the horrible realization he had crawled right over them. They must have tried to escape but never made it past the door. They remained huddled there together. They had died there. He knew they were long dead before he kicked that door in, but the fact that he had crawled on top of them weighed heavy.

This one had made the papers. Fire deaths were more dramatic than shootings and the media usually reported on them. An unauthorized dealer had sold crack cocaine from the first floor. Someone torched his apartment to send a message. No thought was given to anyone who lived upstairs. Two small children perished that night, along with their father.

Their faces, distorted by flames with eyes calling out, remained visible for a time before eventually fading back with the others and disappearing altogether. Though no longer in front of him, the weight of their presence lingered.

The glittering signs and garden paths slowly reappeared. He returned his glass to the table and turned toward Gina. Seeing him turn, she quickly closed her eyes. Carl went to the sink and filled a glass with water, drinking it down, feeling hot in spite of the air conditioning. These visions rattled him to the core and left him exhausted. Too tired to think, he would have to wait until morning to wrestle with the cause of these hauntings. There had to be a reason, he thought. Or was his soul simply cleansing itself of its demons.

He slipped into bed and closed his eyes. Gina wrapped an arm over his chest and folded her leg on top of his thigh. The comfort she provided had him at rest immediately. Now she lay awake and wondered.

29

Gina insisted on ironing Carl's suit, as well as her dress. "I'm embarrassed enough, Carl. Checking out without any luggage and still wearing an evening gown. People will think we were up to something sleazy. At least our clothes won't look like we slept in them."

Carl considered this statement for a moment. "Honey, if they thought we slept with our clothes on, how could they think we were up to something sleazy?"

She smiled, her eyes sparkling at him. "Carl, you're such a dufuss. You know what I mean."

He chuckled and said, "This is Vegas, hon. No one will notice anything. It's a twenty-four hour town. No one cares if we're wearing evening clothes in the morning." She continued ironing, and Carl watched without complaint.

They ate a light breakfast at The Atrium, an elegant, glass domed, café brimming with tropical plants, and then stopped by Sandy's office to ask about Charlie.

"Hi, love birds." Sandy greeted her parents with a knowing grin.

"That's enough, young lady. Your father was just trying to make up for leaving me alone so much lately. It was very romantic. Thank you for helping out. I had a wonderful evening."

Sandy noticed her mother's dress. "Mom, that dress is

gorgeous."

Gina's face was free of make-up, and her hair was no longer up; but the dress looked the same, and she felt the same wearing it.

"Thanks, Sweetie. We've already had breakfast, and we're going to stop by and get Charlie on our way home. How was he?"

Sandy seemed to melt and made a set of puppy-dog eyes herself. "Mom he's sooo adorable. He slept on the pillow next to me. I felt bad leaving him in a box this morning. He's in the kitchen. I put some towels and newspaper in with him. I hope he's alright."

Carl thought he'd mentioned that he was trying to 'cage train' Charlie. Sleeping in bed with Sandy would probably set the training back a few days. Oh well, he thought. He would just have to remember this incident when she has children some day and sends them over to Grandpa's house for a visit.

They left her office and Carl told Gina that he wanted to look in on the poker room for a second to check on something. "I'm not even going in. Just a look over the rail. I'll be back in five minutes."

"Alright, Carl." She took a five-dollar bill from her purse and sat at the nearest twenty-five cent video poker machine. "Let's see if you can get back before I go through this."

He walked off at a brisk pace. "I guarantee it."

From what he could see, the room looked free of any of the cheats. *Dmitri must be moving quickly on this. He probably wants to clear things up before it gets back to his brother.* The thick-necked floor supervisor spotted Carl and motioned for him to wait where he was.

He seemed a little more disagreeable than usual. "What are you doing here? You are not working today."

Carl tried to seem friendly. Maybe it would rub off. "I know, Boss, I'm not playing either. My wife and I had dinner at Vito's last night and drank too much wine, so we decided to get a room."

Dmitri fixed his eyes on Carl and thought, wasteful American; he has a perfectly good house just a few miles from here. "Yes, yes, I see." He continued to glare at Carl, nodding his head rapidly as if the motion helped him to absorb information. Anxiously he asked, "Did you talk to anyone else about the cheaters?"

Carl, still trying to remain light and cordial, replied, "No. You're the supervisor, right?" Maybe stroking his ego a little would make him lighten up.

"What about your wife?"

Carl suddenly grew tired of his boss's company, and he didn't like the idea of Dmitri even knowing he had a wife. He boiled inside at the idea of this thug asking about her in any context.

"I might have mentioned something to her. What difference does that make? It looks like you started rounding them up already. I don't see any of them in here."

Dmitri's eyes flared; he wasn't used to having people speak to him in that manner, but he managed to suppress any other reaction. "Of course, you don't see them. Did you think I was going to waste time?"

Carl had had enough and didn't pretend at being cordial anymore. "Okay, Dmitri, I'll see ya later. I gotta go."

Dmitri's eyes narrowed and he muttered under his breath, "Yes, go to your woman. Enjoy this day. It will be the last you ever have."

Dmitri had, in fact, acted quickly. As soon as Carl revealed his discoveries, he had gone to his team leader and told him to call everyone off. They would be suspending operations until further notice. It shouldn't be for more than a day or two, but with Leonovich due soon, any interruption in cash flow was unacceptable. He had advised his man to keep his phone with him. They would resume operations as soon as possible.

Gina saw her husband approaching and pressed the cash out button on the machine. It ejected a voucher for eight dollars and fifty cents. Carl's irritation with Dmitri disappeared when he saw his wife smiling over her winnings. She snatched the voucher and said, "C'mon, hon, let's go get Charlie."

Carl kept his promise and spent the whole day with his wife. Gina for her part, suspended the practice of giving orders, and treated him as an equal. A day spent at the gym and having a quiet dinner at home (no wine tonight) was capped off by taking Charlie for a walk in the relative coolness of the evening air and an early trip to bed.

With her husband asleep at her side, Gina, growing weary of her book, set it down and reached for the lamp on the nightstand. With a turn of the switch and a sharp click, the room was cast into darkness.

Less than a hundred feet from the Braun's bedroom window, in a car parked near the curb, sat two men who also saw the room go dark.

30

With eyes fixed on the house, Dmitri spoke to his disinterested partner. "Look, the house is dark; they go to bed early." Viktor seemed more concerned with finding a comfortable position for his pudgy body. He heard what was said and smiled to himself, thinking of the pretty woman lying in her bed. What a shame, he thought again. But why should he care? America was full of pretty women.

Viktor considered his companion to be poor company, speaking little, and watching the house with fierce intensity.

"It is 10:30 now. We will give them two hours to be sure."

Dmitri looked into the back seat to confirm that the newspaper and cigar were still there. Pointing at the paper with his thumb, he spoke to his confederate. "I soaked the inner pages with lighter fluid. They have mostly dried, but the effect will be the same. We will know quickly if he has repaired the smoke detectors. That would be very unlucky. I have to guess that the other doors are open again. With a window open, that should make little difference."

If Dmitri had taken his eyes off the house for a moment, he might have noticed that Viktor had stopped listening as soon as he heard the words 'two hours.' Even though he slept away much of the day, he found he was still tired from last night's lengthy vigil and decided to risk sleep, hoping he wouldn't incur the wrath of his partner. Maybe Dmitri wouldn't even notice.

With his head against the window, he drifted into an uneasy sleep, but snorting like an asthmatic hog, soon gave himself up. Dmitri glared at him, and with disgust in his voice mumbled, "Is this what has become of Russia? I tell them to send me only those who speak English, but they send me anyone who can speak it, regardless of his quality. Everything better go according to plan. I do not think he will be much help if I have to use this." He rested his hand on the bulge under his sport coat and returned his gaze to the house.

Shortly after 12:30 a.m. Dmitri elbowed Viktor in the ribs. He delivered the forceful blow apparently as much out of cruelty and disdain as to awaken his accomplice. "Wake up you fool. Clear your head. We have an important job to do. We can not afford to go in there half asleep."

Viktor sputtered to catch his breath. The sharp jab had achieved its intended goal. By the time he had regained his ability to breathe, Viktor was anything but half asleep.

Each occupied home in the area had long since gone silent and dark. The Russians approached the Braun's front door with more stealth than necessary in the sleepy neighborhood. Already familiar with the lock's trivial peculiarities, Dmitri had them inside even faster and more quietly than on the previous night.

Charlie recognized the scent of the approaching man and let out three high-pitched barks. He didn't have time for more. Dmitri quickly slid the latch on the cage, grabbed the puppy, and pressed the palm of his hand over Charlie's face. With a grin, he used his other hand to clamp down on Charlie's throat. The puppy twisted and clawed at the sleeve of Dmitri's jacket.

"Damn this dog; he will ruin my coat." Dmitri snapped his arms in a quick downward motion, breaking Charlie's grip. The puppy hung in mid air trying to wiggle free, his paws groping frantically in the darkness. His struggles lasted only a short time. Dmitri placed the motionless body back on the padding and re-secured the cage.

Carl took his arm away from Gina's waist and rolled over in bed. With his mind clouded in slumber, the barks penetrated only deeply enough to make him wish Sandy hadn't taken the puppy into her bed last night.

Feeling her husband part from her, Gina rolled over and snuggled against his back. Carl felt her there and sleep was primed to regain its complete hold on his senses.

Dmitri crept back into the living room and signaled to Viktor to open the window.

He seemed surprised at how quietly Viktor managed to crank open the casement. Ah, they are new windows, after all, he thought. Even a child could do it in silence.

He tucked the treated newspaper between two cushions and placed the lit cigar along side of it, striking a match to help things along. The paper burst to life and the cushions quickly followed suit. They waited a minute or two just to make sure, then closed the door behind them as flames rolled across the ceiling and caught the newly hung curtains. Within minutes, flames had filled the entire room. They sped through the first floor, consuming everything in their path, and as if desperate to survive, groped for more.

The spacious floor plan meant the fire would most likely have had enough air to achieve Dmitri's goals without the open window, but with it open, things progressed at an alarming rate.

With the bay window now fiendishly glowing orange, Dmitri's face shined with exultation at the success of his plan. He drove off confident that Carl would not be coming to work in the morning. With one problem solved, his mind, in callous business-like fashion, turned to another: The problem of contacting team members at this late hour and getting them into the casino. He could not afford to waste anymore time.

He let Viktor off at the same corner, warning him against being late for tomorrow's work, and made a quick call to his man telling him to have the team ready by morning.

The rising heat swept the raging inferno to the stairs. The synthetic carpet fibers on each stair melted and bubbled in turn before turning black and erupting in flames pushing destruction further into the house.

Carl's eyes snapped open. A familiar smell he hadn't encountered in weeks. He flung the covers from the bed, reached behind him, and snatched his sleeping wife to the floor. She awoke with a scream. "Carl, what are you doing?"

"Stay by the bed." He crawled toward the door, feeling the temperature rise with each step.

Trying to avoid the heat, he kept his head so low to the ground that his right ear skimmed the floor. He peered out toward the stairs. The searing heat made him withdraw immediately. Pain from the left side of his face registered as he slammed the door shut.

Turning back to the room, his mind's eye perceived more than the darkness before him, a panorama of cherubic faces contorted in fear pleaded with him to do something. He had grown accustomed to their appearance in desperate situations, situations that most men rarely faced. For good or bad, Carl had made a career on the desperation of others. Now he was in peril, and the faces silently groaned with that much more anguish. The sight of those wretched images never failed to compel him.

He sprang to the window "Come here, Gina! The whole house is on fire. That door will only buy us a minute or two."

The casement windows were narrow, but Carl lifted her, and Gina's slim frame slid through without trouble. "I'll lower you as far as I can, honey, but I'm gonna have to drop you. Try and land on your feet and roll."

Carl held onto both of her hands and lowered her as far as his body would allow. "Okay, hon, I'm gonna let go now." Gina gasped breathlessly as she fell. To Carl she seemed suspended in space, until she came to a sudden stop. She didn't roll. The sun-baked soil under the desert grass did little to cushion her fall. He thought she landed at an awkward angle.

"Carl, I think I hurt something."

Carl's thoughts raced as he turned back toward the door.

Hot smoke and flashes of orange pumped through the doorframe. It rattled on its hinges and rapidly burnt away at the top. Flames began to force their way in with increased vigor. They could taste the air from the open bedroom window and wanted more. The air sucked past Carl. Experience told him that his time was about to run out.

He shouted to his wife, "Gina, move away from the house." She rose to her feet and hobbled away. He could hear her cries of pain over the noise of the fire. Carl doubted he would fit through the opening. He grasped the casement with both hands and bracing his back against the window frame, pushed for all he was worth. The vinyl near the hinges twisted and split. The mounting hardware, bent beyond use, finally ruptured entirely and released the window. It fell to the ground, cracking on impact.

Thinking of 9-1-1, Carl reached for the nightstand and tore his cell phone from its charger. He lowered himself through the window, coming to an abrupt stop when a twisted hinge ripped into his shoulder and held him in place. He looked up at the door, the children of his mind looked up, also, and recoiled in horror as the door burst open and hell sped toward them.

Heedless of his shoulder, Carl's reflexes took over, and he pushed free of the building. His flesh gave way, tearing loose from the grip of the jagged metal shard.

With blowtorch-like fury, the inferno roared through the broken window and singed his hair as he fell. In spite of his sudden release from the window frame, Carl landed on his heels and rolled backward harmlessly. He came to his feet and turned. Gina limped toward him.

Her hands clasped over her heart and tears flowing, Gina sobbed, "Carl, what about Charlie?"

He didn't think her question needed an answer but gave her one anyway. "He's gone, honey. There's no way anything could have survived in there." Now wasn't the time to tell her he would get her another puppy. She held out her arms for an embrace.

Her hand slid across the sticky dampness that coated his lacerated shoulder. "God, Carl, you're bleeding. Oh, my God, your shoulder is cut wide open."

He scooped her up in one swift motion and hurried away from the house. He knew modern building techniques didn't stand up well to intense fire loads and didn't want to be close if the home collapsed.

The nearest occupied house stood half a block away. Still carrying his quietly sobbing wife, Carl passed the building sites of the uncompleted homes and reached his neighbor. It took several pushes of the button and several energetic raps on the door to get a reaction from within. A curtain slid open and a man Carl recognized, but had never had a chance to meet, looked out at them. The man's attention was drawn away from the pathetic couple by an eerie glow that illuminated the night sky.

"Holy shit." Carl could hear his neighbor's reaction muffled by the glass of the closed window. He looked over his shoulder and nodded to himself as he recognized the signs of structural failure and imminent collapse. The roof sagged low in the middle and the front wall bulged like a woman in her ninth month. It wouldn't be long now.

The man jumped to the door and opened it in a panic. Carl assured him that, regardless of their appearance, they were mostly okay. His neighbor went to his phone and dialed 9-1-1, telling the operator that he needed an ambulance as well as the fire trucks.

Carl set Gina in the nearest chair. His neighbor returned from making the call with a roll of paper towels. He apologized for not having anything better to cover Carl's wound. Carl apologized for dripping blood all over the new carpeting and then introduced himself and Gina saying, "I know this is a hell of a way to meet. Thanks for letting us in."

Carl figured the man to be in his mid-thirties and he seemed very anxious. He brushed off Carl's thanks by saying "Oh, please, I'm just glad you're not hurt any worse. How did you get out of there?"

Before Carl could answer, the man's wife burst into the room. "Chris, the house down the block is on fire!" She caught sight of the injured couple. Gina sat on the easy chair, holding a paper towel over Carl's shoulder, while he knelt and examined her ankle. The woman summed up the situation and admonished her husband. "Chris, is that all you could find for them?" She left the room and came back moments later wearing her robe and carrying a clean towel for Carl.

Chris introduced his wife, Renee. She wasted no time asking what she could do for Gina. "I'm fine, really," Gina replied, rubbing her right ankle. "I think I just twisted it. But my husband is going to need some stitches."

Renee asked if Chris had called 9-1-1 just as Carl heard the sirens. "Honey, I'm going back for a minute to tell them what happened."

Gina watched him go and called out with little hope in her voice, "Carl, see about Charlie. Please." Carl wanted to let the company officers know that everyone got out okay. He didn't want any of the firemen to get hurt searching for victims in an empty house.

Walking toward his house, Carl watched as the roof finally gave way. It crashed with a deafening rumble into the burning mass below. He didn't have to worry about firemen getting hurt inside there anymore. They could only make an exterior attack now.

He caught up with an officer and told him as much as he could. The officer made a call on his radio to ensure that the ambulance headed to Chris and Renee's house. Carl told him about the puppy and asked to be informed if they recovered his body. For the first time, he wondered why he hadn't heard the smoke detectors. He knew they worked. He had tested them himself the day they moved in.

Renee asked if Charlie was the puppy she had seen them walking. When Gina said yes, Renee went to her with a hug. Gina's eyes welled up with tears all over again. Carl reached the front door just as the ambulance arrived.

The paramedics packaged Gina on the stretcher and splinted her leg. Carl sat on the bench seat next to her. As they drove away, he caught a glimpse of the firemen pumping water onto the remains of his new home. They turned the corner, and as their neighborhood faded behind them, Carl gazed at the cloud of smoke hanging heavily above the young trees.

His shoulder needed a number of stitches. Gina looked at the bandage and reflected on his already scarred body. The doctor applied a temporary cast to her leg and made an appointment for her to see an orthopedic specialist later in the day. Her ankle was fractured, but the bones weren't displaced and should heal fine in several weeks' time.

They spent the long hours of early morning waiting in the hospital. Carl declined a cot for himself, opting instead to sit with Gina on her cot. They discussed all they had lost. She asked hopefully if the items that remained packed in cardboard boxes and stacked in the garage might still be okay.

Carl gently stroked the hair away from her eyes and shook his head explaining that even if the flames and heat never reached the boxes, the amount of water the fire department pumped into the house would have ruined everything inside of them.

She accepted his explanation in silence, but found some relief from the fact that they had turned over many of their keepsakes to Jim and Lori before they moved.

Carl reflected on countless examples of personal devastation he had witnessed over the years–People sobbing, at times wailing, in the streets as he and his men re-bedded hose and prepared for the next run. He considered how those losses must have driven many families to utter ruin. Their losses, very often, were complete. Carl always recognized their suffering with humility, but now he experienced it on a more intimate level.

Sandy was about to leave for work when her weary father called to tell her what had happened. He asked for a ride back to her place. Stunned by the news, and not yet told about Charlie, Sandy said she would be at the hospital in a few minutes.

"Take your time, honey. It's over now and your mother and I are fine. Listen, before you leave, give Meg a call, and tell her I won't be in today. I almost forgot I was on the schedule. Tell her what happened. I'll give her a call tomorrow." Sandy said she would call right away and heard her father hang up just as she started to ask about Charlie.

Meg sounded very concerned when told of the fire and the injuries to Carl and Gina. She offered to help in any way she could. Sandy assured her that she would let her know if there was anything she could do.

Concern wasn't the word for Dmitri's reaction when Meg informed him that his newest dealer would be off the schedule for a while.

31

Peter, Dmitri's handpicked team leader, arrived at the poker room first. Anxious to get things rolling again, the disappointment showed on his face when told to stop the others and send them home before they came into the casino. "I thought you took care of that guy. Aren't we good to go yet?"

Dmitri was in no mood to be questioned, not even by his right hand man. His reply came quickly and with poorly suppressed anger. "Somehow they escaped. I don't know how. The house was raging when I drove off. Do not waste my time with questions. Stop all of them, but that fool, Viktor. I want to speak with him."

Viktor, briefed on Dmitri's mood, approached the sign-in desk timidly. Every vein in Dmitri's head seemed ready to burst, and he stood like a coiled spring, his hands clenched on top of the desk. His knuckles, beyond white, had turned purple. Viktor was reminded of the color he saw in the mirror and was glad they met in a public place.

Viktor stood and listened in silence. "It didn't work. They were injured. Only minor things. Now our problem has grown. We must act fast. I do not think he will discover the cause of the fire, but he is no fool. We are out of time. We were out of time yesterday. Meet me on the same corner at dusk. I will think of something."

Viktor turned and walked away. Dmitri's rage scared him.

He recalled the stories of him from St. Petersburg and spent his day considering what would be the best course of action. Dmitri blamed him for this situation. That wasn't good. Although not familiar with serious crime, he sensed things had gotten out of hand. What they did last night was extreme for him. But then again if it had worked, all would be fine today.

It didn't work. That was unbelievable in itself. *How could they have possibly survived? The heat was severe even before we got out ourselves. Dmitri may be losing control of this situation.* Viktor thought about fleeing. Where would he go? He had little money and no connections. He quickly abandoned that idea as hopeless. No, running was not the answer. Dmitri would know how to handle this. He would take care of things once and for all. There would be no playing around this time.

Not completely aware yet of the seriousness of the fire, Sandy's first question was of Charlie. When informed of his fate, she and her mother embraced, in tears. Carl looked on with a furrowed brow. He felt bad for the pup. He liked the little fellow, but too many years of death and tragedy had passed before his eyes to allow him to get upset over the death of a dog, even if the dog did belong to his wife.

Gina had just filled Sandy in on all the horrifying details. Their escape had been narrow. She stood stunned. The thought that she had almost lost her parents began to sink in. Sandy pushed Gina's wheelchair to the door of the hospital, too shaken to talk.

She was young and her life had remained untouched by

tragedy. Thoughts of mortality remained in the distant future. In her mind, her mother would always be there to love and care for her, and her father would always be tall and strong and ready to keep her from danger. Last night, they had been seconds from being gone forever. It chilled her.

Carl retrieved the Mustang from the lot. He came to a stop under the canopy, and Sandy helped her mother into the front seat.

Carl didn't say much all day. Sandy implored him to allow her to take Gina to the specialist, but he wanted to take her himself. "No thanks, Sweetie. You've done enough already by going to the store and buying all these clothes."

Sandy tried again. "Oh, Dad, it's just a few things to help out until you guys can replace your own stuff. Now let me take mom; you must need some rest."

Carl didn't feel like resting. His first concern was making sure Gina was okay, but he couldn't take his mind off of those damn smoke detectors. He didn't want to wait around for the fire investigator's report. He knew a thing or two about fires. As soon as Gina settled in, he was going to do some investigating himself.

Evening approached before Carl and Gina returned from the orthopedic surgeon's office. It had been a long day. He helped her into a chair in Sandy's apartment. The specialist had set her leg in a cast. The plaster felt hard enough, but it was warm and still curing. The doctor told her to stay off her feet until the cast hardened enough for the walking boot. Gina became agitated and restless as the doctor explained what she had in store. He encouraged her to be patient. She would be as good as new in six or seven weeks.

Depression set in as she considered her predicament. She hated inactivity. The baby would be coming soon. What good could she be to Lori and Jim with a cast on her leg? Their house, the cars, and poor little Charlie. A lifetime of keepsakes. What a mess.

"Are you comfortable, honey? What can I get for you?" Carl propped her leg on a stack of pillows and stroked her forehead with tenderness and care. Gina took his hand, silently kissed it, and pressed it against her cheek.

Sandy stood in the kitchen doorway watching the display of affection between her parents. A feeling of warmth, that she hadn't experienced since she went away to college, cascaded her senses. Her father rarely allowed a glimpse of his affectionate side, but she had caught examples of it over the years, and somehow it always helped to make her world seem secure. She cleared her throat and came into the room with a glass of water for her mother.

Gina took Carl's hand away from her face but continued to hold it tightly. "I'm fine you guys. I just want to sit still. It's throbbing a little. I want to give it a rest. Carl, how's your shoulder?"

"Don't worry about me, hon, please. It's just a cut." It was more than just a cut, and Gina knew it. It was a deep jagged tear. She remembered thinking it would never stop bleeding, but she let it go. Injuries had become a part of life to him, and he didn't like the attention.

"Listen, hon, I want to go back to the house and look

around, see if anything survived the fire. I have a few things I want to clear up in my mind."

Gina also wanted to know more about what happened and seemed anxious for Carl to report back. "Okay, hon. Don't be too long. I'll wait up. I want you to tell me what you find."

It had been an incredibly taxing day. Calls to the doctors and to two different insurance agents. A police report and an interview with a fire investigator. The wait at the hospital and later at the orthopedic center. All on almost no sleep. The constant activity and medical concerns gave them little time to reflect on what had just happened to them.

As Carl prepared to go on his errand of discovery and to leave Gina for the first time since the fire, it suddenly hit him that she could have been killed last night. What if he hadn't awakened when the familiar smell of smoke reached him? What if Charlie hadn't jarred his mind in the first place? If he hadn't been awake to close that bedroom door, their time would have run out fast. Another minute or two at the most.

Before he turned to leave, their eyes met. The sensitivity and softness of her gaze captured him. It lasted only a moment but the understanding that passed was clear. He kissed her gently on the lips. Words weren't necessary.

Carl felt funny asking his daughter for the keys to her car. He realized he was now dependent on her for shelter and support. *This is one hell of a town. Maybe I should've stayed in Chicago after all. At least I had that place figured out.*

"Here, Dad." Sandy handed him the keys. "I'll have the patient all fed and bathed before you get back." The hesitant smile on her face showed that she could feel her parents' spirits sinking and was trying to lighten the mood. "Looks like Mom and I will have to start shopping all over again."

Carl forced a smile. Gina flinched as if she didn't like being referred to as 'the patient' but managed to force a smile. Neither of them fooled Sandy.

Her car was parked in front of the apartment building. Across the street from it, parked in front of a trendy café, sat a plain, windowless, white panel van. Carl took no notice.

The occupants of the van noticed him though, and it didn't sit well. "Now what? They just came back. Where is he going?" Dmitri had a decision to make and he had to make it fast.

32

Viktor arrived at the familiar street corner early and waited, as the sun receded from view. He didn't notice the white van stopping in front of him. It wasn't the vehicle he was used to. Dmitri had to hit the horn to get his attention. "Get in you fool." Viktor opened the door and gave the van's interior a quick glance before sitting down. It had no windows, and was empty in the back, except for a shovel and some quilted blankets. His mind filled with questions, but he faced forward and kept silent.

Dmitri started to lay out the plan he had devised over the course of the day. The anger that had possessed him in the morning disappeared, to be replaced with agitation. He seemed a bundle of nerves. Viktor had never seen him like this. He spoke as if trying to convince himself of the plan's merit and potential for success.

"He has a daughter who also works at the Majestic. She lives in an apartment not far from here. Meghan says they are staying there for now. We now have three to get rid of." He paused to hand Viktor a 9mm automatic, identical to his own and fitted with a silencer. "I assume you know how to use that. You can not be completely incompetent."

Viktor shoved the gun under his shirt and assured his boss that he was familiar with its use.

"With three of them now, it would be better if you were

armed, also. I will go to the apartment and say I need to talk with him in private. I will make some excuse related to the cheating he reported and lure him into the hallway. Once alone I will pull the gun and tell him to come quietly or the women would get hurt, also. With that on his mind, I do not think he will put up a fight."

Viktor's mind raced. This was not another fire in the dark. Dmitri intended to shoot this family in cold blood. His eyes widened with fear and doubt as he realized just how accurate Dmitri's reputation was proving to be.

"You will wait outside the building. When you see us pass, you go to the apartment door and make sure they do not follow. Do what you must, but I do not want them killed in the apartment if we can avoid it."

Dmitri nodded his head. His faith in the makeshift plan was growing. "As soon as I get him into the van, I will shoot him in the head. Always in the head, you know. It is most effective. Even if they are not killed right away, it makes them unconscious. I will cover him with a blanket and meet you at the apartment. The women should come quietly when I tell them that Braun is waiting in the van. As soon as they are in the back, I will shoot them, also."

Viktor didn't like the idea of shooting the women. But he liked the idea of angering Dmitri even less.

"We will drive the bodies to a remote area in the desert. The moon is almost full, and it will make it easier to see where we are going. You will dig a hole deep enough for the three of them."

Dmitri looked at his pudgy partner as if assessing his

ability to perform the physical labor. "I did not want it to go this way. They will be missed and a search will be made. But if we conceal the grave well enough, the crime should go unsolved. It will be understood that they were taken, but why, and by whom will remain unknown. You see how much more complicated things have become?"

They had stopped across the street from Sandy's apartment building only minutes before the Mustang pulled up. "I will give them a little time to relax and get comfortable before I go up." Viktor, remained silent and only nodded. He did not share Dmitri's growing confidence.

When Carl re-emerged from the building and got into the car, Dmitri's waning nervousness came back with a vengeance and quickly evolved into a state of panic. "This is bad." His mind raced for a solution; he must maintain control of the situation. The family had to be contained. Options and possibilities came and were rejected by him rapidly. He turned to Viktor and snapped a question. "Can you drive?"

"Yes, yes of course."

It was the answer he had hoped for. Dmitri opened the door and got out. "Follow him. See if he goes to the police. If he goes to the Majestic, follow him inside and see who he speaks to. Above all, do not let him see you. I will watch from this café. We will get him when he returns, before he goes back into the building."

The van pulled away from the curb and Viktor quickly caught up to the Mustang.

Dmitri entered the café after checking to make sure the

automatic was safely concealed. The silencer increased its bulk and made it more difficult to hide under his coat. He sat near a window overlooking the street and ordered coffee, hoping the wait wouldn't be a long one

Dmitri sipped his coffee and tried to hide his anxiety. He reviewed the situation. It had grown more desperate than he thought possible. He squirmed in his seat and kept looking from his cup to his watch and to the building across the street. He didn't like sending that young fool to follow the American, but he liked the idea of leaving him with the women even less. He seemed in awe of these American tramps. Surely they would cloud his judgment. The daughter was young and sure to be pretty. No, he couldn't trust him. Again Dmitri shook his head at the quality of men they sent from back home.

All he had to do was follow and watch. Once they had Carl in the van, the women would be an easy matter.

The trials of this tiresome day began to take their toll on Carl. He tried to rub the fatigue from his eyes as he drove away from Sandy's apartment. He hadn't felt this drained since his last bad night on Engine 51. His mind kept reliving the day's events. He drove on, as if in a trance.

Even if rested and alert, he probably wouldn't have noticed the van that followed him.

He knew it wouldn't be easy to find much valuable information in the rubble of his house. Most everything, including evidence, had been buried in the collapse. All he really cared about was finding one of the smoke detectors more or less intact, and seeing if he could discover anything from it.

He resurfaced from the depths of his thoughts and came to a stop in front of the house.

The sight made him grimace. A hollow and charred mass of twisted building materials, strewn here and there with the remains of their possessions. He stepped over a crumpled wall and entered the sodden remains.

With a full moon and a flashlight, borrowed from Sandy, he figured he'd be able to see well enough. He was too occupied with his search to notice the white van as it rolled to a stop down the block.

With a quizzical twist on his face, Viktor looked at Carl. *Why would he come back to this scene of devastation? He must be tired. Why didn't he go to bed? He seems to be looking for something.* As Viktor watched Carl's efforts in the moonlight, he began to consider the possibility of altering the plan.

This neighborhood was still deserted. He could take the American right here and no one would see. It would be safer than taking him in front of a well-lit apartment building across from a busy café. Dmitri would certainly be pleased if he came back with the American already dead. They could then take the women as planned and continue into the desert. He knew Dmitri had become frustrated and unhappy with him. This would set things right.

He started the van and pulled it close to the front of the red car. He went to the convertible, hoping to find the keys in the ignition. He leaned past the steering wheel, a smile growing on his bruised face. Viktor began mumbling, apparently growing proud of himself for coming up with such a clever idea. "Dmitri often called me a fool, but I am no fool. There is no reason to be nervous or anxious at all. This is a good plan. The 9mm will make handling the rugged American a thing of ease. Perhaps I really am cut out for this type of thing. No keys. Oh, well, that does not really matter."

Carl held a blackened smoke detector in his hand. He found it in the foyer that led to the garage. That particular section of the house wasn't as severely damaged by the flames and collapse.

He had mounted the detector in that location himself, in addition to the ones already installed by the building contractor. Many house fires start when fire spreads from an attached garage. He wanted to be sure they had plenty of warning if that happened in their house. The plastic parts of the device had fused together by the heat, but Carl managed to twist them apart. He looked in wonder when he saw the battery was missing.

Impossible. He had checked all the detectors on their first day in the house, but specifically remembered installing the battery in this one.

His mind began to unravel the puzzle, and he looked up from the small device suddenly bewildered by a realization. Carl had never been a policeman, nor had he ever worked in the Fire Department's office of investigations, but he was no idiot either. The missing battery meant the fire must have been set intentionally, and the disabled smoke detectors meant the arsonist's purpose was to kill.

Alarm bells went off in his head and adrenalin rushed as if he were responding to an emergency once again.

Why would someone want to kill him? His eyes narrowed beneath his knitted brow as he wrestled with this new and unimaginable question. Gina's words came back to him. "Won't they be ticked?" The cheating team. It had to be them. Who else could it be? But how could they know he was the one who discovered them? Could Dmitri really have been that careless?

The truth hit him like a punch, leaving him dazed. *Dmitri, the accents, Russians. Goddamn it, how could I have been so blind? They are Dmitri's crew. He is the ring leader.* His head began to pound and he muttered, "That bastard tried to kill me. He tried to kill Gina."

Carl was never quick to anger, but rage grew rapidly inside him. All of a sudden he became aware of the van parked so close to Sandy's car. "What the hell's on that guy's mind, and what's he looking for in the car?"

He dropped the smoke detector and walked impatiently toward his waiting assassin. All at once, the panorama of children became visible to him, their hands held up to their faces in silent horror. He shook his head in anger trying to rid his mind of the distraction.

Clearly Viktor didn't want to scare off his victim, so he let Carl approach to within a couple of steps before drawing the gun. Carl saw the gun and recognized its owner at the same time.

Viktor raised the gun, but was unprepared for the quickness of his victim. Carl swept away his arm and shoved with all his might. Viktor's portly body became unbalanced, and he sprawled backward across the hood of the Mustang. He didn't drop the gun, however, and while still on his back, swung his arm in a clumsy motion and fired toward Carl.

The muzzle flashed brightly in the night air and Carl recoiled. The bullet whistled past his head. While struggling to regain his feet, Viktor tried to steady his aim and fire again. Carl backed away from the gun and fled for shelter. Again he heard the pop, pop of the silencer but didn't feel the sting of pain. Imitating what he had seen in many police movies, he ran in a zigzag pattern, hoping to make himself a more difficult target.

As he ran past the houses still under construction, he realized that the end of the block was only a couple of hundred feet away. Once he passed the last house, he would be left exposed in open desert with the bright moonlight making him an easy target.

He looked over his shoulder and saw Viktor giving chase and trying to aim at the same time. The faces of the children were still present but no longer a distraction. Carl hardly noticed the terror in their eyes as he tried to find safety. All his attention was now directed to his survival. He came to the last house and rounded the corner. A bullet slapped into the wall about chest high, shards of brick exploding in every direction.

He could go no further. He heard Viktor running toward him. The children became a distraction again, their faces a reflection of the dread that pursued him.

If he had cover for safety, he knew he could escape the out of shape young man, but in the open, it was just a matter of time before one of the bullets found its mark. Flight was no longer an option. He looked around for something, anything, to defend himself with. On the ground at his feet, amongst an odd assortment of construction debris, he spotted a piece of brick. It filled his hand. He gripped it tightly, the sharp edges digging into his palm.

Viktor skidded around the corner, running as fast as balance would permit. He grabbed the corner of the wall with his right hand in an effort to steady himself in the turn. His right hand also held the gun. That was a mistake. He had a split second to realize his error, but no more than that.

Carl swung with all the force his enraged six-foot, one hundred eighty-five pound body could summon. He slammed the chunk of brick against the left side of Viktor's face with such force that the pudgy man's body lifted off its feet and flew backward. Carl could feel his pursuer's face cave in. A geyser of blood sprayed from Viktor's cheek splattering Carl's arm.

Viktor landed on his back with a sickening thud and lay motionless, still clutching the butt of the gun. Carl could see that he still breathed. He kicked the gun away and pushed it under some debris with his foot. He didn't want to touch it.

With his chest heaving and his heart racing, he stared down at his would-be killer. The man who wanted to kill Gina. Who wanted to take away everything he had.

Wrath and frustration possessed him. His hands began to tremble, his mind, spinning in a whirlwind, revisited the terrors he had spent his career trying to put right. Terrors caused by men like this, who preyed on the weak and consumed the innocence of children.

No longer able to contain his fury, it burst free in the form of savage kicks. Viktor's defenseless head lolled back and forth as each kick hit its mark with disturbing accuracy. Carl didn't stop until his body, drained of emotion, grew too tired to strike out again.

Blood oozed from Viktor's grotesquely injured face and soaked into the dry earth.

With the Mustang blocked by the van, Carl dropped the transmission into reverse and hit the gas. Before the car came to a complete stop, he slammed it into drive and tore away from the curb, squealing the tires.

With effort, he managed to calm himself and concentrate. Truly out of his element now, he knew of only one thing to do. Get Gina and Sandy to safety. If they knew how to find him, they surely knew how to find his family.

He recalled Dmitri asking about his wife. *Damn, what an ass I've been.* Beyond getting his family to safety, he wasn't sure what to do. He took his cell phone from his pocket and hit Sandy's number on the speed dial. Her phone rang, then it rang a second time, then a third. Damn it. Where is she? Sandy picked up on the fourth ring. Carl let out a deep breath relieved his call hadn't gone into voice mail.

"What's up, Daddy? I was just helping Mom into the bathtub."

Carl tried to remain calm. He wasn't directing a probationary fireman at his first fire; he was trying to save his wife's and daughter's lives without causing alarm. Almost in a panic himself, he struggled to suppress his emotion. "Listen, honey, I want you to stay calm but do exactly as I say."

Sandy seemed to pick up something in her father's voice. Try as he might, he couldn't conceal his anxiety.

"I'll explain later, but get your mother dressed right now. Just put anything on her and wait for me. We're leaving. All of us. Make sure your door is locked and don't open it until you hear me. If anyone but me shows up, call the police. Do you understand?" Carl's effort to avoid causing a panic had not been totally successful.

Sandy became thoroughly rattled and it showed in her voice "I understand, Daddy. What's the matter? You're scaring me."

With as much patience as he could muster, he tried to nudge his daughter to action. "Not now, Sweetie. Just do like I said and hurry. I'll be there in a few minutes. Now goodbye." He shut the phone and dropped it on the seat.

He put the sports car to the test, driving as fast as possible while trying not to be reckless. His thoughts turned to Viktor. He had still been breathing after he hit him with the brick, but he wasn't so sure after he finished kicking him. He thought about calling the police, but what would he say? "I just beat a man to death over on Sun Valley Drive." No, he had to see about his family's safety first. He could sort out the rest later. He would bring them to a motel for the night. Any motel. He just wanted to be anonymous and safe.

He stopped in front of Sandy's apartment building and realized he could have to defend himself again. He looked around for something to use as a weapon. Nothing. He wished he had kept the brick. For the first time, he noticed the blood. Viktor's blood, all down his right arm. The skin on the palm of his right hand was split and bleeding, an indication of the force he put behind that piece of brick. If the girls opened the door and saw him like this, they would have a fit. Blood was smeared on the steering wheel and had dripped onto his jeans.

He looked around for something to clean up with and found some napkins on the backseat. It was no use. The blood had practically dried already. He was wasting time. He had to get the girls out of here.

Sandy removed the chain and slid the deadbolt. When she opened the door, she reacted as Carl expected. "Dad, what happened? Are you alright?" She looked queasy.

Carl said, "Hang in there, honey. It's not my blood. I'm fine. Now let's go. Lock up the door and hurry." Sandy decided to hold her questions until later and did as her father said.

Gina seemed to sense the seriousness of the situation and hobbled along in silence, using Carl's arm for support. Even with his help she moved very slowly. They only went along that way for a few feet before he swept her up and rushed quickly to the elevator. Sandy edged past the closing doors with fright growing in her eyes.

Carl took a quick look around before joining the women in the car. He missed seeing Dmitri standing at his table in the café. Carl pulled away, deciding to drive for several miles before selecting a motel. He wanted to be sure they weren't being followed and didn't think he would have much trouble finding a motel room anywhere in town.

Gina and Sandy fidgeted in their seats. Apparently the silence was becoming unbearable. They looked into each other's eyes, as if hoping to glean some hint of what had happened. Wordlessly they agreed to leave Carl to his thoughts.

33

Time seemed to stand still, and Dmitri started to worry. Hiding his anxiety nearly became an impossible task. He thought every eye in the café was on him. He forced himself to sip the coffee slowly, and gaze casually out the window. Three cups of the strong, dark roasted blend had an ill effect on his already agitated demeanor.

The red Mustang re-appeared. The time had come. Dmitri placed his hand under his coat and hurried from the café. He looked up the street expecting to see the van. Timing was everything. No van. He crossed the street and hid in the shadows of the building. Carl seemed preoccupied with something in the car. That was lucky. By delaying, he gave that fool a chance to catch up. Dmitri looked up the block again and slammed his palm against the brick wall. *Still no van. Where is that fool?*

Carl remained in the car fidgeting with something. He gave Dmitri more time than he could have hoped for, but still no van. Finally, Carl left the car and walked toward the building's lobby. Dmitri looked up the street in desperation, then withdrew deeper into the shadows. No van. The opportunity had passed. *Damn that fat fool.*

He went back to the café and ordered more coffee. They would just have to revert back to the original plan. *Maybe this will be better after all. It is later now. Less activity on the street. Where the hell is that boy?*

The cup fell from his hands with a crash. Dmitri jumped to his feet, gaping in horror, as Carl and his daughter helped the injured woman into the car and sped off.

He rushed from the café only to watch the car turn the corner and disappear. Dmitri's eyes bulged from their sockets and burned red, but his mind didn't stop groping for solutions. He would not give up. Braun had slipped away again, but there was still time.

Several more minutes passed before the white van appeared. Dmitri had regained his composure and actually grew calm. *Now at least I can eliminate one of my problems.*

Viktor pulled the van up to the curb and stopped next to Dmitri. Dmitri stepped quickly to the driver's door and opening it, told the younger man to move over.

He slipped his bulk into the vacated seat and glanced at his confederate for the first time. Dmitri could never be described as a squeamish man, but what he saw caused him to flinch. The purple bruise he'd left on Viktor's cheek the previous day was hardly noticeable on his ruptured and inflamed face.

His lower jaw no longer lined up with the rest of his face. A flap of flesh that had once been his cheek hung loosely against his chin. Dmitri could see Viktor's upper teeth through the gaping hole. Three of his lower teeth were missing, and his left eye had swollen shut and continued to seep blood. His head, neck, and chest glistened red. Dmitri wondered how he had driven back at all.

"My God, what happened to you?" Speaking seemed

difficult and painful to Viktor, but Dmitri was not one to be put off. With garbled speech, and occasionally choking on his own blood, he told his boss how and why he tried to take Carl at the house. The result of his attempt appeared obvious.

Dmitri found new respect for the American, and asked with a hint of awe, "He did this with his bare hands while you tried to shoot him?"

Viktor examined himself in the rear view mirror and grimaced. The discovery of his hideous appearance appeared to shock him. "Ya, I sink so. Are ya gonna take me to da doctor?"

Dmitri brushed off the question and asked about the gun. "Do you still have the 9mm?"

Tears rolled from Viktor's open eye as he attempted speech once again. "Ya, Ya, I stumbled on it. It was under rubbish." Dmitri took the gun.

Dmitri drove, steering away from civilization and toward the vast desert surrounding the city. He addressed the question regarding a doctor. "Yes, of course, I will take you to a hospital; I know you are in pain, but we still have to finish this. It will all be settled soon. Then I will see that you get proper treatment."

He looked at his passenger and cringed before continuing. "Our mistake was in trying to take them too early in the evening. We will wait until much later, but we are not going to waste time sitting in front of their building. We will use the time to make things ready. It will be very late then and they will all be asleep when we return. After all, they can not stay awake forever."

Viktor didn't seem convinced. He thought that the family would certainly be on guard after his attack on Carl, but speaking was too painful, so he kept his concerns to himself. Dmitri would do as he pleased, anyway. His only choice was to do as told so he could get to a doctor as soon as possible.

"We are going out to the desert and will spend this time digging a hole. I know you are hurt, but you must do the digging. Make it deep enough for three of them. When you are finished, we will return to the city. It will be an easy matter by then. Try to get some rest. We have much work to do."

Viktor rested his head against the window, smearing blood on whatever he touched. Dmitri only hoped he wouldn't die before he finished with the hole. He had no desire to do the digging himself.

Dmitri brought the van to a stop about half a mile removed from the dirt road, the isolation so complete that not even a coyote could be heard. Dmitri reached behind his seat and retrieved the shovel. "Get started, Viktor. It is getting late."

Viktor's head throbbed. His cheek still seeped blood along with his swollen left eye, and he was sure his jaw was broken, or worse. Still, Dmitri had never called him by his name before. Maybe he had finally come around. Maybe he appreciated his effort and sacrifice this evening in spite of the way things turned out. Maybe.

Viktor took the shovel, got out of the van, and started digging, but after only a few minutes of work, he stopped to look at his hands. Dmitri leaned out of the window and said, "Those are blisters. You have the hands of a woman. Keep working or we will be here all night."

Blood continued to drip from Viktor's face, the crimson drops making tiny craters in the dry dusty ground. Though weak, he pushed on. The work went slow, and he became angry at his boss, wondering why he refused to help, but he held it in. He was in no position to make a stand.

The pain and loss of blood numbed him, making him dizzy. Dmitri watched as Viktor's strength gradually faded. He decided it might be time to examine the pathetic young man's work. Dmitri stepped from the van and approached. Viktor climbed out of the hole and stood swaying on its edge as Dmitri assessed his work. "It is more than a meter now; I guess that will be enough."

Viktor sighed and seemed relieved to learn that his work had come to an end. As always, Dmitri made the decision, but he doubted the hole was deep enough for three people, even if two of them were women.

With his work over, Viktor's body relaxed and made him acutely aware of the brutality he had suffered. Seeking relief from the intense pain, he found comfort in thoughts of the women they would be taking soon. He had never seen the daughter, but assumed she must be very pretty. The mother, though older, was still very pretty. The younger one must be beautiful. Perhaps, he thought, he might convince Dmitri not to kill them right away. Surely he had earned at least that much. He wouldn't ask for much time. What did it matter? They were only going to kill them, after all.

Dmitri raised his arm and placed the barrel of his gun near the base of Viktor's skull. For the second time in the space of just a couple of hours, a geyser of blood sprayed from the young man's face. This time, however, a copper-jacketed projectile led the way. As it emerged from just above Viktor's lip, it brought chips of bone and broken teeth with it.

The bullet sailed unmolested into the desert night, but the teeth, bone, and blood landed neatly into the waiting hole, followed very shortly by the lifeless body of the young Russian.

Dmitri refilled the hole, laughing at himself for wishing he could have kept the young fool around long enough to do the refilling himself. His humor proved short-lived, however, and his thoughts returned to Carl and the women. He wasn't exactly back where he started. Two days had passed, and now because of this fool, the American must know everything.

This problem required some real concentration. He might need to go to others for help now, go to a higher authority. It didn't look good for him, letting things go this far. He must take care of this once and for all. They were losing money everyday now, and he doubted he had enough cash on hand to satisfy Leonovich. The organization in St. Petersburg, he feared, would not look kindly on his situation.

34

Carl drove until he found a motel he considered distant enough to provide the safety they needed. He checked in and took a room on the second level. In time, he started to feel secure in their safety. After a lengthy vigil, he sighed deeply and moved away from the window. Sandy had just helped Gina to bed. He thought of showering and cleaning himself up. He rechecked the locks and told the women of his intentions.

They could take his silence no longer. Gina spoke up. "Honey, I think you better tell us what this is all about." Carl had been so deep in thought that telling Gina and Sandy what happened had never occurred to him. He nodded his head and sat on the only chair available in the meagerly furnished room, a stiff wooden desk chair. He collected his thoughts and took a deep breath.

Sandy and Gina sat in their beds listening intently as Carl told all he knew and all he suspected. He went into detail about the mechanics of the cheating scheme, and how he'd had suspicions from his first day on the job. He talked about Peter and Viktor and how the inexperienced team member had become distracted by Mindy and gave up the initial clues. He also told them of his suspicions regarding the Beria brothers.

He explained why the missing batteries meant the fire was surely a murder attempt.

Gina shuddered when told that Dmitri asked if she knew

anything.

His anger built anew as he told how Viktor had tried to shoot him.

They gaped when he told of the way he'd dealt with his attacker.

By the time he finished, both members of his audience clutched their bed sheets to their chins, their eyes opened as wide as their mouths. He thought they looked ridiculous. Like kids listening to ghost stories around a campfire. He almost laughed in spite of their dire circumstances.

He looked out the window, and checked the locks again before going to the shower. He didn't realize how safe they really were. The man who wanted them dead had no idea where they had gone.

Carl may have been amused by his family's expressions, but the women were not amused by what they had just heard. "Mom, did you hear what he said? Do you think he killed that man? I just can't picture Dad doing something like that."

Gina knew her husband had spent a lifetime working in a profession that challenged a man's courage and strength. Other than that understanding, she knew little of his life outside the home. "Well, Sandy, he had to defend himself." Gina realized her words sounded weak.

"I know, Mom, but he said the man went down when he hit him the first time."

"Look, honey, it's not easy for me to say this, but I don't know much more about your father than you do. Over the years I've read accounts of horrible things in the paper and knew your father was there, but he never talked to me about them. Sometimes I caught a few words when he talked to his friends and filled in the blanks on my own. Who knows what that neighborhood made him capable of?

"All I knew was the way he treated us. I came to accept his distance concerning certain things. It hurt. I wanted more. It always seemed he was locking things inside, hiding demons, but what could I do?"

"I know the way he is to us, Mom. That's what makes what he said seem so unbelievable. If a man pointed a gun at me, I would've froze. No way could I have fought and escaped. I'd be dead."

"Honey, I guess most people would freeze. Your Dad spent almost thirty years reacting. It's what he's conditioned to do."

Sandy sat in silence for a moment before asking, "Do you think conditioning explains everything he told us?"

Gina answered as much to herself as to Sandy. "I don't think there's any other way to explain it."

As the stingy showerhead sprayed him lightly with lukewarm water, Carl tried to decide on his next course of action. The soap caused a stinging pain on the right side of his body, and he noticed three superficial lacerations. The bullet-splintered brick came to mind. He paid extra attention to the area when washing and thought again how easily it could have been him lying out there and not the pudgy young Russian. He considered that he might have a lot of explaining to do if they found Viktor lying dead down the block from his house. Self-defense only went so far.

He was sure Dmitri was the leader of the cheating team. He couldn't go to Meg now. He might put her in jeopardy, and he didn't trust anyone else at the Majestic. He didn't know how high this thing went. After all, Dmitri's brother ran the place, and the great Aleksandr Beria had brought Dmitri to this country. Aleksandr could be the real ringleader. Why else would he keep that jackass of a brother around, even promote him over more qualified people?

Maybe they systematically sent money back to Russia. He had heard of the growing power of the Russian Mafia. The state of Nevada had implemented procedures and regulations that made old-fashioned skimming a thing of the past. A subtle but advanced cheating method, sanctioned and abetted by the casino administrators, and implemented by trained players planted in the poker room, was brilliant. With steady consistent play, the take must be huge.

Carl knew that unless he showed security personnel exactly what to look for, the surveillance equipment, no matter how advanced, was useless.

He had to turn to someone. He continued to concentrate on the problem. The water rinsed down, becoming ever cooler, losing any hint of warmth before he settled on a decision.

The State Gaming Control Board. He would bring his complaint directly to them. The cheating, after all, was the root of Dmitri's crimes. They would be compelled to act, launch an investigation. With the information he supplied, they couldn't help but see the truth. They would see that the fire was set to silence him and his wife. He would wait and see about Viktor. If the police found a body, he would just keep quiet for awhile.

At least until the cheating scheme was out in the open.

Cheating is a felony, one taken seriously in Nevada. The integrity of the gaming industry had to be preserved. When the Gaming Board confirmed the team's existence, they would round up the members in a hurry. Carl and his family would be out of danger.

In the meantime, he had not only lost his own house but had to flee for his life from his daughter's apartment, all in a little over twenty-four hours. With weariness returning, he wrapped himself in a dry towel and left the bathroom. He hadn't slept since the fire and found the women already sound asleep. He checked the windows and door once again and went as far as to wedge the desk chair under the doorknob.

He believed that the obscurity of the motel probably provided all the protection they really needed, but he wanted to play it smart, as always, putting the odds in his favor as much as possible. Life seemed to take on the appearance of one big poker game at times.

He slipped into bed and pulled Gina against him. She moaned softly, and rubbed her plaster-encased leg against his shin. He would have to be careful. He kissed the back of her head, inhaling the sweetness of her silky brown hair and soon joined her in sleep.

35

Uneasiness penetrated his slumber, and Carl woke before the women. He was in no mood for inaction and went to the door to retrieve the chair. Sitting at the desk, he searched the local phone book. 555 East Washington. He took his cell phone from the nightstand and dialed the number. A recording told him that general office hours didn't begin until eight o'clock. The illumination on the phone's LCD read 6:30 a.m.

He sat and tried to piece out a plan of action. He would start with the Gaming Control Board, but he knew he might have to go to the police eventually to report the arson. It would be better if the fire investigation revealed that the blaze was set intentionally, but he knew that the condition of the house would make the investigation difficult, and possibly wouldn't produce conclusive findings.

What could I tell the police, anyway? The missing battery alone won't convince anyone. Just because I'm convinced of the facts, doesn't mean the authorities will necessarily be convinced as well. He took a deep breath and tried to remain positive. *Perhaps all I have to do is get the ball rolling.*

The Gaming Control Board. I'm sure once they knew of the cheaters, it will be easier to go to the police and show them that the arson was a result of my threat to the team. Then they could charge the gang with attempted murder, as well. But charge who? Carl put his elbows on the desk and rested his face in his hands. The seeds of exasperation and doubt grew in him.

How can I tie Dmitri into all this? He never played at the tables himself. The surveillance tapes might give no indication of his involvement. Sure, he seated the team players, but he seated everyone on the day shift. And what about Aleksandr? He's even further removed. Carl admitted that he actually had very little.

I can show that cheating took place, and the team would be picked up and charged, if they can be found. Dmitri probably has them scattered already.

The only things he had that would tie Dmitri to the arson or the attack was the fact that Carl had gone to him alone with his discovery. No one else knew he knew, and yet someone had tried to kill him. The fact that the cheaters were all foreigners, probably Russians, was the only other connection Carl could think of. He bit his lip and shook his head in doubt. *The authorities must surely see these connections. But is it enough?*

No, in truth Carl couldn't envision a time in the near future when he might feel safe again. He would drive past the house on his way to the Gaming Control Board's offices. If the van was gone and he found no evidence of Viktor, he would feel free to tell about the attack. Viktor, after all, wouldn't go to the police about the cause of his injuries.

He knew at this point all he could prove was the cheating, so he decided he would start his counter attack there. Once the investigation began, hopefully it would take on a life of its own and everything would fall into place.

Carl's ideas and plans seemed disjointed to him. He rested his head in his hands once again to try and steady his thoughts. His head spun. It had been spinning since they moved to this town; he felt the dizziness about to overtake him.

Sandy woke around 7:30 and looked at her father with questions in her eyes. Carl held a finger to his lips, "Let your mother sleep." He quietly gave her a brief run down of his plans for the morning. "I'm going to the Gaming Control Board first. I'll tell them what I told you last night. I don't think I'll go to the police just yet. I want the gaming people to confirm my story about the cheaters first. Then my theory about the fire will have more credibility."

Unsure of this course of action, Sandy shook her head slowly. "Daddy, what about the man who tried to kill you last night?"

Carl rose to leave but stopped at the door. "Honey, I have no proof that it ever happened. Let me hear what the gaming control people have to say about it. Keep your phone on. I'll update you as soon as I can. I won't be long. When I get back, we can go out and get some breakfast. Don't forget to lock this door."

Carl drove into the morning sun, his mind racing, intent on doing something to get control of his life back. He rolled past his house, relieved to see no sign of the van. He continued along, creeping slowly. Construction crews worked across the street, but the house at the end of the block was devoid of activity, another good sign.

Before he reached the last house, he spotted his neighbor, Chris, who waved to him from the end of his driveway. He stopped the car. "Hey, Carl, how are you and your wife making out? Is her leg okay?"

Suddenly Carl considered that he might have a witness to last night's attack. "Well, actually, Chris, her ankle is broken. But it's not bad, and they say she'll be fine in a few weeks.

What's been going on here?"

Carl didn't want to come right out and ask if he had seen someone try to shoot him last night. He figured his neighbor would volunteer that kind of information on his own. Chris stroked his goatee and answered as one endowed with valuable information. "Not much, really. Renee stayed home yesterday. She said that a fire investigator was over there for a little while. Then the construction guys poked around some."

The conversation continued in that vein for several minutes, mostly stuff about salvage, insurance, rebuilding, etc. Chris volunteered to do whatever he could, assuring Carl that he would keep an eye on things. Carl entered Chris's number into his cell phone directory, convinced that neither he nor his wife witnessed anything.

He really wasn't surprised. He knew that at this time of year everyone had their windows closed and air conditioners going full blast. On top of that, the gunman had used a silencer, which only made a popping noise. The commotion caused by the attack couldn't have lasted more than a minute. No, it was unreasonable to think someone in this sparsely populated area might have been disturbed by the attack.

Carl thanked his neighbor and continued up the block. He reached the last house and peered around the corner with trepidation. Nothing. Not even the gun. He could see that the drywall scraps he'd used to hide the pistol had been tossed aside. Apparently his attacker still had the presence of mind to search around for his weapon before he fled.

As he left the sub-division and headed for the Gaming Control Board's offices, Carl was relieved he hadn't killed anyone. Not that the guy didn't deserve it, but now at least he could tell the gaming control agent about the second attempt on his life. It should help bring a sense of urgency to the investigation.

Carl reviewed the directory in the building's lobby and rode the elevator alone. He found what he wanted and informed the thin, red headed receptionist that he wanted to report a team of cheaters. She slid her glasses to the end of her nose and directed him by aiming a sharply filed fingernail. With an easy western drawl she advised him to take a seat. "An agent will be with ya shortly."

An office door marked 'Enforcement Division' stood several feet down the corridor. Two stiff chairs were provided outside of the room. Carl didn't feel like sitting. Now that he had arrived, he wanted to get things going and return to his hiding family. He knew they would be worried about him and decided to check in while he waited.

The office door opened just as he pulled the cell phone from his pocket. A man, who seemed not much older than Sandy, stepped into the corridor and offered Carl his hand. He stood as tall as Carl, had short dark hair, and a strong grip. Carl thought he overdid it with the grip. Maybe he wanted to project a sense of power. This relatively common trick to establish dominance had never impressed Carl, but he let it go, deciding to allow this young agent a little more time before he formed an impression of his character.

The agent was dressed in business clothes, a plain white shirt, and brown tie. "Hello, I'm Agent Eric Casper. The receptionist said you had a complaint about cheaters working in a poker room." Carl confirmed this and introduced himself, adding that he was a dealer in the poker room. Agent Casper held the door open and asked why he didn't bring this information to his floor supervisor first.

Carl took a seat, across from a black steel desk in a cramped windowless office. "I did. That's when the trouble began. The floor supervisor's in on it, and he's spent the last two days trying to shut me up by making attempts on my life. I knew there was a whole team of cheaters working at a number of different tables, but apparently this thing is much bigger than I suspected. That's why I came to you."

"Whoa, Mr. Braun, you've said a mouth full. Why don't you back up a little and take it from the top, beginning with the name of the casino you work for and the name of your floor supervisor." The agent took a yellow legal pad out of a drawer and clicked the top of a plastic pen.

Carl watched the young agent closely as he prepared to take notes, hoping to spot anything that might give an indication of his ability. Eric's expression was one of concern. Carl couldn't sense any hint of dismissiveness in his demeanor. He seemed to be taking this seriously.

Eric looked up from his legal pad. The intensity of Carl's scrutiny seemed to make him doubt if he had managed to establish any authority over Mr. Braun.

Carl deemed the young man worthy of his confidence, so he began to unfold his story.

He went into detail about the manner in which the chips were manipulated to send information. He explained that he believed the lower limit tables were used as a training ground. Carl described Peter and told how Viktor had become the weak link that made him suspicious in the first place. Agent Casper wrote as fast as he could but held up his hand from time to time to get Carl to slow down.

"I tested my theories three days ago. I sat at table number

eight. You can watch me on the surveillance tapes. I picked up their system quickly and used it against them."

Without looking up, agent Casper asked, "How did you do?"

"I can tell you the system works. It worked better for me than it did for them. I knew the hole cards of three players. The best they could do was two. It was like I couldn't lose. Watch the tapes, you'll see."

The young agent stopped writing and inquired about his winnings, although Carl didn't understand what difference it made. Carl told him about the church. Agent Casper rubbed his chin and resumed his note taking.

When he began explaining his theories on the Russian connection and on Aleksandr Beria, Eric put his pen down and looked up with disbelief in his eyes. "Are you telling me that this Dmitri is the brother of Al Beria?"

Carl wanted to make sure that Agent Casper completely understood this point. "Yes, that's what I'm telling you. Al Beria's been in this country for a long time, but he only brought his brother over a few years ago. Dmitri is a real son of a bitch, and this Al promoted him to floor supervisor against everyone's better judgment. Don't you see? Al has to be the brains behind this thing."

Eric picked up his pen and asked Carl to tell him about the attempts on his life. Carl couldn't shake a growing sense of impatience, but pushed on. He started with the fire and admitted that the missing battery might be considered thin evidence, but insisted that the detector had been installed properly. He described Viktor and the shooting and how he escaped and took his family into hiding.

At the conclusion of the long narrative, agent Casper let

out a deep breath and arched his eyebrows, "Mr. Braun, if this thing is all you say it is, I think we're going to cause quite a commotion. I'm going to take this to my supervisor right away and see what he thinks. My guess is he's going to want us to review those tapes ASAP. If it's only been three days, they should still be in the surveillance room. Wait here. I'll be right back."

There wasn't going to be any 'wait here', Carl stopped the young man before he reached the door. "Hold on there, Agent. I'm out of time. I told you what my family and I have been through the last couple of days. My wife and daughter are still hiding out. We have to get some food. We lost everything we owned in the fire, and now we can't even go back to my daughter's apartment. We've been surviving on her credit card. I know they're worried sick about me, and I'm going back to them right now."

Carl reached for the pen and legal pad. "I'll sign your notes and write down my cell phone number. That will have to satisfy your boss for now."

Eric offered a word of protest. "I'd really like you to have a word with my boss. We can send a car for your family."

Carl smiled at the thought of some strange Agent trying to get Gina to open the door.

Any inklings of dominance the young Agent thought he might have established were summarily dispelled.

Carl scanned the notes, signed, wrote his number, and dropped the pen on the pad. As he moved past Eric in the doorway, he held out his hand and said, "I wasn't opening a discussion on the subject, Agent Casper. You seem like a good man. The ball's in your court now. Don't let me down."

They shook hands and Carl searched the younger man's

eyes once again. His grip was noticeably less firm.

"Take my card and call if you need anything or think of anything else." Carl accepted the card, slid it into his back pocket, and left without saying another word. Eric picked up the legal pad and hurried to his supervisor's office.

The Mustang was parked on the street, facing away from Carl's intended destination. Out of patience, he saw his chance, took a quick look around for the police, and hit the gas. He spun the steering wheel, and the sports car responded by performing a perfect u-turn in the middle of the block. There were no police around to witness the audacious move, but it did draw attention. The squealing tires had every head turning.

Dmitri couldn't believe his luck. The noise and flash of red made him abandon his thoughts and take notice just like everyone else around. But unlike everyone else, he recognized the driver. The roof on the convertible was up, and the car turned away in an instant, but it was enough. He had been fixated on that face for days. He could not be mistaken–no matter how quickly the face flashed by.

36

Gina woke to the sound of Sandy sliding the safety chain in place. With sleep in her eyes, she surveyed her surroundings, confused by the strangeness of the room. A dull ache in her leg and the weight of the plaster cast brought her thoughts up to date.

After a quick look around, she decided the room appeared much shabbier in the daylight than it had last night. The minimal furnishings consisted of two queen size beds and a modest nightstand that barely fit between them. With the heavy window curtains pulled shut, their sole source of light came from a cracked ceramic lamp, topped off with a faded lampshade. The small desk and chair stood near the foot of Gina's bed. A nineteen-inch TV took up most of the space on the desk. The out-dated wallpaper curled away from the wall in several places. Pretty meager surroundings, she thought, hoping she wouldn't be there long.

"Where's your father, Sandy?"

Sandy dropped the curtain and turned suddenly. "Oh. Sorry Mom. I didn't wake you did I?"

Gina sat up and rubbed her eyes. "No, honey. My leg is bothering me a little. Do you have an aspirin or something in your purse?"

Sandy searched through her purse for a minute before handing her mother a packet of extra-strength Tylenol. "Here,

Mom. I'll get you some water." She filled the plastic pitcher from the bathroom sink and poured into a glass on the nightstand.

As Sandy set the pitcher on the desk, Gina repeated her question. "Where did your father go?"

"He said he was going to the Gaming Control Board to report the cheating team."

Gina shook her head. "What's he doing that for? Why doesn't he just go to the police? What's this Gaming Control Board stuff all about?"

Sandy didn't know how to answer. She didn't seem to understand exactly what her father had on his mind either. She sat on her bed and tried to give her mother an answer, using the most reassuring voice she could manage. "I don't know, Mom. He seemed like he knew what he wanted to do. He said the cheating was the only thing he could prove, so he was starting with the Gaming Board. I don't think they have a large agency like that in Illinois, but out here they function like another police body."

Gina finished her glass of water and folded her arms across her chest. "Oh, please. This is just like your father. He thinks he has us tucked away all safe and sound, and now he's free to throw himself at this problem. Who does he think he is? Tell me. He's no policeman. Let the police department find the proof. That's what they do, isn't it?"

Sandy raised her eyebrows. Even though her mother still asked questions, they were clearly rhetorical.

"Are you telling me that even though someone tried to shoot him last night he's not going to the police?" Sandy didn't answer. "I'm telling you, Sandy, the thing that scares me the most about your father is that nothing scares him. This is just like him. I can't tell you how many times I asked him to leave that neighborhood he worked in. We had more...." Gina paused and looked at her daughter before choosing the right word, "discussions about him transferring to a slower firehouse, but not him. Not Carl. Now look at what he's up to. This isn't what we planned on when we left Chicago. I wasn't supposed to feel like this anymore. He's supposed to be retired."

Gina turned away from her daughter and wiped at her cheek with the back of her hand. Sandy had seen this motion before. Carl never spotted it, but Sandy, like most children, saw much that her parents never realized. A look around the room told her that she wasn't going to find a Kleenex box. She went to the bathroom and brought her mother a piece of tissue from the roll. Gina accepted it with a silent nod and took a deep breath to calm herself.

Sandy sat on the edge of her mother's bed and watched as Gina regained her composure.

Gina saw the confusion in her daughter's eyes.

"Look, honey, you don't know what it's been like all these years. Your father went off in the morning and I had no idea what might be happening to him for twenty-four hours. You can't imagine what it felt like to have the phone ring at 5:30 in the morning and see Christ Hospital on the caller I.D. When he was younger and you kids were all babies, it seemed as if he was constantly getting hurt. Broken bones, surgeries, stitches, and it seemed as if he always came home with some kind of burn. To make matters worse, he never talked to me about any of it. I had to be like Sherlock Holmes if I wanted to find out what happened. I've had years of guessing and being kept in the dark. If I hadn't been so busy with you kids and teaching, I think I would have gone out of my mind.

"That was all supposed to be behind us now. We came out here to get away from that world and reconnect with each other. Now look at this mess. And there goes your father running off again, leaving me in the dark."

Sandy sat unmoved. Gina's words seemed to come as no surprise to her. She had never heard it spoken out loud before, but she had grown-up with her parents and the tension had intruded upon her childhood from time to time.

"I know this is a mess, Mom, but it's not like this is the way your lives are going to be forever. Once this stuff is over, things will be the way you hoped. Dad loves you like mad. You already have more than most women ever get."

Gina didn't reply to her daughter's comment. She kept her arms folded in front of her and continued to wear a sour expression, but she had gotten some things off her chest and that alone had helped put her at ease.

"Would you help me to the shower, Sweetie? My bath last night was kind'a cut short."

After doing her best in the shower, Gina put on the cut off sweat pants and tattered 'Bears' jersey that Sandy had hastily tossed at her the previous night. "Sandy, I know beggars can't be choosers, but these things are awful. They make me look like a bum."

Sandy laughed. "Dad said to just throw something on you and get you ready to leave. Those are my housework clothes. At least they're clean."

Gina wondered out loud why Carl hadn't called yet.

Sandy told her mother that he said he would, and that they would all go to breakfast when he returned. They resumed their places on the beds. Sandy picked up the remote, and said with a sigh, "At least this place has a TV"

She flipped through the channels, and Gina watched with disinterest until a commercial for the 'Regis and Kelly Show' zipped across the screen. "Hey, put that back. I like her."

Sandy raised an eyebrow and returned to the channel her mother wanted. "Mom, you like all the petite women."

Gina sat up straighter in bed and replied to her daughters comment. "You will too one day. Not all of them, just the ones who've made it good. Most people look at us and write us off. We can be a lot tougher than we get credit for. Believe me; if she made it in show business she's tougher than she looks."

Sandy turned to her mother with a smile and seemed impressed by her spirit. "I know you're pretty tough, Mom, but I wish Dad would get back just the same."

Gina returned her daughter's smile and agreed. "Yeah, hon, me too."

A rap on the door brought Sandy to her feet, Gina's pulse bounded. Sandy went to the window and Gina called out, "Is that you Carl?" Sandy confirmed that it was her father and unlocked the door. Carl entered carrying three Styrofoam cups on a cardboard tray. "Here ladies, let's have some coffee while I tell you what I've been up to." He handed his wife a steaming cup and kissed her on the cheek.

Sandy swung the door closed. The room number became visible once again to the outside observer. And he made a note of the number.

37

The digital clock on Meg's desk read 8:25, Saturday morning. She decided the time had come to make a call. Aleksandr's secretary put the call right through.

"Good morning, Ms. O'Meara, what can I do for you?"

This aspect of Meg's managerial responsibilities made her uncomfortable. More than a year ago, Aleksandr had asked her to keep him informed of any peculiarities in his brother's work habits. The request seemed and imposition to Meg. She felt perfectly capable handling any peculiarity in the work habits of anyone who worked under her, even if that person was the general manager's brother. She had made a few calls the first month, but didn't have to call again until the last few weeks. Out of the blue, Dmitri's work habits began to lag seriously. Aleksandr said he would speak to Dmitri about it, but things seemed to be getting worse.

"I hate to bother you Mr. Beria, but Dmitri was due in at eight, and he's not here yet. As we discussed, this has been happening more and more lately. As a floor supervisor, his absences are very troublesome. Maybe he could use a vacation to get himself together."

In typical, monotone fashion, Aleksandr asked, "Did you try reaching him, Ms. O'Meara?"

Meg answered, hoping to end the call quickly. She was covering for Dmitri herself and didn't feel like being there at all.

"Yes, sir. The only number I have is his home number, and he's not answering."

"Thank you. I'll try to reach him myself and will inform you of my results." The call ended as quickly as Meg hoped.

She returned to her duties and considered the fact that even though she didn't have to work every Saturday, whenever she did, Al Beria was there as well. *Don't these Russians ever take a day off? Aleksandr probably didn't even know what I meant by 'vacation.'*

Dmitri's fingernails dug into the steering wheel's vinyl covering. Trying to avoid detection, he followed the red car as closely as he dared. Fate had presented him with a golden opportunity and had restored his hope. Determined not to let this opportunity escape him, he still wasn't sure how to exploit this lucky break. The situation might be contained yet, and he believed he could hold off a little longer before seeking outside assistance.

Still, he would need some help, but from whom? He had no real organization here. His teams of cheaters were not hardened men; just boys he had trained to do tricks, like monkeys in a circus. Only one choice offered any real potential. Peter.

Peter was more American than Russian. He had come to this country as a boy and had attended American schools. His parents, professional people of some sort, traveled with him to the Motherland on occasion. On one of these occasions, he had met Dmitri. Peter, being rather rich and idle, ran with a fast crowd that had put him in the younger Beria's path.

Dmitri became interested in him because of his apparent wealth. Initially, his intentions had been devious, but when he learned that Peter came from America, he decided to nurture a relationship. He had just accepted his brother's invitation to join him in the States and thought he might need some friends in the new country.

When he formed the cheating team, Peter stood out at once as the most adept. In time, Dmitri came to depend on him and look to him as the leader of his team. Now he would find out how much value his American friendship really had. He picked up his cell phone and was about to call Peter when the phone rang in his hand. He recognized the number blinking on the display. "Damn."

"Yes, Yes, Aleksandr, I know, but I was up all night. I have not been feeling well lately, and my illness was at its worst last night. When I finally slept, I did not hear the alarm."

Aleksandr suggested that he should have called in as soon as he woke and realized he would be late. "Yes, Brother, I apologize for that. As I said, I have not been myself. I will call Ms. O'Meara myself, and I will be in as soon as I can."

Aleksandr paused. He had heard this excuse before and seemed unconvinced. "Dmitri, you must take your position more seriously. I feel compelled to inform you that I have been under some pressure concerning your employment here. Please do not give your detractors anything more to complain about, and do take a moment to call Ms. O'Meara. I'm sure she will appreciate your call. Goodbye."

Dmitri slammed his fist against the passenger seat. "That

bitch. Always watching me and reporting to my brother. I look forward to the day when I can deal with her." He bit down on the inside of his mouth and tried to keep focused on his grave task. Precious time was slipping away. He mumbled. "Where is he going?"

Carl stopped at a convenience store and seemed to take forever before coming out with a tray of coffee cups.

"I must get to the casino. Aleksandr is losing patience with me. This is the second time he has spoken of replacing me. I could lose my work Visa, and that tramp will be wondering where I am. How much longer must I follow this American?"

He picked up his phone and punched in the number to Meg's office. He informed her, with a less than friendly tone, that he had spoken to his brother and would be in shortly.

Meg didn't care if he came in or not. She tolerated him only because of Aleksandr Beria. As far as she was concerned, a day without the rude Russian was a day off for everyone else. She thanked him for his call and ended the conversation.

Carl pulled away and Dmitri resumed his pursuit.

A few blocks later, the red car turned into the parking lot of a run-down motel. A sign standing on a rusted pole read 'The Lucky Roll'. 'Vacancy' was painted at the bottom without provision for the word 'no' to be added in front of it. A picture, flaking away but still visible, depicted a pair of dice rolling across a pink bed.

Dmitri smiled thinking, "Where is he staying, a whore house?" The structure had two stories with exterior entrances to each room. The second floor rooms could be accessed by wrought iron stairs located at either end of the building.

He watched as Carl carried his coffee to the second floor and entered a room in the middle of the walkway. Room 212. In keeping with his habit, Dmitri nodded his head as a way of convincing himself that the number had been committed to memory. He desperately wanted to stay and observe but knew he must return to the casino. Time seemed to fly past. He must go. He could not afford to disappoint Aleksandr again.

Peter received a call from his agitated leader and was told, in no uncertain terms, to remain near his phone. "I will be calling you soon. As soon as I figure out what we must do."

He didn't like the sound of that and spoke up. "I thought Viktor was helping you with these Americans. I'm not into heavy work, Dmitri, I'm just your little card cheat, remember?" Dmitri was beyond negotiating and made that point clear.

"Listen, you American son of a bitch, that fat fool was useless. He is out of the picture. You have made a fortune for yourself these last two years. Don't you think we must protect our incomes? There are more people depending on our revenues than only you and I. They will not tolerate an interruption in their cash flow much longer. Now stay by your phone and do as I say, when I call."

Peter liked the sound of that outburst even less. *Out of the picture.* What was he getting himself into here? He had little doubt about his boss's intentions and he shivered, breaking out in a cold sweat. He stayed near the phone nonetheless.

Well past nine o'clock, Dmitri arrived at the poker room. He appeared more distracted and ill at ease than Meg had ever seen him. She used his arrival as an excuse to take a break.

"I'm glad you're here, Dmitri." The lie wouldn't fool anyone. "I'm going for some coffee. Are you ready to take over here?"

The Russian bent his thick neck to indicate a positive reply and Meg took her leave.

Dmitri filled a couple of empty seats with waiting patrons, then wasted no time going to the file cabinet in Meg's office. He knew it was a brazen play, but the time for caution and subtleties had passed. If this thing blew up in his face, he would have more to worry about than the feeble American judicial system. There were his brother and the people from back home.

He found Carl's personal file without trouble. He scanned it quickly, something he should have done days ago. A fireman, retired after twenty-nine years. That explained a few things. Cell phone number. He copied the number, returned the file to the cabinet, and returned to his post with time to spare.

Time continued to speed past as his mind searched for an answer. He tried to sort through the questions that kept surfacing in his brain. *Where had the American gone this morning? He must have told someone else, but who? If he went to the police, why haven't they come to the casino yet to make an arrest? Did the American really have much he could tell the police?* Dmitri knew he had no answers, but he understood that he had let things go too far. One way or the other, he must end it tonight or his only choice would be to flee for his own safety, and Dmitri Beria was never one to flee.

In the middle of the afternoon, Meg approached the sign-in desk with a message. "Dmitri, your brother just called down. He said he has to leave early today and wants to speak with you before he goes. Would you run up there please?"

What now? I was only an hour late and I told him I had been ill.

Dmitri saw that his brother's secretary had already left for the day and that the office door stood ajar. He knocked and entered, leaving the door open.

Aleksandr's office, located at the back of the mezzanine level, overlooked the casino floor. The office was tasteful, but in keeping with Al's personality, not overdone. A large ebony desk sat near the floor-to-ceiling, tinted glass panel windows. The windows permitted a tremendous view of the mountains and the lavish pool area below. The uncluttered desk faced the mammoth oak door. A bar, stocked with one of Russia's finest vodkas and a rarely used leather couch completed the décor.

Aleksandr's briefcase sat closed on the desk, his car keys sitting on top of it. He really did appear to be leaving early, something Dmitri never knew him to do. There must be some special occasion.

Aleksandr stood near the bar and had just finished pouring from a green-labeled bottle of Moskovskaya Special. He filled two small glasses and handed one to his brother. "Have a drink with me, Dima. Remember, today is little George's birthday. Robin is having a party, and I am leaving early to be with my family. You didn't forget, did you?" Dmitri accepted the glass and raised it to his lips, downing the burning liquid in one gulp.

He cursed himself for forgetting his nephew's birthday. Though of no importance to him, he knew what it meant to

Aleksandr, and he needed to keep up appearances. Small beads of sweat appeared on his forehead. He fumed inside whenever his brother referred to him with the familiar form of his name, Dima. At least Aleksandr was in a good mood. He appeared to have forgotten about Dmitri's tardiness.

Dmitri's knuckles turned white as he squeezed the empty glass. *Who does he think he is? He left me with aged parents to grow up in a country that had nothing left to offer. I made my own way and became what I have become. Now, after all these years, he wants us to be like family. He has his family, an American princess and two spoiled brats. He can keep them. I will do what I must for the sake of business, put up a good front, and do it for as long as I must. I've always done what must be done.*

Aleksandr watched his brother stare into his glass and spoke. "Are you feeling better? You don't look yourself."

Dmitri used his brother's observation to make an excuse. "No, Sasha, I am still not feeling well. I don't know what it is, but I'm going home to rest when my shift here is over. Tell George that I will be with him before his party is over." Dmitri hated referring to his brother with the familiar form of his name more than he hated being on the receiving end of that treatment, but he was intent on keeping up the front.

"Yes, I can see that would be best. But do come before the boys go to bed. You know Robin is an only child. You are the only uncle they have and they love having you visit. You really must come by more often, Dima."

In his present state of mind, Dmitri found this line of conversation difficult to tolerate. Sweat rolled past his temples.

"Yes, Brother, I know. I wish I could come by more often myself. I will make a greater effort in the future."

Aleksandr accepted his brother's word. "Yes, of course you will. Good."

About to say goodbye, he heard someone knocking on the doorframe. Aleksandr recognized the older of the two men standing in the open doorway. Noah Gibson was a supervisor with the Gaming Control Board. Thin, tall and about fifty, he was almost completely bald and wore thick black rimmed glasses. Despite the fact he had spent years working in law enforcement, he had a pleasant and disarming face.

"Yes, Mr. Gibson, what can I do for you?"

Noah cleared his throat and spoke. "I'm sorry to bother you, Mr. Beria, but there was no secretary here so I took it upon myself to knock. I wanted to give you a courtesy call. This is Agent Casper."

Aleksandr interrupted, "One moment, Mr. Gibson, perhaps we had better step outside for a moment."

Aleksandr led the men to the outer office and pulled at the heavy door behind him. The lock failed to catch and the door remained open a few inches. Noah Gibson, with a habit common to many men in a position of authority, spoke with a loud, commanding voice. Some would say too loud, but not Dmitri.

Remaining near the bar, he heard everything.

"A man, claiming to be an employee of yours, came into our offices this morning and told quite a story to Agent Casper here. The story concerned a team of cheats operating at the Majestic. He gave us some very specific information but wouldn't stay long enough for me to interview him. He didn't produce any identification and according to agent Casper, was in a hurry to leave. The story sounds rather extreme to be coming out of the blue in this way, but the name he gave did appear on your most recent employee list, so I thought we had better look into it. We're going to spend some time in the surveillance room reviewing a couple of tapes. I've already spoken to your Surveillance Director, but as I said, I also wanted to speak with you about it. If we find anything on the tapes, I'll call the man into our office in the morning and take an official statement."

Aleksandr had been in this business a long time. Dealing with the Gaming Control Board was part of doing business, and he always treated the Agents with respect and courtesy. This respect was appreciated and returned.

"Certainly, gentlemen, if there is anything I can do please call. I'm sure this will prove to be nothing. My security staff misses very little. I'm sure they would have noted any large cheating organization."

The men shook hands. "I will be leaving shortly for a personal engagement. Here is my card. My cell phone number is listed. Please call me at once if you turn up anything unusual."

Noah put the card in his shirt pocket. "I hope it turns out to be nothing, sir. I won't be happy if I have to come in tomorrow."

The Agents hadn't reached the elevator before a plan formed in Dmitri's mind. Aleksandr retrieved his briefcase and said goodbye to his brother, inviting him to help himself to another drink. "Yes, Sasha, goodbye. I will be with you this evening." As soon as his brother left the room, Dmitri took out his phone and punched in Peter's number.

Peter had spent the last few hours hoping this call would never come. When he saw Dmitri's name on the caller I.D., he considered ignoring the call, but decided against it. He did not want to make an enemy of Dmitri. He did not want to be 'out of the picture.'

In a shaky voice, he answered. "Yes, Dmitri, I'm here."

Dmitri understood that the drama was about to reach its climax. He spoke with excitement in his voice. "Peter, get a pen and paper and listen closely."

Peter did as he was told. "Go ahead, I'm ready."

Dmitri read off Carl's cell phone number. He also told him to write down the names of the two Agents.

"Use your most American voice and call Braun on his cell phone. Tell him that you are the older agent Gibson. He is a supervisor, and you have reviewed the tapes and can confirm his accusations but you need to conduct an interview yourself. Tell him you need his signature on an affidavit before you can proceed any further. Tell him that Aleksandr Beria is very concerned over this, and the three of you should meet in the general manager's office for the official interview. Say agent Casper will be there, also. Say whatever you have to. You can be very smooth when you want to be. I have seen you. Just make sure he comes to Aleksandr's office."

Peter interrupted, "What if he knows it's not this Gibson's voice."

Dmitri snarled, "He has never spoken to him. He only

spoke to Casper. Do you think I am a fool? Do not interrupt me again."

"Before you call, go to the parking lot of 'The Lucky Roll' motel on Starlight Boulevard. Do you know the place?"

"Yes, it's a real dive."

Dmitri continued. "Make sure their car is still parked in the lot. It is a red sports car, a Mustang. When you get there, watch room 212. Make the call and watch for the man to leave. When he is gone, go to the front desk and tell them your wife left with the key and you need the spare, or bribe the clerk, or steal the key. I do not care how you do it but get into that room and kill the women. I will take care of the man when he gets here. When you are done, lock the door and meet me back at my brother's office to help me remove the American's body. Do you know where the office is?"

Peter pulled the phone away from his head and looked at it as if it were some strange foreign object. The room began to spin. Was he hearing things? Did Dmitri just say what he thought he said?

Dmitri knew that his team leader would be shaken by his order. He listened closely for a reaction. He needed Peter and he had to make sure he would hold up.

"What do you mean women? I thought there was just the wife. How am I supposed to kill them? Why don't you just go to the motel room and kill all of them all at once?"

Dmitri would not consider going to the hotel and attacking the three of them at once. He remembered all too well what Carl did to Viktor. He had no intention of allowing Carl to get within arm's reach of him. The process of forcing the hotel room door would give him too much time to react. He couldn't have that. He would kill Carl in the privacy of his brother's deserted office. There would be no eyes or surveillance cameras in there.

The young man had panic in his voice. Dmitri sensed that he might be losing him. He knew the quickly hatched plan was desperate, but his options had run out and so had his time. If his day of reckoning had come, he was determined to at least take the cause of his downfall with him, no matter the cost. As desperate as the scheme sounded, it still had a chance to succeed. All they needed were cool heads and ruthlessness.

Dmitri acted quickly to shore up his man's courage. His voice becoming velvety and relaxed, he took Peter into his confidence. "Calm yourself, comrade. Let me explain our situation to you, so you will understand the importance of what we must do tonight. When I came to this country, I was not only trying to avoid the police. I had fallen into debt with a certain organization. I was at the end of my rope. They decided to dispose of me. A man had already been chosen to take my place in the organization. I became desperate for a solution to my problem.

"I told them of my brother in America and convinced them I could establish an interest for them there. We agreed on a timetable and a system of sending payment. It went well at first, but in recent months, through no fault of my own, the payments have fallen off. I have been sending all I could, but they are unsatisfied. Last week, they contacted me and said a man would be coming to me within days to settle with me one way or another."

Dmitri failed to admit that while the team was growing and making a fortune, he had started giving himself totally to the temptations of excess, the same behavior that he so readily condemned in the people of his adopted country.

Dmitri knew that Peter took in all that he was told. The line went silent on his end. "Just as I was starting to amass a considerable sum for payment, this man Braun causes me to halt our operation. Peter, my friend, if we can eliminate the Brauns and resume our efforts, I know I can convince the St. Petersburg organization to allow us more time. I can show them how lucrative our system is."

Dmitri's words twisted the truth. "Your concern in this is as deep as mine. They are aware of you, also. They know that you are my top man and comrade. If they eliminate me, the debt will be passed to you. Do you understand fully why we must act without delay?"

Peter sat dumbfounded. His lightheadedness had become intense and he felt nauseous. He swallowed hard, and tried to gain control of himself.

"Why are there two women now, Dmitri? How am I to kill them?" His voice held acceptance and reservation. "I have never done anything like this before."

Dmitri smiled, feeling his heart lighten. His words had convinced the young man. He answered patiently, "Their daughter is with them now. Don't let the killing bother you. It is now a matter of you or them. Killing is easy. Trust me. They are both small women and the older one has an injured leg. Do it quickly so they will not have time to make much noise. A knife across the throat will keep them silent, and then once in the heart before you leave. You will see how easy it is. You have a carving knife of some sort at your home I assume?"

At first Dmitri was concerned he had no time to get a gun to Peter, but upon further consideration, he decided that the silence and up-close effectiveness of a knife would be better after all.

Peter's answer came without emotion. "Yes, Dmitri, I have a knife."

Dmitri's hopes began to rise. "Good, my friend. You had better get started now."

38

Aleksandr arrived home to a house full of raucous seven and eight-year-olds. Robin greeted him with a kiss and introduced him to the few mothers who had stayed to help with the party. The house had been decorated with streamers and multi-colored balloons. A magician, who performed at one of the Majestic's lounges, had just left, and a clown was about to begin taking requests for balloon animals.

Most of the children were dressed in bathing suits and were dripping wet when the clown had them gather on the patio near his bright yellow folding table. Aleksandr picked his sons' faces out of the crowd. They beamed, Edward's smile just as wide, if not wider, than his brother's. George sat next to the yellow table and had the honor of receiving the first creation: a palm tree, complete with a coconut stealing monkey.

The only one at the party more pleased than the boys was their father. Days like this were the reason he had come to America and worked so hard. He went inside and removed his sport coat and tie. With a healthy glass of Moskovskaya Special in his hand he sat near the pool and watched the rest of the clown's act.

He wasn't much of a cook, and Robin had planned on doing it herself, but Aleksandr insisted on grilling the burgers and hot dogs. He stood before the monstrous, flagstone encased stainless steal grill with all the confidence of a world-class chef. Some of the meat may have been overdone but the children never noticed. They were more interested in the ample supply of chips, pop, candy, and assorted other snacks.

George blew out the candles with one breath, and each child had a slice of chocolate cake accompanied by a rapidly melting scoop of vanilla ice cream. Aleksandr raised the glass to his lips and let the premium vodka slide down, bathing his throat in warmth. He went inside to refill the glass feeling more satisfied than he could ever remember.

He wished he had thought to give Dmitri the rest of the day off. He had already missed singing 'Happy Birthday'. Robin waved at him with a smile from beyond the patio doors, then stuck out her tongue, and slumped her shoulders to indicate how tiring the day had been.

Aleksandr held up his glass as a way of asking if she wanted to join him. She smiled again and mouthed the word "later." He reached for the bottle, nodding his understanding. The phone clipped to his belt sounded its familiar tone. Irritated by the imposition, he set the unopened bottle on the bar. "Hello, this is Al Beria."

"Mr. Beria, this is Agent Gibson. I'm afraid the report we received this morning from your employee was accurate. There is definitely a very efficient cheating team working your poker room. I wouldn't be disappointed with your security people. If we hadn't been told what to look for, we never would have detected them either. They are well practiced and professional, and they seem to go to great lengths to be inconspicuous. Agent Casper and I surveyed the room through the TPZs before we left and none of the team seems to be working at this time. I briefed the security people who were on duty when we left. I want to go over a few things this evening and then try to reach the man who made the report."

Agent Gibson was well aware of the power and respect Aleksandr Beria wielded in Las Vegas, so he chose his next words with care. "Mr. Beria, I want everything to be above board in this investigation, so I have to tell you that the man who came into our office this morning thought that you and your brother were involved. He also said that his life had been threatened. Now I've known you for a long time and your reputation precedes you. I have seen nothing so far that would point to you, and so far the surveillance tapes of your brother are inconclusive. There is a need for further investigation certainly, and everything must be looked into. It seems we'll be working on Sunday after all.

"Mr. Beria, are you there?"

Al had been listening intently. It had been years since his stint in the KGB, but he retained the mind of an investigator. His mental circuits sorted this new information and added it to previous observations. "Yes, Mr. Gibson, I'm here. What you are saying is very disturbing. Could you tell me what time slots you reviewed?" Al wouldn't consider insulting the supervisor by asking for the name of the employee who made the report.

"Yes, sir, day shift. They seem to work mostly on the day shifts, but sometimes they run over into the evenings. It looks like they put in a lot of hours. They work everyday, and aside from a few exceptions, the faces and teams rotate often."

Robin looked in from the patio and saw that her husband's

easy grin had been replaced with a look of grave concern. "Thank you for the call, Mr. Gibson. As always, I appreciate your efforts."

"Thank you, Mr. Beria. It's getting late and I still have a lot to do. I'll be in touch."

All very pleasant and professional, but Aleksandr's mind worked fast. He sat at the dinning room table, facing the patio. Children jumped into the pool and splashed each other, with shouts and screams. Parents had begun to arrive. The children resisted their attempts to make them leave the party. Aleksandr saw none of this, his mind elsewhere.

An occasional cheat or sneak thief was to be expected. Sometimes they encountered small aggressive teams but rarely failed to shut them down quickly. As with every aspect he put into place at the Majestic, Al made sure his security team was the best of the best. Years spent working his way up through the ranks had exposed him to much, and when the time came to build his own organization, he knew where to turn and spared no expense.

Now someone had tried to implicate him in something like this. He considered it a personal attack. An attack against everything he worked so hard to achieve. An attack against his future, his children's future. He would not rest until he had cleared this thing up, and he wouldn't wait for the Gaming Board to get to the bottom of things. He would do that himself. It had become a matter of self-defense.

Al knew only too well how intensely the Nevada authorities protected the integrity of the gaming industry. He also suspected how the Majestic's board of directors might react if this thing went too far. All at once, he realized that he had been thrust into a fight for his professional survival.

With concern on her face, Robin again looked in at Al. She saw him turn away from the bar and retrieve his sport coat. He didn't bother with the tie. As if she knew what to expect next, she excused herself from a set of parents, and hurried through the sliding doors. She met her husband as he picked up his keys. The look on his face told her the matter would not be debated, she simply sought an explanation.

"Robin, you know how much I wanted to be here today, but something very serious has come up. Perhaps more serious than anything I have encountered since I came to this country. I am sorry but I must leave now."

Robin felt the weight of his words and offered no resistance. She kissed him on the cheek and watched him leave. He stopped in the doorway and told her what a nice job she had done with the party and apologized once more, advising her to give his love to the boys and not to wait up for him.

Aleksandr knew where he must begin his investigation. The security room at the Majestic. He would sit up all night if he had to. He speed-dialed his Surveillance Director's number and changed the man's plans for his Saturday evening. This thing wasn't going to beat him.

39

Dmitri went back to the bar in his brother's office and poured himself another glass of vodka. This time he used a larger glass. As he held the mouth of the bottle over the edge of the glass, his eyebrows arched in concern over the way the bottle shook in his hand. He poured with two hands and began his vigil. He had no choice but to sit and wait for Peter to call and let him know if his plan had a chance of succeeding.

Konstantin Leonovich had arrived in New York the previous day. Dmitri received a voice mail message telling him what Leonovich expected, and when he expected it. Dmitri remembered Leonovich. It had been a few years, but he was a man one could not easily forget. He was more than a simple courier, more even than a feared assassin.

Tall and gaunt with a face so drawn it appeared skeletal, Konstantin Leonovich rose through the ranks of St. Petersburg's underworld without ambition or care. The only pleasure he took came from the successful completion of an assignment. His progression came as a natural consequence of the results he produced. In time, he had attained a position of trust. His judgment cold and impartial, he could be counted on to carry out his own decisions.

Dmitri knew that by sending Konstantin, they were telling him he still had a chance to prove himself. He knew Konstantin had the authority to come to his own conclusions and make a decision. The beads of sweat returned as he realized that this decision would be acted on immediately, and it could easily go either way. In fact, Dmitri admitted to himself that the odds lay heavily against him.

Essential that he prove there was good money to be made, he must be convincing. The team must be up and running at full strength, at least long enough to satisfy and impress Konstantin. He could even work the team on the other shifts, around the clock if necessary. Perhaps even make clear his intention to expand to other casinos.

After Konstantin returned to Russia, Dmitri could concentrate his efforts on cleaning up the mess caused by Braun. The American had possibly done enough damage to make remaining in Las Vegas a hazardous proposition. Those Agents had already responded to his accusations.

Dmitri drank hard and set his jaw. Things would still be going well if Braun hadn't caused him so much trouble. The problems with St. Petersburg would have been easily solved, but with no money coming in, he had very little to turn over to Konstantin. He would take pleasure in killing Carl. This American had become much more than a simple thorn in his side.

If all went well, the only difficulty he could envision would be removing the body. Braun was not a small man, but he should fit into one of the Majestic's large laundry karts. There were no surveillance cameras in the office area, but they were located almost everywhere else throughout the building. Many of their locations weren't even required by state regulations. Just like his brother to overdo things. Dmitri shrugged his shoulders and thought it really didn't matter; he had no intention of being the one to push the kart. Peter would do that.

He made a call to the laundry room, posing as Aleksandr, saying he had a collection of bulky things he needed to move from his office. He asked for a kart and a number of blankets to be brought to his office door right away. Dmitri finished his drink thinking that things could work out yet. Much depended on Peter and his ability to see a difficult task through to the end.

Peter was clever. Dmitri had little doubt that he would convince Braun, and that he would obtain the key to room 212. At that point, his confidence in Peter faltered. Once in the room, he would have to steel himself for the attack. The job needed quickness. No hesitation. It had to be done before the women knew what was happening, before they could scream, if possible, or fight back. Yes, much depended on Peter. He should be calling soon.

Dmitri knew he shouldn't be drinking at a time like this. But Moskovskaya was hard to find in America. His brother must have hoarded all of it for himself. In spite of his better judgment, he crossed to the bar.

His phone rang, bringing him to an abrupt halt. Peter's number appeared on the tiny screen. His heart rose to his throat. "Yes, this is Dmitri."

Peter's voice, though tinged with anxiety, remained clear. "He believed everything I told him. He asked a few questions about your brother and using his office for the meeting, but nothing serious. He seemed anxious to press on with the investigation and left right away. I already have the key. There was no one at the desk. All I had to do was go behind the counter and take it for myself."

Dmitri heard the kart being left outside the door. "Good, Peter, very good. Remember, you must do it quickly. Do not give them time to react. Hurry here to the Majestic. I'm already in my brother's office."

Peter took a deep breath and said, "Yes, Dmitri, I'll do it quickly. I want to get this over with."

As Peter started up the wrought iron stairs, a man caused heads to turn at McCarran airport. He did nothing more than walk toward the cab stand along with dozens of other newly arrived passengers. He drew attention simply because of his appearance, so tall and thin, dressed in black, with eyes so light they seemed almost white. The only luggage he possessed was a small black bag suspended over his shoulder by a thin strap. The silent figure stood out sharply from the excited throng of tourists eager to engross themselves in the Vegas experience. He seemed an embodiment of death, the reaper, impersonal and efficient.

Dmitri filled his glass and checked his gun. He positioned himself behind the door and calculated the time it would take the American to reach him. It would not be long. Peter said he was already on his way.

40

Carl passed out the cups, his face reflecting satisfaction with the morning's activities. He told of his drive past the house and said there was no trace of his attacker. After listening to an account of his meeting with Agent Casper, Gina suggested the idea of also going to the police.

Carl explained why he believed the Gaming Board would be more effective investigating something like this. Gina sighed, as if accepting she had no choice but to take her husband's word.

"What about something to eat, Carl, we're starving?"

He acted as if eating were a new idea to him. After a moment's thought, he told them he'd seen a small family restaurant around the corner.

"Honey, it might be kind of hard for you to get around in that cast and I'd still rather we stayed out of sight for now. Why don't I go to the restaurant and bring us back breakfast?"

The thought of remaining cooped up in the dreary motel room appealed to neither of the women, and their expressions were easy to interpret, but they seemed resigned to their fate. Gina tried to hide her impatience from Carl, but did ask how long they had to remain hidden.

"Hon, I'm sure we'll be safe as soon as this is all out in the open. I left my number with the Agent, and he'll call me as soon as they have something."

Carl was happy to see his wife's wry little smirk return.

"Okay, Carl, if you say so. But if you're going to keep us prisoner here, you better bring back some magazines and newspapers."

The limited number of television channels aired nothing but children's shows all morning. After Carl left, Sandy tried again, hoping to find an old movie or something, but dropped the remote in frustration, wishing they already had the magazines.

Carl returned a short time later with a stack of Styrofoam containers and a bag of reading materials. He also picked up a deck of Bicycles and a bottle of Motrin in case Gina's ankle bothered her.

The trio spent the rest of the day reading and card playing. The women seemed more interested in light conversation and reading. Carl sat at the desk trying to practice his card handling skills, but his thoughts were drawn elsewhere.

He believed he had reviewed every possible scenario he might encounter, his brain tired from the concentration. As evening approached; he had just stretched his hands behind his head, yawned, and thought of taking a nap when Gina asked about dinner. Before he could reply, his cell phone rang and presented him with a scenario he hadn't considered.

Peter had spent the day thinking of possibilities, also. When Dmitri called back in late afternoon and told him of his plan, the range of possibilities for him decreased markedly. The plan appeared ridiculously simple. Killing did seem to be an easy matter. Perhaps, he thought, that's why it's done so readily; it seemed to have a way of solving difficult problems.

The young man was indeed smooth. When the time came to implement Dmitri's plan, his natural ability took over, and any sign of inexperience disappeared. He sat in his car across the street from 'The Lucky Roll', and with resignation, made the phone call.

"Mr. Braun, this is Agent Gibson. I'm Agent Casper's supervisor. I believe I have some good news for you. The surveillance tapes bore out everything you told us this morning. We've already contacted the metropolitan police with information about the attempts on your life. We're at the Majestic now and need to interview you again in more detail. Before we can proceed any further, I'm going to need you to sign an affidavit. I'm set up here in the general manager's office. I'd like you to meet me right away so we can start clearing this thing up."

The women watched anxiously as Carl listened, their eyes seemed full of questions. He turned to them, a smile growing on his face, convinced now that he had gone about things the right way.

But why the general manager's office? Carl was willing to accept all he had been told, but he needed to clarify that point. "Al Beria's the general manager. Why are we using his office? I thought he was in on it."

Peter hadn't expected this question but answered without missing a beat. "Mr. Braun, I can assure you that you were on target with most of your suspicions, but you missed the mark with Al Beria. He is a very important and successful man in this town. He wouldn't benefit in the least from a scheme like this. To say this matter is troubling to him would be an understatement. He's been aiding our investigation and is very put out by the fact that the evidence is pointing to his brother."

Carl had never been completely convinced of Al Beria's involvement. He had no dealings with him directly and other than the fact that he was Dmitri's brother, couldn't associate him with the cheating organization at all. The ready answer Peter gave seemed logical and served to allay his apprehension.

"Very well, Mr. Gibson. As I told Agent Casper this morning, the ball's in your court. When would you like me there?"

This was too easy. Peter tried to suppress his delight. "As soon as possible, sir. This is a serious matter, and as I said, we want to clear it up as soon as possible."

The call ended and Carl told the women what had transpired. He stepped impatiently to the door, advising Sandy to lock up after him. "We still have to be careful. This isn't over yet." The subject of dinner was not addressed.

Sandy turned away from the door, a wide grin on her face. After sliding the safety chain in place, she commented that apparently Dad knew what he was doing after all. Gina sighed. "We'll see, honey. I still don't know why he didn't just go to the police first. I can't understand why he thought he needed more proof. I mean they burned down our house, didn't they?"

Sandy seemed unwilling to abandon her trust in her father. "Okay, Mom. Well that man said he called the police, so now both agencies are working on it."

Gina decided not to argue with the idealism of youth. Sandy, she realized, had always had a case of hero worship when it came to her father. Hopefully, Carl would continue to live up to it.

Peter waited until the Mustang drove out of view before he crossed the street and entered the motel's office. The room appeared vacant.

A pink Formica countertop, worn white in places, served as the registration desk. The wall behind the countertop held dozens of hooks, one labeled for each room. Peter simply raised the hinged portion of countertop and helped himself to the extra key for room 212. He exited the office, paused at the bottom of the stairs, and placed his call to Dmitri.

His pulse bounding, Peter took a moment to steel his nerves and conscience for the grim task ahead. Doubt twisted in his stomach. Could he truly slash and stab two helpless women? Driven by the energy of the moment, his world spinning in a surrealistic dream, he put his foot on the first step. His legs, weak and heavy, moved from one step to the next. Yes, it was really happening. This was no dream.

It had become a matter of survival. The thought of killing these women revolted him, but he was no coward and would do what he must to survive. He couldn't let Dmitri put him 'out of the picture'. He didn't want the St. Petersburg people coming after him. He had to protect himself.

He managed to suppress the guidance of his conscience, but his nerves proved another matter. Nausea attacked in waves, but he pushed on, the handle of the knife poking him in the small of his back with each step. His body now seemed to weigh a ton, and he used the handrail to pull himself forward. He reached the landing, discovered the reason for the abandoned office, and had to stop. The clerk was helping a couple carry their luggage to room number 213.

Peter retreated to the car. The delay only agitated his nerves further, but he wanted to make sure the new visitors were settled in before he proceeded. The clerk had to go up and down the stairs carrying each piece of luggage himself. The baggage came complete with a pair of large, leaky coolers. The exercise seemed to take forever and Peter grew disgusted with the pair when they failed to tip the clerk. He considered it ironic that within minutes he would kill two, probably very respectable, women, while these parasites would go on feeding off the world like a set of lazy ticks. *Sometimes Dmitri could be right about Americans.*

Peter, satisfied that things had quieted down sufficiently, started toward the motel. The clerk once again sat at his place behind the Formica counter, fully involved in a magazine. Now that he had time to accept the reality of what he had to do, it all seemed easier. He mounted the stairs, took a deep breath, and for the final time reviewed the way he intended to go about things.

Turn the key and the knob at the same time and shove hard. He had been in outdated places like this before and knew the cheap safety chains they used would fail as soon he applied a little force. Once inside, he would attack in whichever direction opportunity led him. Hopefully, luck would put the daughter in his path first. *The mother should be less trouble what with an injured leg and all. Slice quickly across the throat and then once in the heart, just as Dmitri said. Don't get so worked up that you forget to lock the door behind you. The longer it takes to discover the bodies the better.* It would all be horrible but he knew he could do it.

Gina, unable to find a comfortable position, twisted about on her bed. "It's starting to ache again, Sandy, would you give me a couple of those Motrins?" Gina had accepted the tablets and waited for Sandy to return from the bathroom with the water pitcher when she heard a key slip into the lock.

"Dad must have forgotten something. I better remove the safety chain." Sandy set the pitcher on the desk and stepped toward the door.

All at once the door burst open, ripping the chain free and throwing splinters of wood into the room. A young man stumbled in under the force of his own exertion, but righted himself quickly. He brandished a long bladed knife and slashed wildly. Sandy stepped between the beds and used the desk chair as a shield. The heavy blade made a sickening thud as it gouged into the ancient chair.

Gina screamed and slid herself off the foot of the bed, instinctively coming to her child's aid. Peter pulled his arm back and made ready to strike again. Sandy still held the chair but had been knocked off balance and leaned forward, her head only inches from the glinting steel.

Gina reached for the only thing she could grab and threw it at the attacker.

With the knife already descending toward Sandy's neck, Peter redirected his blow and swiped at the water-filled pitcher. This left an opening for Sandy. She righted herself in an instant, hoisted the chair, and swung with all her might. The chair struck him full on the back, knocking him to his hands and knees.

Peter looked up at Gina, the knife still clutched in his hand. She detected a look of shock in his eyes, and now running on nothing but adrenaline and instinct, kicked out with her plaster casted leg. The blow glanced off Peter's head, opening a gash. The novice killer gasped and reached for his bleeding scalp.

What Gina did next had nothing to do with instinct or reflexes. It was a response born of quick thinking and self-preservation. Turning away from her attacker and bracing herself between the desk and bed, she raised her injured leg to her chest and kicked back with a force that defied her limited stature.

Peter couldn't help but see it coming; perhaps he might have brushed it aside or moved his head if he could. Certainly he at least would have closed his eyes, but there was no time.

The mule-kick struck him right between the eyes. He let out an abbreviated grunt and collapsed into unconsciousness, his wounds seeping blood into the dirty carpet. Gina turned and took possession of the knife.

Sandy stood awestruck, the chair still raised over her head. "Mom, you saved my life. He was going to kill us both. Oh, my God"!

Gina, eyes wide with horror, looked at her trembling daughter. She hobbled past the prone figure and reached out for an embrace. "Get your phone, Sandy. I'm going to call 9-1-1. I think your father would say we have enough proof now."

The emergency operator told the women to leave the room and close the door behind them. A police car was right around the corner and would be there in seconds. Gina's ankle throbbed so much Sandy had to help her down the stairs. They reached the parking lot just as the squad car arrived. It screeched to a halt, siren blaring and emergency lights flashing.

When Peter regained consciousness, his eyes searched the empty room. He opened the door, now thinking only of escape, and staggered out in disbelief. It should have been so easy.

Sandy pointed up at the bleeding figure and shouted, "There he is. He tried to kill us." As she spoke, Gina dropped the knife at the officer's feet. A second squad car arrived. Seeing the officer racing up the stairs, Peter put his hands above his head and awaited his fate.

The two occupants of room 213 stood at their door, munching chips, and gaping at the unexpected drama, as if the scene had been performed for their own entertainment. Their eyes had followed Sandy as she supported her injured mother, and in unison turned back to Peter. Gina heard the woman screech in outrage. "What kind of man would try to hurt those defenseless women?"

A policeman secured the prisoner in handcuffs and led him to a waiting squad car. Peter had fully regained his senses, but didn't have the courage to look at the women he'd come to kill. He kept his head down as he walked past Gina and Sandy. Then something occurred to him. Because of the determination of these two women, he was guilty only of attempted murder, or possibly only of assault.

The strange truth about American justice was that you could stab a person in the chest, and if they didn't have the good sense to die, you could receive a relatively light sentence. His intentions may have been obvious, but he never actually laid a hand on either woman. If Dmitri killed Carl, the connection to him would be made quickly and he would be charged in a murder after all. As slick as always, Peter decided he had better start talking.

He spoke over his shoulder to a police officer. "You better move fast if you want to stop a killing. That lady's husband is being led into a trap at the Majestic. Someone's waiting to shoot him in the general manager's office."

Gina overheard the remark and quickly did the math. Realization and terror struck her simultaneously. The drive to the Majestic wasn't that long and would take little time if the evening traffic was light. Carl had already been gone a long time. With despair in her heart and tears in her eyes, she clutched Sandy's hand to her chest and cried out, "My God, they could have killed him already."

A police sergeant also overheard what Peter told the officer and asked him to explain. She wasted no time calling in the report, but like Gina, also did the math. When told how long ago Carl had driven off, she realized all they could do was hope.

41

In spite of all he had been through over the last few days, Carl approached the lobby doors of the Majestic with a spring in his step and an expression of pleasure on his face. He had reason to be pleased. He had discovered an organized group of criminals, gathered evidence against them, and effectively reported them to the proper authorities.

Obviously, it wasn't all peaches and cream. The criminals fought back and fought back hard. This was nothing new to Carl. His entire professional life resembled one big fight. On the fire department, he knew how to conduct the battle. Here in Las Vegas, he had been forced into an unfamiliar ring and for the first time the fight came to his doorstep. Gina was injured, and their home lay in ruins. He wouldn't get over those realities any time soon. Still, in the end, he had come out on top, and his ability to adapt and roll with the punches, as always, had seen him through.

It had been a near thing, but soon he would put the finishing touches on a victory he had orchestrated. Traffic had been light and the drive had gone by quickly. Being rather anxious, he had walked swiftly and reached the doors at the same time as the man who had been walking in front of him. The man seemed to sense Carl's urgency and graciously allowed him to pass. Carl looked up at him, about to utter an expression of gratitude, when the words froze in his throat.

Such an odd-looking man, almost a head taller than himself, dressed in black with a sunken face and eyes that glowed like pearls.

Konstantin saw the reaction but paid no attention to it, other than allowing a narrow grin. He had become used to this reaction and even promoted it by dressing as he did. Carl passed into the building without giving another thought to the strange encounter.

Before proceeding any further, the tall Russian wanted to get a feel for his surroundings. He approached the nearest roulette wheel and bought in for two hundred dollars. Playing without enthusiasm, he surveyed the grand casino with deep interest. One of the first sights he took in was that of a man he had studied in earnest before making his trip to America, the brother of the man Konstantin came to deal with. His eyes followed Aleksandr as he passed toward the elevators.

Carl watched as a crowd of people jammed into each of the first two elevator cars. He didn't care to be crammed in like a sardine so he waited for the third car. A set of doors glided open and he stepped into the empty car. The doors were about to shut when a man approached. Carl held his hand between the rubber stoppers; the man entered, expressing his thanks.

Although Aleksandr did not know Carl, Carl recognized his boss at once and thought he had better use the opportunity to introduce himself. Oddly, in the back of his head, Carl could sense the children gathering for an appearance.

"Hello, Mr. Beria. My name is Carl Braun. I imagine Agent Gibson told you I would be meeting with him in your office?" Aleksandr Beria was a man used to being in control of his world, but this man's words baffled him.

"No, Mr. Braun, I spoke to agent Gibson a short time ago, and he said nothing about a meeting in my office. What exactly is this concerning?"

The elevator doors opened. It was Carl's turn to be baffled. Aleksandr led the way to his office, and Carl tried to explain his question. The children were now completely visible, their faces ripe with anxiety. Again, Carl found them distracting.

"Mr. Beria, I'm the man who's been under attack for reporting a team of cheaters to your brother. Agent Gibson told me to meet him and Agent Casper in your office for a formal interview; he told me that you were cooperating with the investigation."

Al listened, continuing his practice of gathering information and adding it to the observations already stored in his methodical brain. They passed through the outer office and reached the closed door to Aleksandr's office.

The sound of the doorknob turning surprised Dmitri. He had naturally assumed the American would knock before he entered. Still standing behind the door, he raised his gun and held it shoulder high. His lips curled into a sneer, his eyes became glowing slits. *What a grand day–two lives. This will be a day to remember.*

Aleksandr pushed the door open. "Mr. Braun, I make it a practice to always cooperate fully with the Gaming Board, but I can assure you that no meeting has been scheduled to take place in my private office. Please come in, I think we have much to discuss."

With eyes down, rubbing his temples in a vain attempt to

rid his head of growing pain, Carl followed Aleksandr into the office. He struggled to see past the anguished, pleading faces, but the vision intensified and would not relent.

Dmitri, stunned to hear his brother's voice, kept the gun raised until he saw that it really was Aleksandr who pushed the door open.

"Dmitri! What is this? What does this mean?" Dmitri backed away from his brother, stopping in front of the glass panel windows. Al crossed the threshold and moved to his right, as Carl continued into the room.

"Dmitri, does this have something to do with the accusations made against me?"

Carl shook his head and looked up to see a gun pointing at him from just a few feet away. His mind suddenly cleared and he realized he stood between the brothers.

With desperation in his voice, Dmitri pleaded, "Yes, Brother, and this scum is the cause of our trouble. I will kill him now and take him away in that kart. It is a simple matter–a task I have been forced to carry out in the past. Leave it to me, Sasha. It is only a small thing."

Dmitri lowered the gun to his side and with a quick nervous voice, continued to implore his brother. Aleksandr listened, his eyes narrowed, processing the new information.

Carl's mind raced as well. Dmitri was armed and stood too far away to attack. Even if he could reach him, Al would surely come to his brother's aid. Al stood between Carl and the door, so retreat in that direction was out of the question. There would be a struggle which Dmitri would end with one shot.

Carl saw the children drop their heads in quiet resolution.

He felt lightheaded as a cold wave passed over him and he realized the clarity of his fate. He had been led into a trap from which there was no escape. He was at his end.

Strangely, he sensed a certain calm take over his mind almost as if he had already left his body. His surroundings no longer appeared real. Dmitri and Aleksandr seemed as figures merely playing out a scene like actors on the stage. He was about to be released from his torments. There would be no more hauntings, no more pain. He thought of his father and could even see his face. He lowered his head and stood silently in anticipation. Dmitri's voice grew distant, like an echo coming from an unseen place.

His thoughts turned to Gina. The harshness of the world crept back. She would be crushed by his loss. They had been together for so long. Their lives were as one. He tried to allay his fears for her by telling himself that she would still have the kids and soon a grandchild. She would survive.

Carl lifted his head to face a stark reality. They had tried to kill Gina as well. His mind grappled with this new horror. After Dmitri killed him, he would naturally go after Gina. He could not allow that to happen.

With the same collected calm and precision employed throughout his life, he saw the only way to prevent this and steeled himself for action. As soon as Dmitri began to raise the gun, he would rush him and force him through the plate glass window.

Dmitri would certainly get off at least one shot, but Carl knew his strength and momentum would carry him through. The fall would surely be fatal, fatal to both of them. But with the attention drawn by this very public and very violent spectacle, Gina would be safe. It would be impossible to keep his murder a secret. He would not be hauled away anonymously in some laundry kart. He would still have his victory, but the price was going to be much higher.

"Don't you see, Sasha, it is the only way." Dmitri's eyes left his brother and settled with malice on Carl's face. Carl met his enemy's glare, but his own eyes remained wide and determined, free of the hatred that drove his rival. Every muscle in Carl's body strained for release.

He concentrated on his enemy's right hand and waited for the first sign of movement. But Dmitri's left hand grabbed out.

Carl heard a deafening report and watched as Dmitri groped pathetically toward his brother, a red stain spreading on his chest. He ripped open his shirt revealing a torrent of blood that pulsed weaker with each heartbeat.

Dmitri's malice found Carl once again and he struggled to lift the gun, but drained of strength, it fell from his hand. His eyes flashed to his brother and he muttered, 'Sasha,' before collapsing to the floor.

Carl never flinched, but allowed his muscles to relax as he watched an evil man die. He had been with many innocent people when their lives ended. Death was not an unfamiliar sight to him, but this was different. His heart held no remorse for this man and he stood unmoved by his death.

Aleksandr walked to his desk and placed the smoking Glock 17 on the leather pad. He removed his wallet, retrieved his permit and blue registration card, and in very business like fashion placed them on the pad next to his gun.

Carl turned from Dmitri and watched Aleksandr, who leaned against his desk and rubbed his eyes. He breathed deeply and for the first time since entering the room, spoke to Carl, his voice somber and dejected. "I have no doubt that he was about to shoot you, Mr. Braun. I had such hopes for my brother when I brought him to this country. I guess I always knew that I hoped for too much. The die, as they say, had already been cast."

The shot had rung out just as the elevator doors parted and two police officers stepped onto the mezzanine level. They raced to the office with guns drawn.

Aleksandr seemed confused by the promptness of their arrival, but accepted the fact. "Mr. Braun, I believe these fine officers are going to require some of our time."

Roulette is an ancient European game that can be played with very little attention to detail. That is why Konstantin Leonovich chose it. The game occupied his thoughts only slightly. When he saw that his chips were depleted, he merely placed two more hundred-dollar bills on the felt and asked for more.

His attention remained fixed on his surroundings and he missed little. He watched as two police officers sped along in the same direction he had seen Aleksandr Beria going only minutes before. He heard the echo of the gunshot, a sound he was very familiar with. He watched as many more police officers arrived and walked through the casino with restraint and affected calm. They all moved in the same direction as the others.

With his second chip purchase exhausted, he decided it was time to look around and satisfy some of his suspicions. The casino staff could be heard circulating rumors. Mr. Beria had just shot his brother. Konstantin listened with interest as many offered their opinions of the younger Beria. He wandered outside and saw the arrival of a forensics team, and saw personnel from the coroner's office park their plainly marked vehicle in a place usually reserved for high rollers.

Konstantin had seen enough. He went to the registration desk and checked in. He dined at Moy's, sitting alone in a secluded corner. He tipped the waitress generously before retiring to his room for the night.

A quick review of the morning papers completed the store of knowledge he needed before returning to St. Petersburg. Aleksandr Beria had killed his brother in an act of defense. The man he defended was also an employee of the hotel. The deceased had recently come under investigation in a number of criminal allegations. No charges were to be filed in his death.

Konstantin folded the article, tucked it into his bag, and took a cab back to McCarran.

42

Carl and Aleksandr rode to the police station in separate cars. Noah Gibson and Eric Casper waited for them as they arrived. Carl and Aleksandr were led to individual interrogation rooms. Agent Gibson accompanied the officers who were interviewing Aleksandr, and Agent Casper accompanied the team interviewing Carl.

Aleksandr and Carl learned more than they were able to tell. Noah Gibson informed Aleksandr in detail of the preliminary results of his investigations and how they confirmed Carl's assertions, especially concerning Dmitri. The surveillance tapes implicated Dmitri more than Carl suspected they might. Noah told Al about the fire and the attack Viktor made on Carl.

Aleksandr had been silent and upright throughout Agent Gibson's narrative, but now held his head between his hands in shame when Noah informed him of the injury to Gina and the attack at 'The Lucky Roll.' He was filled with remorse over his own stubbornness. His remorse stung all the more when he reflected how hard he had strived to handle every aspect of his life, paying meticulous attention to detail. When it came to his brother, he realized he had overlooked much. His blind desire to have Dmitri join him in pursuit of the American dream had cost these innocent people so much, had nearly cost them their lives.

At that moment, Aleksandr lifted his head and made a silent oath. He would use his great energy and position to ensure that the Braun's lives were restored, as much as possible, to their previous state. He swore to himself that he would take full responsibility for the acts committed by his brother.

Aleksandr reviewed and signed his statement. His interview session ended before Carl's, but he didn't plan to leave the police station until he had a chance to speak with his unfortunate employee. While waiting, he asked Agent Gibson about the condition of Mr. Braun's family.

Noah explained that Sandy Braun had suffered no injuries. He asked if Al recognized the name, and told him she worked as a middle manager in his hospitality department. Aleksandr nodded his head. He considered it important to stay familiar with as many members of his staff as possible, especially his managers. He recalled that Sandy was a personable and capable young executive and made a mental note to consider her for advancement.

Noah told him Gina was in the hospital emergency room having her leg x-rayed and having her broken cast repaired. Aleksandr asked for the name of the hospital.

He excused himself from Agent Gibson's company, and made a series of phone calls. The first were made to the Majestic and Meghan O'Meara. Aleksandr became intrigued by his part time poker dealer, and wanted to know more about him. His mind replayed the scene in his office. His thoughts settled on how calmly Carl had stood as he faced death, and how calm he had remained when it was violently dealt to another.

He told Ms. O'Meara of all that passed that evening and asked her to describe what she knew of Carl and his background.

Meg felt a little guilty at the gladness that came to her when she learned of Dmitri's demise. Putting that aside, she told as much about Carl as she could.

Aleksandr listened and combined the information with his own observations. He had extensive experience in dealing with men of every kind and was sure that he had enough data to make certain assumptions about the fireman from Chicago. Carl was a man of rare qualities and one deserving of his respect.

Carl, for his part, had repeated everything he'd told Agent Casper that morning to the metropolitan police. He knew the task was arduous but necessary. Once again, he summoned his patience and went over the whole story, detail by detail. He began with his earliest suspicions on his first day at work and ended with the police officers' entry into Aleksandr's office. He read the statement and signed, glad that his business with the police was finished, and he would soon be able to return to Gina and Sandy.

Carl's cell phone hadn't been on a charger since the night of the fire and had finally gone dead. He turned to an officer and asked, "Can I use a phone officer? My wife and daughter are still at that dive, and I want to call them and let them know I'm alright."

The looks that passed between the officers and Agent Casper left little doubt in Carl's mind that something was wrong.

Agent Casper spoke up while the others stuttered to each other and made excuses. "Carl, I can't believe no one has told you."

Carl abruptly reached the limits of his patience. He had suffered the tedium of these legal formalities with tolerance, but now realized that something was amiss with his family, and it had been kept from him. It didn't matter to him if the omission was inadvertent or by design. He stood suddenly and leaned toward the Agent, his fists clenched on the top of the table. "Tell me what?"

Agent Casper pushed his chair away from the table and spoke quickly. "They're okay. No one was hurt. They're fine."

Carl restrained himself and waited for more. The other officers picked up their paperwork and left the room with haste. They seemed more than happy to leave the task of making the explanation to their colleague from the Gaming Board.

"Mr. Braun, please relax. Your wife broke her cast in an attack that occurred at the motel. She and your daughter defended themselves and actually knocked the attacker unconscious. I guess your wife kicked him with the cast. Other than the shattered plaster she suffered no injuries."

Carl wanted out. His business there was over. He flung the door open as Agent Casper voiced an offer to drive him to the hospital.

Aleksandr overheard the offer and interjected swiftly. "That won't be necessary, Agent Casper." He rose from his seat and approached Carl. "Your wife is already on her way to the Majestic. I spoke to my limousine driver only moments ago, and he informed me that he had already dropped your daughter off at her apartment. I was completely apprised of your situation and took the liberty of reserving a suite of rooms for you and your wife for whatever length of time is necessary. My driver has been instructed to give your wife this same information, and to inform her that accounts have been opened for her at each of our shops."

Carl's response came without hesitation. "Mr. Beria, I can assure you that that is completely unnecessary. We will manage very well on our own. Thank you anyway."

Carl could be a strong-willed man, but in this case Aleksandr proved determined to have his way. He asked Carl to move with him to a corner of the room for privacy and there expressed his regret over what happened and how he was responsible to a great extent. Carl accepted this, but firmly maintained his position.

Aleksandr saw his resolve. Even though he thought it was hitting below the belt, he revealed just how strong a hand he held.

"Mr. Braun, my driver has informed me that Mrs. Braun could barely contain her joy at the prospect of staying as our guest for a time. Please find it in your heart to reconsider for her sake."

For the second time tonight, Carl, knew he was trapped. This time, however, there truly was no escape. He wondered if he would ever be in control of his own life again. He thought of Gina, and all she had been through. "Very well, Mr. Beria, I can see you have me beat."

Aleksandr accepted his victory with grace. "I can assure

you, Mr. Braun, that I take no pleasure in imposing something on you against your will. I do know, however, that our facility can be very accommodating, and you and your wife will be presented with the very best we have to offer. I respect a man who can sacrifice a principle for his family. I will make every effort to ensure your sacrifice will not be in vain."

They rode to the Majestic in Aleksandr's private car. Carl sat in silent reflection as the lights of the Strip passed by. He had survived after he thought all was lost. With his thoughts clear once again, he sensed the suggestion of his past lingering stubbornly in the dark corners of his mind.

He turned his eyes away from the window and stared at the floor. His mind struggled with the notion that perhaps the trauma of death never leaves. Hopefully, the pain dulled with time, lost its edge. He knew the years, with their volume of tragedy, meant the pain might need much more time to lose its grip. He sighed, realizing that maybe it never would.

He guessed he could carry the weight a while longer. After all, he still had Gina and his family, and soon there would be a grandchild. Life renewed itself. It wasn't all tragedy. Surely those times were behind him now.

They reached the top of the circle drive. A uniformed valet opened Carl's door and escorted him to the top floor of the hotel. Their suite towered over the gardens. Carl explained to the valet that he had nothing to tip him with, but was told that tips would not be accepted from either him or Mrs. Braun anywhere in the resort.

He inserted the keycard, smiled at the promising click, and pushed the door slowly. Gina called out, "Is that you, Blue

Eyes?" She'd dimmed the lights in the suite, but Carl could still make out the lavish setting.

"Yeah, hon, where are you?"

"Look around, Carl, this place isn't that big. You're really cold right now."

The sound of his wife's voice, after having accepted that he would never hear it again, caused a knot to form in the pit of his stomach. He was sure she didn't know what had nearly happened in Aleksandr's office, he didn't think he would tell her.

"C'mon, slow poke, what's taking you so long?" Carl followed the sound of her voice and found himself in the master bedroom. Much to his disappointment, he found the bed empty.

"You're getting warmer."

The playfully tempting voice came to him from a far corner, the area lit only by candles flickering around the mirrored perimeter of a large Jacuzzi spa. Her casted leg hung out over the side with the rest of her body hidden in a cloud of bubbles.

He walked toward her, dazed by desire. Her eyes, moist and black as night, glimmered in the candle light. Entranced, he was drawn to her side.

"Oh, honey, you're getting really hot now."

She had no idea.

THE END

Kevin Helmold is a twenty-year veteran of the Chicago Fire Department and has spent his entire career as a Firefighter/Paramedic in one of the most challenging areas of urban America. He's stood witness to a panorama of violence and despair that few outside of his profession can match. Kevin's debut novel, "Echoes of Torment," is a story laced with examples from this panorama.

Kevin's interest in writing stretches back to childhood and to date has consisted of short story and extensive journal writing. With his four children well beyond the "baby stage" Kevin felt the time had come to take his writing to the next level.

The son of a Chicago Firefighter, Kevin has lived his entire life, including the last twenty plus years with his beautiful wife, on the south side of Chicago. His interests extend beyond family and writing to include the challenges physical fitness, summer time athletics, and poker playing. His literary interests range widely and he has read everything from Dostoevsky to Stephen King and from James Fennimore Cooper to Ken Bruen. Some of his particular favorites include the works of Ernest Hemingway, Arthur Conan Doyle, and Edgar Allen Poe.

After having completed a number of short stories, Kevin is currently working on his second book.

You can visit Kevin's web site at

www.KevinHelmold.com